Sarabande in Blue

Doreen Hinchliffe

To Pat,

with best wishes,

Doreen Hinchliffe

First Published in 2020 by Blossom Spring Publishing
Sarabande in Blue Copyright © 2020 Doreen Hinchliffe
ISBN 978-1-9161735-9-0
E: admin@blossomspringpublishing.com
W: www.blossomspringpublishing.com
Published in the United Kingdom. All rights reserved
under International Copyright Law. Contents and/or
cover may not be reproduced in whole or in part without
the express written consent of the publisher.
Although inspired by a true story this is a work of fiction.
Names, characters, places and incidents are either
products of the author's imagination or are used
fictitiously.

In memory of Rene Pedley and Ann Jonas, without
whose love, support and encouragement
this book would not have been published.

Chapter 1

'Be upstanding in court!'

The assembled throng rose in unison, and a hush descended on the courtroom. All eyes turned towards the door from which the judge would soon emerge to pass sentence. Alice glanced down nervously from her place in the crowded public gallery, trying desperately to catch the eye of her friend, who stood impassively below, head bowed, as if she were completely unaware of what was going on around her. She looked so small, so vulnerable, so incredibly ordinary. It was still impossible to think of her as 'the accused'.

'Could I have done more?' Alice asked herself for the hundredth time. 'If I'd only known what was happening a bit earlier, could I have saved her? Could I have saved them all?'

The silence was deep, prolonged, broken only by the rustle of the judge's robes as he took his seat, and by the brief buzz of anticipation that swept through the courtroom when, prompted by the court usher's nod, all those in attendance settled themselves on the long mahogany benches. Dreading what she might be about to hear, Alice closed her eyes and gripped the rail in front of her.

The judge stared down at the diminutive figure in the dock beneath him, at her double-breasted coat with the silver brooch in its lapel and her neat black hat held firmly in place by a large silver hatpin. She was standing completely still, as she had done throughout the proceedings, seemingly lost in a world of her own and unable to say anything in her own defence. For the first time, he noticed a few wispy strands of grey hair trickle across her brow as she slowly raised her head.

Aware of the judge's scrutiny, she stood stiffly to attention, force of habit dictating that she adopt a deferential stance towards such a figure of authority, although she knew whatever sentence he pronounced would make no difference. Her life had ended months ago; only time, empty endless time stretched out before her now, waiting to be walked across.

She watched the judge carefully adjust the sleeves of his robe, watched him deliberately pause to reflect before he finally spoke. In that brief moment, she allowed herself a glimpse into a past as unremarkable as a hundred thousand others.

She saw herself a child again, bowling her wooden hoop across the cobbles in a world before the Great War changed the map of everything, heard the laughter of her friends and the playful taunts and chants of the grinning boys who would poke their heads round the corner of her street and shout after her –

Eliza Bell, Eliza Bell –
does 'ter know tha's going to hell?

Eliza Bell, Eliza Bell –
does 'ter know tha's going to hell?

Chapter 2

A fast-flowing river gushing over stones, the constant smell of smoke and steam, the high-pitched wailing of a siren that signalled the beginning and end of the working day – these were Eliza's first memories of life.

They intermingled now with a host of others from her early childhood – the smell of fresh bread from the kitchen; the sound of the milkman's horse clip-clopping over the cobbles at dawn, his metal churn rattling against the step as he poured milk into the jug they always left outside the front door; the brief flicker of a candle beside her bed, casting dark shadows on the wall until the rush of her mother's breath blew it out; the sound of Mrs. Lumb, the knocker-up, tapping her long wooden pole against the bedroom windows to wake the street at five o'clock; the laughter of her brother George, who came home every Sunday from the farm where he worked and once took her back with him to witness the birth of a calf.

She must have been only four or five at the time, but for some reason, this memory remained as clear as day. George had held her hand as they stood together by the barn, looking over a low wooden fence at a square enclosure where a brown cow was pacing around, agitated. All at once it stopped and began to strain and breathe noisily, its head swaying uneasily from side to side.

Eliza had never seen the birth of anything before, so the arrival of a tiny calf took her completely by surprise. It slid out quite suddenly, head first, covered in what seemed to be a watery balloon, and slithered to the ground in a series of jerks and lunges. Then, wet and trembling, it lay beneath its mother on the straw-covered ground, flapping its ears back and forth on its neck. Fascinated, Eliza watched the mother as she began to lick it all over, transforming it as she did so from a quivering sticky mess into something resembling a tiny image of herself.

'Is that how you and me were born, George?' she asked, wide-eyed with astonishment.

'Ay, a bit similar,' he replied, amused by the question. 'Only we don't have to be licked all over and we certainly can't stand up after a few minutes like they can.'

Eliza pondered for a while, then said dogmatically

and with absolute certainty, in the way that only small children can, 'I'm going to be a mother!'

'Not for a good while yet I hope,' grinned George, but this comment was lost on Eliza, who was now totally absorbed in watching every movement of the baby calf.

Eliza's early years were happy ones. She was close to her mother and loved to help her with the daily chores. By the time she went to school, she was an expert in scouring the front steps and black leading the hearth. She would help with the weekly wash, pummelling the dirty clothes in the peggy tub before her mother fed them through the wringer and hung them out to dry in the back yard. Occasionally, her mother would let her roll out the pastry for tarts or knead the dough for bread. These were the golden hours, the two of them covered in flour and chatting happily together in the cosy warmth of the kitchen.

'You're a very lucky lass being able to live in Saltaire,' her mother used to say as she hung out her washing on the line that was permanently strung across the street between the backs of the houses. 'A lot of folk would run through fire and water to be in a place like this.'

Mrs Bell, like all the other inhabitants of Saltaire, was immensely proud to live in the unrivalled model village that stood beneath the giant textile mill, built in 1853 by the great Victorian philanthropist, Sir Titus Salt.

His was indeed a unique vision. Three miles from Bradford, on the waving cornfields near the banks of the River Aire, he created his new industrial community. His mill was the largest and most modern in the whole of Europe and reflected his determination to cut down on all forms of industrial pollution, in particular the sulphurous fumes from factory chimneys, which had turned Bradford into the unhealthiest town in England. Noise in his factory was kept to a minimum because the shafting which drove his machinery was placed underground. Large flues removed the dust and dirt from the factory floor, and the tall factory chimney, built in the style of an Italian campanile, was fitted with the latest smoke burners that significantly reduced the amount of sulphur produced.

For his three thousand five hundred workers, he built eight hundred and fifty terraced houses in long, narrow streets. Two of these streets were named after the reigning queen and her consort, the others were all given the name of one of his own children. He also built shops, a school, a park, bath houses and a hospital. Fresh water was pumped into each house from Saltaire's own reservoir, gas was laid on to provide lighting to each dwelling, and unlike other mill families in Bradford, every family in Saltaire had its own outside lavatory.

No pubs or pawn shops were allowed in the village, since one of Salt's main concerns was to provide for the moral and spiritual welfare of his workers. To this end, he commissioned architects to design a Congregational Church in the same Italianate architectural style as many of the other buildings in the village, a church which he expected his workers would attend each Sunday and from which he hoped they would draw strength. To help them relax and improve themselves, he also built an educational institute, complete with library, reading rooms, lecture halls and a fully equipped gymnasium.

In this community Eliza grew up and spent her formative years. She was born in Albert Road, exactly twenty-one years after the death of Sir Titus, too late ever to see him stride proudly into his mill, but not too late to feel the benevolent shadow he still cast over the villagers, most of whom, despite working long hours in harsh conditions, remained grateful for their inheritance. Eliza loved listening to her mother's memories of Sir Titus and to her conversations with other women in the village about what life used to be like when they were children. Mrs Bell had left school at the age of ten to work half days on one of the looms in the mill and it was there that she had met Eliza's father. She had married at seventeen, and a year later, Eliza's brother George had been born. He was thirteen years older than Eliza and had never wanted to follow his father into the mill. As a boy, he used to love to work on the farm owned by Tom Walker, an old friend of the family. Tom taught him lots of farming skills, including how to milk his cows and shear his sheep. It was no surprise, therefore, when George was taken on as one of his farm labourers as soon as he was old enough to leave school.

Unusually for a small girl of that time, Eliza had never experienced the birth of a baby in her house. In between George's arrival and that of herself, there had been two miscarriages and a much cherished daughter, Martha, who had died of diphtheria when she was only two. Although her parents rarely spoke of their first daughter, Eliza could sense that the deep pain of her loss had never left them. Sometimes, when her mother sang her to sleep, Eliza saw her eyes fill with tears, as if she were remembering a time when she had sung the same lullaby to someone else.

Eliza's father was inevitably a more remote figure than her mother, working as he did for five and a half days a week. He would leave home at half past five in the morning and often wouldn't return until nearly seven at night, by which time he was far too tired to do anything much except have his tea and sink into the fireside chair. On Sunday mornings, though, she walked with him hand in hand up the steps of the church and down the aisle to the front, where he and her mother took their place in front of the great golden pipes of the magnificent organ. She loved to stand beside him and listen to him sing the hymns, all of which he knew by heart. Unlike him, she didn't find it easy to remember the words but she did know every verse of *Onward Christian Soldiers*. This hymn was her favourite, mainly because it went faster than all the others and had a strong pulsing rhythm you could march to. It seemed to be driving her onward, driving her forward into a life of fulfilment and excitement and unimaginable happiness.

On rainy Sunday afternoons, her father would often sit down at the piano and vamp a wide variety of popular songs. He came from a musical family and took great pride in telling people how his grandfather had played the cornet in Sir Titus Salt's famous Saltaire Brass Band, which had come second in the national brass band competition held at Crystal Palace in 1860. His own father, too, had been in a band for several years and had taught all his children to play the piano.

After listening to him go through his repertoire for about half an hour, Eliza would always make the same request.

'Play *Onward Christian Soldiers*, pa. Go on.'

He would usually do as she asked, laughing at her as she marched energetically all round the living room, keeping in step with its insistent four-four time.

At elementary school, Eliza's best friend was Alice Chadwick, a rather dumpy girl with curly dark brown hair, an open face and a beaming smile. She lived at the other end of Albert Road and had lots of brothers and sisters, which Eliza secretly longed to have too.

Alice's father was a warehouseman in the mill and her mother had her hands full bringing up a family of five boys and three girls.

Whenever Eliza went round there, Alice's home was always buzzing with activity, children of various ages running in and out, chattering or arguing with each other. Alice was closest to her oldest brother Laurie, a good-looking boy with a cheeky grin and strong sense of mischief. But she got on well enough with all of her siblings and they would often play games together after school.

Eliza loved to join in, hopscotch and marbles being her favourites. The skipping games were fun, too, though. They all took turns to hold the rope, chanting a variety of songs and rhymes passed down through the generations: *Raspberry, strawberry, gooseberry jam, tell me the name of your young man,* or *Bluebells, cockle-shells, eevory-ivory-over.*

Sometimes, they joined hands for *Ring a Ring of Roses* but the boys soon got bored and broke away to start up games on their own. Laurie was usually the organiser and Eliza was amused by the way he confidently took charge, his hands on his hips and his flat cap pulled down at a jaunty angle.

'Come on, lads,' he'd call, undoing the top button of his waistcoat as if to get ready for some action. 'Let's play pickaback!'

This was a more boisterous form of leapfrog where the boys leapt over each other's backs down the whole length of the street. It finished at the wall near the end, where the first boy would squat low, and then everyone else would pile on top of him, shouting and giggling and throwing their caps in the air with excitement.

Eliza really wished that she could play too, but even if the boys had allowed it, she knew her long skirt and petticoats would have made it impossible. She and Alice would stand and watch, though, cheering the boys on and shrieking with them at the end.

Sometimes, Laurie would drag an old wooden shoe box out of the house and jump on top of it, shouting, 'I'm the king of the castle. Get down you dirty rascal!'

Then his brother Harry would push him off the box and repeat the rhyme and so they would go on, the game getting rougher and rougher until one of the little boys started to cry. At this, Alice's mother would appear to call a halt to the proceedings and the whole family would be made to troop indoors, leaving Eliza to walk back home on her own.

When not at school or helping her mother at home, Eliza spent her free time with Alice. They picked wild flowers together, played bowl the hoop and whip and top in the street, shared their secrets behind the boat sheds in the park, and best of all, on summer Sunday afternoons, often went up to Shipley Glen. Usually, they walked up along a steep path strewn with buttercups. Sometimes, though, they would treat themselves to a ride on the magical Glen Tramway, a tiny tram powered by a gas suction engine that had opened to the public two years before they were born and had since ferried thousands of enchanted customers up the quarter mile of wooded track to the very top of the moor, where a fairground awaited them.

One Sunday in late summer, Alice and Eliza carefully packed their jam sandwiches in paper and headed through Victoria Park towards the foot of the glen. They were both nine years old now and had begun to get a halfpenny a week pocket money. Often, they saved this up for a month so that they had tuppence to spend on whatever they wanted. Today, they intended to use a halfpenny on the tram fare to the top and then spend the rest on rides or amusements.

'Come on Eliza,' Alice called as she rushed to get a seat on the crowded tram, 'I'll save you a place next to me.' She was adept at weaving her way through the crowds and usually managed to find a seat on one of the tiny wooden benches, immediately placing both hands on the seat next to her until Eliza succeeded in joining her. They wriggled with excitement, impatient for the operator to signal it was time to move off. At last, the departure bell rang and the tram then rumbled up the hill, the girls being careful to avoid any overgrown branches from the trees that lined the route. Alice knew the names of all the wild flowers that grew beside the track and loved to point them out to Eliza.

'Look!' she said. 'There's a red campion and those tall purple ones are foxgloves.'

'What about that curvy white one that looks like a weed?' said Eliza, pointing to a clump of tall straggly flowers rising above the undergrowth.

'I don't know its real name,' admitted Alice, 'but

my gran calls it a stepmother blessing 'cos it reminds her of the bit of white skin that sometimes hangs down from her finger nail.'

By this time, they were nearing the end of their journey. They had to wait for the tram to come to a complete halt before they were allowed to disembark, but as soon as the guard called, 'All off now for Shipley Glen!' they raced through the gate at the end and onto the vast expanse of land that had become such a famous local pleasure ground.

At weekends, the place was usually full of mill workers and their families, keen to spend some of their hard-earned money on having a good time. There was plenty to attract them, including a giant camera obscura, a cable car operating between two high towers and a wooden switchback ride, known rather grandly as 'The Royal Yorkshire Switchback'.

The biggest attraction, however, was the aerial glide. Built in 1900, it consisted of a series of steel towers with an overhead gantry and rail from which chairlift-style cars dangled. The creator of the ride had skilfully used the contours of the land to ensure that gravity would propel the cars ever faster down the u-shaped track until the lowest point was reached, when they naturally came to a slow halt, only to be hoisted back up the incline once the occupants had jumped off.

Chattering excitedly, Alice and Eliza joined the end of the queue. It seemed a long time before they reached the front, but the attendant finally settled each of them in turn onto a chair, then lowered the safety chain in position to fasten them in.

'Are you ready then?' he called, hardly waiting for the cry of 'yes' before he gave a firm push, first to Eliza and then to Alice behind her. Off they went down the steep slope, picking up speed all the way until they hurtled round the turn at the bottom, at which point they both screamed and gripped the arms of their chairs as tightly as they could, convinced they were about to be tipped over the edge of the steep escarpment and down to the woods below. Once round the turn, the car gradually lost speed, and relieved to be in one piece, the girls giggled all the way to the foot of the incline. An attendant stationed at the bottom removed the safety chain and then they had to get out and walk all the way back up to the top again. They felt this didn't matter at all, though, since the ride was so exhilarating and well worth the halfpenny they had to pay.

Afterwards, they made straight for the brightly painted wooden swings, six of them arranged in a long line, each shaped rather like a small curved boat. There were seats at either end, and after paying another halfpenny, Eliza and Alice clambered in and sat opposite each other, holding on to two long ropes that dangled in front of them. To make their swing move, they had to pull alternately on these ropes. The harder they tugged, the higher the opposite end of the swing would go. They both loved the sensation of being flung high in the air, so they would keep on tugging away at the ropes until their tiny arms became tired. Sometimes, they screamed with delight, imagining that their swing was in danger of flying off on its own, taking them with it as it soared above the glen.

Their adventure on the swings over, they decided to buy a ha'porth of sweets from one of the stalls at the entrance to the fairground and then spend the whole afternoon walking over the rugged moor. They walked on and on, picking their way through the well-worn paths with the wind blowing through their hair, laughing and talking together about everything and nothing. After about an hour, they began to feel tired, so they took out their sandwiches and ate them sitting on one of the glen's huge stones from which they could look down on a vast expanse of hills and moorland that stretched for miles, as far as the eye could see.

'Do you think God put these big stones on the glen so we can flop down on them whenever we feel tired and look across at all them green moors?' asked Alice, her mouth still full of bread.

'Maybe,' replied Eliza. 'From what they say about him in Sunday School, I reckon it's the sort of thing he might do.'

'Our Norman says he doesn't think there is a God,' continued Alice, 'says what they spout on about in Sunday School is all made up. I don't think he's right, though. He's always talking a load of nonsense according to my ma.'

They continued eating quietly for a while.

'Let's write our names in the rocks,' said Eliza suddenly, noticing how many others had done so in the one they happened to be sitting on.

They looked around for some sharp stones that would serve as a carving tool and each of them solemnly carved their initials – *EB. AC.*

'Let's put the date as well,' said Alice, so they added it – *26 August 1906.*

'There,' said Eliza as they sat down again to finish their lunch, 'now we'll live forever.'

They sat in silence again and looked across the valley. The clouds were making sculptures of faces over the distant hills and all the shifting colours of the windswept moors were bathed in the light of the late afternoon sun.

'Look at yon cloud,' said Alice. 'Who do you think it looks like?'

Eliza considered the cloud's shape for a moment.

'It's like your pa, Alice. Look! It's got a little curly beard and a long neck. And that one following behind's your ma. Can you see its long nose and pointed chin?'

Alice laughed.

'Your ma and pa are nice, Alice,' continued Eliza. 'Do you think *we'll* be like them when *we* grow up? You know – married, with lots of children.'

'I don't know,' mused Alice. 'I'm not sure I want to get married. I'm happy as I am.'

Alice was quiet for a little while and appeared to

be deep in thought. Then she turned back to her friend with a look of excitement on her face.

'Eliza,' she cried, 'what if we never got married at all? What if we never had to wash clothes or scrub floors or cook or feed loads of babies? What if we could just come up here every day and go on them swings and sit and watch clouds and write messages in them rocks?'

'Aye, it'd be grand wouldn't it?' Eliza paused, trying to imagine herself and Alice as middle-aged women trekking across the moors or riding on the swing boats. 'We'll have to get married and have children some day, though, Alice. It's what grown-ups do.'

'I know but grown-ups aren't always happy when they're married, are they? Billy's parents next door aren't happy. They're always rowing and fighting. I often hear his ma crying in the back yard.'

'Well, *my* ma *never* cries,' proclaimed Eliza, realising even as she finished her sentence that this wasn't strictly true. There were actually two occasions when she'd seen her cry.

The first was when Eliza was about five years old and had heard moans coming from the yard. She had rushed out only to discover her mother collapsed in the outside privy in a pool of blood which was seeping from the back of her skirt. Unable to speak and trembling with fear, Eliza had just stood there rooted to the spot for what seemed an eternity until her mother shouted at her to go next door for Mrs Pollard. Later that night, Eliza had listened outside her parents' bedroom. She heard her mother sobbing and her father comforting her. He was speaking very softly, so it was impossible to catch exactly what he was saying, although Eliza thought it was something about them being 'unlucky again'.

The second occasion was more recent, and Eliza blamed herself for being its cause. It had occurred one Sunday afternoon the previous year when, trying to be helpful, she had offered to dust the furniture in the two bedrooms upstairs. She always enjoyed removing the various ornaments from her mother's dressing table and was particularly fascinated by the glass trinket box full of brooches and hatpins, some worn by her grandmother or even great grandmother.

After polishing the wood until it shone, she carefully put back each object she had removed and then turned to the huge walnut wardrobe with its heavy mirrored door that opened on a treasure trove of drawers and secret nooks and crannies. Summoning all her strength, she pulled hard on the brass handle, releasing intoxicating scents of cedar wood and mothballs. Unable to resist a peek inside a particularly inviting-looking compartment that was tucked behind one of her mother's coats, she reached inside and prised it slowly open. Her tiny hand felt around for its secrets and soon came across a picture frame, which she immediately took out. She knew there were no photographs at all in their house because her parents always said they could never afford them, so why had they never mentioned this one? Holding it gently in both hands, Eliza gazed down at the picture in front of her. It was a photograph of her mother holding a tiny child wrapped in a shawl. The child's face looked gaunt, its eyes lifeless and staring. In the bottom right corner, her father had written, in black ink, *Martha after death, 5th October 1893.*

It was at this moment that her mother chose to enter the bedroom to check how Eliza was getting on.

'What are you doing? What are you doing?' she screamed, seizing the photograph from Eliza's hands and holding it tightly to her breast. 'Never touch that photograph again, do you hear? Never!'

Terrified by the vehemence of her mother's rage, Eliza had fled downstairs, pretending to her father that she needed a fresh cleaning cloth. She stayed in the kitchen for a few minutes, trying to compose herself, then crept back up to the bedroom to peep through the crack in the open door. Once again, she heard her mother weeping, but softly this time, with her head bowed.

These memories of her mother's tears took only seconds to pass through her mind but to Eliza the seconds were more like minutes. Conscious that, after such a long silence, her friend seemed to be staring at her, and feeling guilty that she had lied to Alice about her mother never crying, Eliza quickly changed the subject.

'Do you want to come up to the glen again next week, Alice?' she asked. 'I love this place. We can say what we like up here.'

'Course I do,' her friend exclaimed. 'I want to come up here next week, and the week after that and the week after that, forever and ever Eliza. I never ever want to stop coming up here with you.'

Alice jumped up then and leapt onto a nearby stone. She lifted her face to the sky to feel the wind full on her face and raised her arms, as if she were about to take off, like a bird. For a few seconds she stood there, perfectly still, her dark brown hair blowing back to reveal her wide forehead.

Eliza, not wanting to be left out, clambered up and stood beside her. The wind was getting stronger now and they each gripped the other's hand, imagining it might actually blow them over. Many of the ramblers and pleasure seekers had already gone home, so the two little girls had the end of the glen to themselves. They loved it like this. Complete silence was rare in their lives and it felt wonderful to be free for a while from the constant demands of school and housework.

Turning to Eliza, Alice said vehemently, 'Cross your heart and promise you'll always keep on coming up here with me – even when we're grown-up, even when we're married with a dozen children, even when we're old!'

'Don't talk so daft,' said Eliza, giving her friend a gentle shove. 'Come on! Race you to the bottom of the glen!'

Chapter 3

Eliza's schooldays were not particularly happy. She enjoyed playtimes with Alice and her other friends but found lessons hard work and often boring. Every day, Standard Four chanted their multiplication tables and learned new spellings, every day they recited rhymes or the names of kings or famous battles, every day they were given lists to copy down on their slates or poems to learn by heart. They sat crammed together on benches behind small wooden desks arranged in long rows, kept warm in winter by the wrought iron hot water pipes that ran along the walls and in summer by the rays of sunlight slanting through the long, high windows.

The teachers were always strict and she rarely liked them. Each year, a new one would take over her class but whoever it was always seemed to have the same harsh tone, the same stern face and rigid stance.

Although no dunce, Eliza was usually in the bottom half of the class. Two boys who sat behind her would often stop her concentrating by pulling her hair when the teacher wasn't looking, the same boys who sometimes hid behind a corner as she walked home from

26

school and jumped out at her, yelling abuse.

'Is your head ringing Eliza?' they'd call or they'd chant cruel rhymes, often poking fun at her name: *Eliza's not silver, Eliza's not gold – Eliza's a bell that's never been tolled.* After this, they would try to pull her pony tail as if it were a rope attached to the end of a huge bell.

'Stop it!' Eliza would cry. 'Stop it or I'll tell my ma.'

They ran away then, too scared to really do her any serious damage, though she would often hear the mocking chant of 'tell-tale Bell, tell-tale Bell' fading into the distance.

She never told her parents about this bullying. It didn't happen that often and she hated the thought of telling tales. When Alice was there it never happened at all, but there were odd occasions when Alice couldn't walk back with her because she had to run errands for her mother, and it was at these times that Eliza felt most vulnerable.

'I'll just have to put up with it,' she kept telling herself. After about a year, however, the boys grew tired of what they now began to see as a childish game, preferring to play football with some older lads from

Standard Five.

From the moment Eliza started school, Mr and Mrs Bell were keen for her to take full advantage of the educational opportunities that had been denied to them and were proud each time she passed the annual exam to move up to the next standard. Literacy and numeracy were important, they knew. Even more important though, was that Eliza was well prepared for marriage and motherhood so, as the years passed, she was given more and more responsibility for chores in the house.

Every day had its own allotted tasks. Monday equalled washday in Eliza's mind. She would walk home from school past endless rows of clothes flapping in the wind – shirts and petticoats, blouses and skirts, smocks and socks, white drawers and long johns – all swaying to and fro on the washing lines across the backs. She knew her mother would have been doing the washing all day so, as soon as she got in, she headed for the scullery to see what remained to be done.

The scent of soap and damp linen pervaded the air as her mother struggled to complete the final stages of her task. Usually, the coloureds and most of the whites were completed by early afternoon. It was the sheets that took the longest time, having to be boiled and pummelled and rinsed again and again. After each rinse, they were then put through the mangle to get rid of as much dirty water as possible. Eliza took her turn with this pummelling but the dolly stick was heavy and the whole process made her arms ache. She much preferred to turn the handle of the mangle and watch the bedding mysteriously wrung through its wooden rollers, the excess water dripping into the container below.

On long summer days, Eliza and her mother would hang the sheets on the line. In winter, or if it was wet, as it often was, they would drag the wooden clothes horse into position in front of the fire and drape them over it. Occasionally, if her mother had been unable to complete the ironing of the family's clothes that day, Eliza would now help her to finish this off, too. Usually, though, all she had to do was fold the completed pile of laundry and carry it back upstairs.

Other tasks came round as regular as clockwork – on Tuesdays she helped her mother with the baking, learning more about the art of kneading dough and how to make pies and puddings, scones and rock buns. She loved the smell of fresh bread and cakes that filled the kitchen from late afternoon and lingered on into the evening. On Wednesdays, she scrubbed the floor of the kitchen and scullery, a task she hated but which had to be done, nevertheless. Thursday was darning day, when she mended her father's socks or the sleeves of his jumpers, watched closely by her mother, who always wanted to check she was 'doing it right'. Then, on Fridays, she tidied and cleaned the pantry and on Saturdays ran errands for her mother to nearby Shipley market.

In this way, Mrs. Bell ensured that her daughter was fully prepared for her future life as wife and mother. By the time Eliza was twelve years old, she had a good grasp of what would be expected of her by a husband and was beginning to look forward to her transition from school to work, marking as it did, a new stage in her life, one in which she would be free from the old routines and able, for the first time, to contribute financially to the running costs of her home.

At twelve years old, many of her friends in the upper standards had already started working half time in the mill. She and Alice, however, stayed on full time at school until they were thirteen. Alice's parents, who had worried about their eldest daughter's health ever since she had almost died from an attack of measles, decided to scrimp and save in order to protect her from the rigours of mill life for an extra year. Mr and Mrs Bell, having only two children, were slightly better placed financially than the Chadwicks, and with George beginning to earn more on the farm, they felt they should give Eliza the benefit of a state education for as long as she was entitled to it. As soon as the girls reached thirteen, however, they had to leave school and begin working full time.

Eliza had always been intrigued by the grand building that towered over the village like some enormous beast. She was fascinated by its tall chimney which, like a huge nose, spewed forth clouds of thick smoke all day long; was fascinated, too, by the hustle and bustle that surrounded the place – the crowds of people that flooded through its gates morning and evening, the clatter of the busy looms and shuttles that could still be heard even outside the building in the mill yard, the constant loading and unloading of wool and mohair and alpaca, and the shipping of huge crates from the warehouses that backed onto the Leeds-Liverpool canal.

On the morning of her first day, she got up at five o'clock, trembling with a mixture of fear and excitement.

She pulled on her chemise and stays, then her white drawers and petticoats, then her black knitted stockings and old leather boots. Her mother had left her mill clothes ready for her at the end of the bed – a long dark grey worsted skirt and an old white blouse, plus a white apron that she slotted over her head and tied behind her. After putting them on, she fastened her hair up at the back as all the mill girls had to do in order to keep it out of the way of the machinery. She knew the work would be hard and tiring, the day long and exhausting but she was taking her place in the world, putting her foot on the first rung of a ladder that would lead her onward to a new and different phase in her young life.

She met Alice at the end of the road just before six and they walked together through the great iron gates, jostled by a throng of workers, all seeming to know exactly what to do and where to go next. They paused a moment before entering, overawed by the sheer size of the structure that towered above them, its dark stones now just about visible in the growing light of dawn.

Inside, the place seemed even bigger, with stone stairways leading up to its six floors and passages going off in all directions. They stopped for a moment at the end of a vast, echoing hall and gazed up at the great black looms, feeling like two tiny dwarfs in the presence of an army of giants. In the distance, a man with a long taper was going round lighting scores of now faintly glimmering gas mantles, and suddenly crowds of women were pushing past them, all carrying enamel tea and cocoa cans which they carefully arranged along the steam pipes, apparently to warm them up in preparation for the first brew of the day.

At six o'clock precisely, a loud siren sounded and the factory leapt into life. The looms and great wheels burst into rhythmic motion, the dim gas mantles became fully aglow and everything around them crashed and vibrated and clattered and banged in a demonic cacophony of sound. Despite Titus Salt's innovations to reduce it, the level of noise was still tremendous, especially when experienced for the first time. Eliza put her hands over her ears and she and Alice ran upstairs, unable to comprehend how people ever survived in such a place.

They had been told to go to the first floor where Violet, Alice's cousin, was waiting. Her instructions were to show them round, teach them how to clock on and off, then take them up to the third floor to be introduced to one of the managers.

'Don't worry,' she cried as she knocked on his office door, 'you'll soon get the hang of things round here.'

At the call of 'Enter,' they were led into a small office, its walls lined with dusty shelves. In the middle of the room stood a large desk on which were scattered a variety of files and papers. Behind it was a plump, bespectacled little man with a balding head, a thick moustache and large bulbous eyes.

'This is Mr Porterhouse,' said Violet, then promptly withdrew.

The manager sat back in his chair and eyed them intently, his lips parting in a half-smile to reveal a row of yellowing teeth. Eliza didn't like the look of him at all.

'Well now my lovelies,' he began, 'so you're today's new recruits are you?' He looked down at his notebook for a moment, checking their names. 'I see from my list that you're to be trained as burlers and menders.' He leaned forward and peered at them more closely over the rim of his glasses.

'Do you know what that means, girls?' he

enquired, scanning Eliza up and down, his eyes resting for a moment on her barely formed breasts.

Eliza had heard a little about burling and mending from conversations between her mother and the women of the village and was aware that it involved checking unfinished fabrics for faults. However, she didn't want to seem forward, so muttered, 'Not really, no,' on behalf of them both.

'We'd better show you then, hadn't we? Come along, my dears, follow me and I'll take you out to the sheds.'

He led them down various corridors and flights of stairs, turning round occasionally to pass comments on Eliza's pretty figure and thick brown hair or to say what a 'beautiful face' Alice had. Once outside, he put one hand on each of their shoulders and gave them a gentle squeeze. Eliza immediately felt uneasy, thinking such a gesture somewhat over-friendly at this early stage of their acquaintance.

'Listen to me, my dears,' he drooled, drawing them nearer, one on each side of him, 'I want you to come up and see me if you have any problems, any problems at all in your first few weeks. You know exactly where my office is now so you mustn't be afraid to come and talk to me. You needn't worry, you can trust me with all your little secrets!'

He pulled them closer still then, slipping both hands down until his arms were around their waists. His moustache twitching, he gazed from one to the other, licking his lips as if anticipating a great feast to come. Eliza shivered, desperate to recoil from his advances but not daring to move. Alice, too, remained perfectly still, terrified of doing something to kindle his anger and consequently lose them both their jobs.

They were saved by a couple of mill hands who arrived just at that moment, pushing heavy trolleys full of unfinished fabric for checking in the nearby shed. One of the two happened to be Alice's brother, Laurie, who immediately called out to her.

'Hallo there, our Alice. How are you getting on then?' He stopped for a moment and stood looking over at them, as if sensing Alice might need his help.

Taking courage from the presence of her brother, Alice spoke up.

'We're just about to start work in yonder shed, aren't we sir?' she said firmly, drawing herself up to her full height and daring to look the manager straight in the face.

Unable to proceed as he might have done had Laurie not appeared on the scene, Mr Porterhouse hesitated for a moment, then reluctantly backed off, apparently admitting defeat, at least for the time being.

'That's correct, ladies' he replied, now adopting a less familiar, more official-sounding tone. 'Come along with me and I'll introduce you to the overlooker.'

With a sigh of relief, Eliza followed him and Alice into the long wooden building in front of them. She glanced back at Laurie as she did so, knowing that she would forever owe him an enormous debt of gratitude.

The overlooker proved to be a brisk but cheerful middle-aged man. He put the new girls next to two 'old hands' who, he reassured them, would show them what to do over the next couple of weeks.

'After that, girls,' he said, 'you're on your own and any mistakes you make will have to be paid for out of your wages.'

Eliza soon learned that she had got the right idea about what the job involved. She had to examine unfinished loom-state fabric for faults or for specks of burr or vegetable matter before it was passed on to other sections to undergo a variety of finishing processes. The job involved standing for much of the day, handling long lengths of material that looked like coarse, grey sacking. Any serious faults were corrected by mending but the unwanted bits of matter had to be removed by means of the burling iron, a strange tool which resembled a giant pair of tweezers.

On her first morning, she began to learn how to spot faults and how to remove bits of waste material with the iron. This tool was awkward to use and it took her a long time to work out the best way of twisting it to pluck out the offending bits of matter. Also, the fabric was rough and difficult to manoeuvre into position, so within an hour or two she found that her fingers were stiff and sore.

Although monotonous and tiring, this work did have some advantages in that the shed was away from the noise of the looms, thereby making it less likely that the girls would go deaf in later years. Its quieter location also meant that the common practice of lip-reading was not so necessary, as it was possible to make yourself heard if you shouted. There were thus occasional opportunities for conversation with a fellow worker when the overlooker was elsewhere. During the course of the morning, Eliza spotted a number of these conversations going on but didn't dare venture to say anything to Alice, much as she ached to do so.

At one o'clock, Eliza was startled by a loud buzzer which rang out at the end of the shed.

'That's the midday-break buzzer,' said the girl next to her. 'You've got half an hour to eat your sandwiches.'

Eliza picked up the bag her mother had packed for her that morning and waited for Alice to join her outside. It was a warm day, so they ate their food in the open air, sitting on a wall behind the shed where they worked. They were both relieved to be able to sit down at last. It had seemed a long, exhausting morning. Neither of them was used to standing for hours on end.

'We're going to have to watch it with that Porterhouse chap,' said Eliza. 'Wouldn't trust him as far as I could throw him. He was sizing us up good and proper.'

'Aye, he was that,' replied her friend. 'But I shouldn't worry, Eliza. I reckon we ought to be able to keep out of his way or at least make sure there's somebody else there when he talks to us. I'll have a word with our Laurie tonight and see what he thinks.'

They chatted about their morning's work, how strange everything seemed and how very different from school.

'Do you think we're going to like it here, Alice?' asked Eliza. 'I'm worried I'm not going to manage to stand up all afternoon. And my fingers are sore already.'

'Well, I expect we'll get used to it in time,' her friend replied. 'Everyone else seems to have done.'

The afternoon passed even more slowly than the morning. The overlooker came over occasionally to see if they were getting the idea of what was required. He told them their wages would be four shillings a week to start with but would go up to seven and sixpence after about a year, when they were fully trained. They would be paid in cash every Friday.

'Remember,' he said to them at the end of the day, 'I'll be checking your work regularly, and as I said earlier, any mistakes will have to be paid for. You'll also get money docked off your wages if you're late or if I think you've been time wasting. So, think on, girls, do as you're told and keep your heads down.'

That night, Mrs Bell was waiting for Eliza when she got home. Sensing that her mother was very worried about the injuries she could incur by standing too close to the looms, Eliza told her at once that she was in the burling and mending sheds. She was delighted to see the anxious expression on her mother's face turn immediately to one of relief.

'You must be that tired, love,' Mrs Bell said, smiling now. 'I'll put the kettle on so we can have a nice cup of tea and then you can tell me all about your first day.'

The weeks soon passed and Eliza gradually began to adjust to her new life, accepting its harsh conditions and long hours. She was becoming adept at handling the burling iron and the skin on her hands and fingers, toughened now by constant contact with coarse fabric, no longer hurt her at the end of the day. Conversations with the other girls were possible at break times or when the overlooker wasn't around and she got on well with all of them. Fortunately, Mr. Porterhouse rarely visited their shed, and perhaps because he now had 'other fish to fry' as Alice put it, never bothered them again.

Every Friday, Eliza queued at the little office at the end of the sheds to pick up her wage packet, three quarters of which she gave to her parents. This contribution was proving useful to them as George was about to marry the daughter of Tom's senior farm hand and they all knew that he would need every penny of his wages to pay for the small house he hoped to rent in Baildon.

On Sunday afternoons, Eliza and Alice continued to go on walks together over the moors, more grateful now than ever before to enjoy the fresh air and freedom. Spring was their favourite time, when the woodland below the glen was covered in wild flowers. Alice preferred the yellow ones, pointing out early celandines and primroses and gasping with pleasure if they happened to see the purple and yellow pansy known as 'heart's ease'.

'There you are, Eliza,' she'd say. 'That's the flower you need to pick if you ever have a broken heart. It's supposed to make you feel better.'

Eliza laughed, trying to imagine what it must be like to need such a flower. She had always been fairly happy, or at least not miserable for long, so it was difficult to know what a broken heart would feel like. She had some idea, though, from the way her mother sometimes used to sit alone in the kitchen with tears in her eyes, obviously still grieving over Martha.

'No, Alice, I wouldn't ever pick that one. My favourites are the bluebells. They're the ones I would choose.'

'But they'd die almost as soon as you picked them,' Alice laughed. 'Not much good for a broken heart.'

'I don't care, Alice,' she retorted. 'I'd still want them, even if they only lasted for a minute.' She turned her face defiantly to her friend as she spoke, her brown eyes flashing.

Blue had always been Eliza's favourite colour. Her first hair ribbon was blue and so was her best dress, the one she always wore to church on Sunday mornings. Even the ribbons she was wearing now to tie back her flowing brown locks were a delicate shade of blue, not dissimilar to the colour of the flowers that carpeted the woods around her.

Halfway up a steep incline, as dappled sunlight

caught their faces, it became clear that these two were now no longer girls but young women, both striking in their own way. Eliza was quite short with a slim figure and a rather angular face. She had a small mouth, a slightly snub nose and high cheekbones. Her hair, now always worn tied up at the back, was an attractive shade of nut brown, which set off her fair complexion. Alice's hair was also brown but much darker and curlier, falling in ringlets onto the top of her shoulders. Her face was round, her cheeks full but not chubby and she had an attractive dimple in her chin which, together with her twinkling green eyes, added to her charm.

They walked on through the woods, occasionally catching an admiring glance from the youths who passed by. Neither had yet been out with a boy but both had already been warned by their mothers of the consequences of being too 'forward' with young men. Courtship was a ritual with strict boundaries designed to protect all concerned and should not be entered into lightly. Eliza and Alice knew the rules but were now at an age when their curiosity about the opposite sex could easily get the better of them. They often giggled together or teased each other about a particular boy at work who made eyes at them and wondered who would be the first to be asked out.

One day, about three years after they had first started working in the mill, Alice waited for the overlooker to go to the other end of the floor and then shouted across at her friend:

'Hey Eliza. How do you feel about going out with our Laurie tonight? He wants me to ask you if you'll meet him later on. I think he's taken a fancy to you.'

'What! Your Laurie wants to go out with *me*! You're having me on. He could have any girl he wanted with *his* looks.'

'He does! Honestly he does. He says would you like to meet him by the bridge at seven o'clock and go for a walk in the park.'

'I can't believe it, Alice!' Eliza said, thrilled and excited. (At this juncture, the overlooker was spotted on his way back.) 'Tell him, yes, I'll meet him at seven,' she called as quickly as she could, 'but don't make me sound too eager or he might get the wrong idea.'

Eliza had always dreamed of stepping out with someone like Laurie Chadwick, who, like his father, now worked as a warehouseman in the mill. He had grown into a handsome young man, tall and dark with a rugged face and thick black moustache. She could hardly believe he had shown an interest in her, especially as she had seen so little of him since he rescued her and Alice from the manager on that first day.

After a hasty tea, Eliza washed and changed into her best blouse and skirt. She brushed her long brown hair and stared ruefully at her reflection in the dressing-table mirror.

'If only I wasn't so plain,' she thought to herself, turning her head to one side. Her nose seemed to her small and ugly, her cheeks far too bony and her mouth, instead of being curved and beautifully rounded, a mere slit, not dissimilar to the sort into which you inserted a coin in the penny arcade. She had never particularly worried about her looks before but now they suddenly seemed all-important. A few minutes later, realising there was no time for further adjustments to face or hair, she hurried downstairs and out into the street, anxious not to be late.

'Bye ma,' she yelled as she closed the door behind her.

'Good luck, my lass,' her mother called after her, pleased that a boy had asked her out at last and delighted that it was someone she both knew and trusted.

Laurie met her, as promised, on the stroke of seven, and they walked together along the far bank of the river Aire, enjoying the last of the setting September sun. The trees had already begun to change colour and the sun's rays filtered through leaves of amber and russet red, creating delicate moving patterns and lending them a beauty Eliza had never noticed before.

They talked for hours, getting to know each other, feeling hesitantly for all the things they might have in common. The longer they talked, the more they grew to like each other. Eliza loved the sound of his hearty laugh and his sense of fun; Laurie, in turn, admired Eliza's optimism and zest for life. He walked her home at ten o'clock, and as they strolled down Albert Road, they both fell silent, each listening to the rhythmic click and tap of the other's shoes across the cobbles, each knowing instinctively that they were on the brink of something new and exciting.

On the doorstep of her house, Eliza turned her face up towards him so that he could see her eyes shining in the flickering gaslight.

'Why do you like me, Laurie?' she said. 'I'm not beautiful, like some of the others you've been out with.'

'Maybe not. But you're damned pretty and you've got a spark in them brown eyes o' yours and a fire in your spirit. I like that. I want a girl that'll help me move up in life, move on. I've got dreams, ambitions. I don't want to stay round here till I'm old and grey and bitter. I don't want to look back and think that all I've done is slave away to end up deaf in yonder mill. I want to find a job with prospects and make a bit of money and travel. There's a whole world waiting out there Eliza, and I want to see it all.'

'So do I, oh so do I!' she cried. 'Take me with you, Laurie. Promise me you'll take me with you wherever you go!'

'Steady on lass!' he laughed. 'We've hardly been going out two minutes!'

He grinned then, and kissing her gently on the cheek, bid her goodnight.

They saw each other almost every day after that. On Saturday afternoons, they would go to the animated picture shows at the Prince's Hall Theatre in Shipley.

There was a matinee every week and Eliza loved the short picture-plays and the wonderful moving pictures of important news events. Two years before, she had been there with Alice to see a newsreel of the coronation of King George V. It seemed amazing that the whole scene could be relived like this, could unfold before their eyes as if they were really there. Only a year later, they had been astounded by another newsreel, this time of the Titanic in harbour followed by shots of relatives and survivors after the sinking. Such news items usually prefaced the main item and Eliza wondered what today's news item might be.

Laurie had been attracted to the film they were paying tuppence to see, not just because it was a thriller, but because he thought the two ladies on the poster outside were incredibly beautiful. *An Unseen Enemy*, the poster read, introducing Dorothy and Lillian Gish.

They settled themselves in the pit stalls and waited for the pianist to take his seat. Soon afterwards, the programme began with a news item entitled *Epsom Derby 1913*. As soon as she saw the title, Eliza knew what was to come. The papers had been full of the story of Emily Davison, the suffragette who had thrown herself in

49

front of a galloping horse and had died four days later. At the critical moment, Eliza averted her gaze, unable to bear the sight of another woman's violent end. Laurie squeezed her hand when it was safe to look again and then kept hold of it for the rest of the show. Another newsreel followed, *The Funeral of the Woman Who Dared,* showing Emily Davison's coffin carried through the streets of London, accompanied by six thousand women, most of them suffragettes who had come out with banners in support of Emily and her sacrifice.

Finally, it was time for the short thriller. Dorothy and Lillian Gish proved to be even more beautiful than the poster had indicated and Eliza could see that they had entirely captured Laurie's heart. He stirred in his seat when a gun was pointed at their heads, as if he were about to leap onto the stage and come to their rescue.

Eliza teased him about this as, with crowds of others, they descended the steps into the grey dusk of an October evening.

'By hell, I thought you were going to put a stop to the show for a minute there. I hope you'll do as much for me if a robber ever points his gun in my direction.'

'I shouldn't think I'll need to,' he laughed. 'We'll

never be like Americans over here.'

As they walked back home, they talked about the newsreel and how life was changing. People were beginning to assert their rights far more – the suffragettes, the striking miners and seamen and transport workers – all were causing the government a lot of problems. New inventions were transforming the world. They had only to look in the streets around them to be aware of enormous differences. Motor cars were now increasingly seen and the patient clopping horses with their carriages were beginning to be pushed ignominiously into the side streets, the main thoroughfares becoming the domain of the new and exciting electric trams.

On Saturday nights, Eliza and Laurie would often take such a tram to the Rolarena in Manningham Lane, where roller-skating was enjoying a resurgence in popularity. The enormous building could accommodate two thousand skaters at a time, its Maplewood floor being half the size of a football pitch. This was *the* place to go and meet others and the rink was full of young men showing off their skating skills in the hope of impressing a particular girl. Laurie would help Eliza onto the floor, and to the blare of music from a brass band and the joyous screams of fellow skaters, they would race around the huge arena, Laurie holding on to her hand and shouting, 'Come on, Eliza, faster, faster.'

The sheer thrill of moving at such speed with Laurie's arm around her waist and a blur of other bodies whizzing past was something Eliza would never forget. Laurie was a wonderful skater, so beautifully balanced and sure of himself. He was never afraid of falling over and never did so.

'That's it Eliza,' he called one evening as they performed an elaborate turn in the middle of the rink, 'you just hang on to me.' She gripped him tighter, reassured by his confidence and amazed at her new skill as they began to waltz around, weaving their way through the other skaters and occasional prostrate beginners. As they slowed and came to an abrupt stop, their bodies slamming against the hand rail, Laurie threw his head back and laughed. It was the same infectious laugh Eliza remembered he used to have as a child, only now it was deeper of course and much more appealing.

When the time came for them to leave, Eliza had difficulty keeping her balance amongst the jostling crowds on the way up the ramp to the exit. Seeing this, Laurie moved up close behind her, and folding her gently in his arms, shielded her with his body. She loved the sensation of his strong arms around her and secretly wished they could stay like this forever.

'Are you really as strong as you seem, Laurie?' Eliza asked, half teasing, after he had escorted her off the rink and they were walking hand in hand to the tram stop.

'I am that!' he grinned. 'You've got to be strong if you're a warehouseman. I'm plenty strong enough to protect you from any of the lads round here. Any more trouble with a chap like that manager and you've only got to say the word – I'll knock him for six!'

They laughed together and Eliza thought how lucky she was to have someone like him by her side.

Mr and Mrs Bell couldn't help noticing how animated and happy Eliza had been since Laurie had started inviting her out. They liked and respected Laurie, whom they had known since he was a boy, and both dearly hoped that a wedding might be in the offing. However, they said nothing of their hopes to Eliza, not wanting her to rush things.

'She's a sensible lass,' said Mr Bell to his wife one Saturday night, puffing on his favourite pipe. 'I don't think she'll be too hasty. She'll want to be sure before she decides.'

'I know, I know. But she can be impulsive and headstrong sometimes and so can he, I reckon. They're full of life, the pair of them and well matched, I don't doubt, but you can't help worrying.'

'Nay lass, you can't put old heads on young shoulders. We'll just have to sit tight and let things be. I'm sure everything will work out all right. You were worried about her injuring herself when she went into the mill at thirteen but she came to no harm.'

At this, Mrs Bell remained silent and went on with her knitting. She remembered the arguments they'd had before Eliza left school. Her husband had felt they should take the risk and let their daughter go straight into factory work, whereas Mrs Bell was worried by the number of often fatal accidents suffered by children working long hours amongst dangerous machinery. Her neighbour Mrs Pollard had told her how one of her daughters was in service with a rich family in Ilkley and might be able to get Eliza a place there when she left school.

Knowing this would be much safer than the mill, Mrs Bell had begged her husband to think about the idea. But Mr Bell wouldn't hear of it, not wanting Eliza to leave the family home until she was married. She came from mill stock and ought to go into the mill, he argued, especially as her brother George hadn't carried on the tradition set by generations of their family. Naturally, Mr Bell had the final word but his wife had never forgotten the anguish his decision had caused her.

Their silence was broken by Eliza's return from a visit to the Rolarena with Laurie.

'What are you two doing then?' she called, taking off her bonnet. 'Shall I put the kettle on?'

'Aye, that'd be grand love,' her father said, smiling proudly. 'Have you had a good night?'

'Champion, pa, champion.'

'And how was Laurie?' her mother asked, deciding it was time to break her silence. 'I expect he was the handsomest man on the rink.'

Her wry smile was not lost on Eliza, who merely shook her head by way of admonishment and went to put the kettle on the stove.

That autumn, Eliza and her parents attended George's wedding in the little village church not far from Tom's farm. They all liked his new bride and Eliza was pleased to see how happy her mother was on the day. After tea and cakes in the church hall, Eliza saw her mother sidle up to George and whisper something in his ear. He looked at her and laughed, then nodded energetically. Later, Eliza couldn't resist tackling him about it:

'What on earth did ma say to you to make you laugh so much?'

'It's a secret,' grinned George and turned as if to go, but Eliza knew he was teasing and persisted.

'Come on, George,' she cried, ruffling his hair in the way she used to do as a child. 'You've got to tell me. You know you can't keep secrets. You never could.'

'All right, all right. But if I do tell you, you'll have to promise me you won't breathe a word to our ma.'

'I promise,' she said, placing her hand jokingly on her heart.

'Well,' her brother began, then paused a moment, dragging the whole process out as long as he could to annoy her even more. 'Well... ma said how her and pa hoped we'd all be going to *your* wedding soon.'

'She never did!' cried Eliza.

'She did and all, our Eliza, and I must say I couldn't agree with her more.'

They laughed together then and hugged each other warmly, delighted to think that, in the same year, they had each found someone they loved.

Secure in the knowledge that she had her parents' blessing, Eliza continued to meet Laurie on a regular basis. Their stepping out soon passed into courtship and they were often seen walking the streets arm in arm, their faces glowing with happiness.

One Saturday evening, on the way back from the picture house, Laurie asked Eliza to meet him the following morning at the Titus Salt statue in Victoria Park.

'You've got to be there by seven o'clock,' he urged.

When she pressed him as to why he wanted her there so early, he wouldn't say anything except that it was a secret and she mustn't tell anyone about it.

Next morning, Eliza was up and dressed at half past six. She slipped quietly out of the house, anxious not to wake her parents and made her way down Victoria Road to the park. Her heart was beating with excitement and she was smiling to herself, wondering what on earth Laurie had in store for her. As soon as she crossed the bridge over the river, she could see him in the distance, waving frantically and beckoning her towards him. She ran straight up to him and they kissed.

'What's all this then?' she said. 'What's the big secret?'

'Ask Sir Titus,' said Laurie, grinning. 'He's got a letter for you.'

He pointed to the statue of Titus Salt. The figure of the great man stood on a huge stone plinth, on each side of which were sculptures of different animals whose wool he had imported for use in the mill. Eliza circled the base of the statue and soon saw that an envelope had been wedged between the ears of the Angora goat. She giggled as she pulled it out and ripped it open. Inside was a small piece of chocolate in fancy paper and a note with a rhyme written on it:

If you think that this is sweet,
Go and look beneath a seat.

'It's a treasure hunt!' cried Eliza excitedly, running

in the direction of the nearest park bench.

Laurie chased after her, not wanting to miss the expression on her face when she made her second discovery.

'It's another one Laurie!' she shouted, scrabbling beneath the seat in order to pick up the second inviting-looking envelope. This one contained two red heart-shaped sweets and another rhyme, with a drawing of two hearts above it:

> *Could these beat as one forever?*
> *Look beside the flowing river.*

Intrigued by where all this was leading, Eliza turned around only to find that Laurie was running away in the distance, heading towards the boat sheds. 'Come on Eliza!' he was calling. 'See if you can find me.'

Clutching the two envelopes to her breast with one hand, Eliza lifted up her skirts with the other and raced across the grass in search of Laurie. She could hear him laughing somewhere behind the boat sheds but couldn't see him.

By now the sun was up, its light flickering across the trees along the riverbank. Suddenly, Eliza caught sight of a white shirt-sleeve sticking out from behind the slender trunk of a silver birch. 'There you are!' she cried, running up to him. 'Found you at last, Laurie Chadwick!'

He chuckled and pointed to another envelope lying near them on the riverbank. 'I wonder what that is,' he said quietly, his voice betraying the excitement bubbling within him.

Eliza pounced on the envelope at once and tore it open as fast as she could. Inside was a neatly folded sheet of writing paper. Her hands shaking with anticipation, Eliza unfolded it slowly. It contained a question in Laurie's handwriting:

Will you marry me?

'Yes! Oh yes!' laughed an overjoyed Eliza.

Laurie took her in his arms and waltzed her all around the boat shed. Then he kissed her again and again, and taking both her hands in his, looked at her solemnly for a moment, his eyes filled with pride and admiration.

'I love you, Eliza Bell,' he cried. 'I'm going to make you so happy – so, so happy for the rest of your life!'

They walked back hand in hand through the park, both of them feeling they were floating on air. Every blade of grass, still wet with dew, glistened like a diamond in the early morning light, and the vivid, varied greens of late spring trembled around them. Eliza felt as if she were seeing the world through new eyes, as if a veil had been suddenly lifted to disclose the quivering beauty of the earth, the sparkle present in each new day.

They wanted to stay longer but feared they would be late for the morning service. Eliza raced back into her house to change her shoes and soon rejoined Laurie on the steps of Saltaire Church, her face flushed with pleasure, her eyes still shining with love.

That afternoon, Eliza and Laurie broke the news of their engagement to their respective families. Everyone was delighted, especially Alice, who was ecstatic about having Eliza as a sister-in-law.

The wedding was planned for early the following year, but in August, war intervened. Posters appeared on every hoarding and wall-end urging young men to enlist, recruiting meetings were held in every public meeting place and the air rang with the sound of military bands, their drums and bugles designed to stir the blood.

Laurie soon found himself drawn by the surging tide of patriotism that was gripping the country. Bored with his life in the mill, he began to view the war as an adventure, a way to escape from humdrum routines and make a name for himself, to show off his strength and courage and give himself the chance of a new job with prospects when he returned.

One evening, therefore, without telling Eliza, he boarded the tram into Bradford to attend a recruiting meeting in the Town Hall. Edging his way through crowds of young men, he found himself a space near the edge of the platform on which were gathered councillors, mill owners and clergymen. Their speeches went on for some while, each more fervent than the last until finally the Mayoress, the only female speaker, raised the roof with an impassioned plea:

'I can assure the lads left behind tonight that they will get nothing like the welcome, when the struggle is over, that will be given by the girls to those who *have* been to war. When I see an able-bodied, well-built young man walking about the streets enjoying himself, I am ashamed of him.'

This struck home with many of them, including Laurie. No longer able to resist the drama of the call to arms which had been tempting him for weeks now, he made up his mind to serve. He signed up with the King's

Own Yorkshire Regiment and the recruiting officer told him to report for duty in the Town Hall Square the following day.

As he left the building, Laurie's heart was beating fast. The thrill of going to war pulled him like a strong magnet and he couldn't hold back his excitement at the thought of boarding a train to London and a ship that would take him off to a foreign land and unspeakable adventures. The only downside was leaving Eliza.

He had told her earlier that he was going to visit an old friend in Bradford that night and would be back on the nine o'clock tram. She would be there, he knew, waiting for him at the tram station in Shipley, expecting everything to carry on as normal. As the tram slowed and eased to a halt, he saw her in the distance and found himself waving to her nervously through the window.

As soon as he got off, she realised something was amiss. He didn't run towards her or throw his arms around her in the usual way but held back, shifting awkwardly from side to side and not looking her in the eye.

'What's up Laurie?' she asked, alarmed now.

He thought it best not to beat about the bush but

come straight out with it. He began slowly, but then blurted out the news as quickly as he could: 'Look, Eliza, I haven't been where I said I was going tonight. I've been to a recruiting meeting in the Town Hall. You can probably guess the rest.'

He heard a little gasp from Eliza, then watched her thin mouth tighten.

'Tell me you haven't, Laurie, tell me you haven't joined up.'

'I can't do that, Eliza. Don't you see, I've got no choice. I'm young and strong and the country needs lads like me. You don't want me to be thought a coward now, do you?'

Eliza was silent. She understood the force of his argument but was trying to suppress the rising fear that caught at her throat and made her mouth feel dry.

'I'm not leaving you for that long, you know,' he said, trying desperately to reassure her and warming now to his vision of a perfect future. 'When I come back we'll get married in yonder church just like we planned. You'll have the best wedding dress money can buy and you'll look a proper picture, I know you will. And I'll wear my uniform with my cap at an angle and I'll have a row of medals across my chest. Everything will be different when we've won this war, you'll see. It'll soon be over and the whole world will be different. I'll get a good job and we'll be able to afford a place of our own and have meals in restaurants like posh folk do, and just think Eliza, we'll be able to go on the kind of holidays you've never even dreamed of!'

He took her in his arms at last and kissed her gently on the forehead. 'I'll make you so proud of me, Eliza. Prouder than you've ever been before.'

The next day, Eliza found herself in the midst of crowds of other women watching the large batch of new recruits muster in Town Hall Square. They had all been given an armband inscribed 'Kitchener's Man' and Eliza saw that Laurie had got one of the blankets donated by a patriotic ladies' committee. He winked at her as he rolled it and tied it 'en banderole' as he had seen the regular soldiers do. Well-wishers passed among them, handing out gifts or sprigs of lucky heather while a few smartly dressed ladies and gentlemen gave out tobacco and chocolate, which the young recruits stowed sheepishly into their pockets.

Recruiting officers soon chivvied the men into

rows and marched them off to Bradford station to board a train. Eliza followed and stood on the packed platform, trying desperately to catch a glimpse of Laurie as he was herded into a carriage. She spotted him suddenly, not far from her, his nose pressed tightly against a window.

'Laurie, Laurie!' she cried above the screams and farewells of others, and realising he had spotted her too, blew him a kiss. Then she waved him off, waved and waved as the train slowly heaved itself out of sight. As his carriage reached the end of the platform, Laurie managed to lean out of the window and shout to her above the hiss of the steam and the frantic cries of goodbye.

'Don't forget, Eliza,' he bellowed through the gathering clouds of smoke, 'when I come back, make sure you're waiting!'

Except, of course, he didn't come back. The telegram boy trudged solemnly down a snow-covered Albert Road almost sixteen months later, and Alice opened the door to him, in tears.

Chapter 4

In the weeks and months after Laurie's death, Eliza withdrew into a world of her own, unable to come to terms with what had happened. Occasionally, she spoke of him to Alice and the two of them wept quietly together but generally she suffered in silence, forcing herself to go through the motions of life. She continued to work in the mill, continued helping her mother at home and sometimes went on walks with Alice but nothing was quite the same without Laurie and almost everywhere she went reminded her of when they were together. Theirs would have been the perfect match, she knew. Never again could she feel as deeply, never again could she find the kind of love she had known with him.

She found the well-meant platitudes of friends ('you'll meet someone else before long, don't worry') and her mother's constant refrain of 'time's a great healer' incredibly painful. Such comments grated and left her feeling more alone, more abandoned than ever. She even began to consider the prospect of never marrying, of being on her own for the rest of her life. There was an old maid in the village who seemed perfectly happy and she wondered if this might now be her destiny, too.

The war dragged on and the telegram boy who had visited Alice soon became a regular visitor to the tiny streets around the mill. Whenever he appeared at the end of their road, women and children would scuttle inside and peer round dingy curtains, dreading his approach, each feeling tremendous relief, quickly followed by guilt, when he knocked on some other family's door.

Over five thousand men from the Bradford area were killed during the conflict and thousands of others wounded. Eliza's brother George was one of the lucky ones. Farm workers, like miners and dockers and others in certain skilled occupations, were exempt from military service. He had to be careful, though, when visiting public places. Once, a group of women pinned a white feather to his chest and accused him of being a coward for not fighting for his country. The accusation stung George deeply. 'I tried to enlist,' he called after the jeering women, 'but they turned me down 'cos I'm a farmer!' This didn't put a stop to their taunts, however. Clearly, they didn't believe him.

Although work in the mill continued, once compulsory male conscription was introduced in 1916, its male workforce was almost halved and more women were drafted in to fill the gaps. Never again did textile production scale the dizzy heights of the immediate pre-war period. Salt's mill, like so many other mills in northern towns, had already had its heyday.

The war made no significant difference to the working lives of Eliza and Alice. They still toiled in the burling and mending sheds all day. However, with the increased need for female labour, the lives of their friends and of many women around them changed dramatically. Alice's younger sisters Nellie and Marian both got jobs driving a tram, while many of their neighbours' girls went to work in one of the munitions factories at Low Mills. They were known as 'canaries' because their hands and faces often turned yellow through handling TNT all day.

It was mostly in the evenings, when she returned home after work, or on Saturday afternoon or Sunday when she was free, that Eliza noticed the biggest changes to her world. The whole mood of the village was subdued, sombre, and it seemed strange to have so few young men around. The nights passed slowly, and though there were occasional sing-songs round the piano, it was hard to enjoy yourself when so many were bereaved or worried about husbands and sons.

As the war progressed, facts grew more difficult to assess. People listened to gossip and rumour of what was happening at the front and shuffled the pages of newspapers in vain to try to get at the truth. On odd occasions, George heard noises and saw lights in the sky at night and Eliza's father feared they might be German zeppelins. Many had heard whispers of food riots in distant towns but the papers never mentioned them.

Food was fast becoming an obsession. Eliza and her mother queued for hours to get the most basic of provisions and the Tuesday baking session was limited to barley scones and a date pudding that Mrs Bell had discovered how to make without flour or sugar. All the rose beds in the public parks were replaced by vegetable patches and part of a nearby golf course was given over to the growing of oats. Accompanied by lots of red tape and an assortment of margarine cards, sugar tickets and meat cards, rationing was finally introduced but still the queues formed and the local shopkeepers became more and more harassed.

Just as the war was coming to an end, a new enemy had to be faced – influenza. The autumn of 1918 saw an epidemic of this disease throughout the world. It was particularly bad in England, where weakened by years of war and hardship, the people were susceptible to complications.

Eliza's parents were already growing old, both of them in their mid-fifties, and in early October her mother fell ill. The virulent strain of flu quickly took hold, soon turning to pneumonia. The doctor came every day for a week, and at first, was hopeful she might recover, but as the days passed and she grew worse, his initial optimism faded.

Mrs Bell lay alone upstairs in the big double bed while her husband slept downstairs in the living room so as not to disturb her during the night. Eliza took a week off work to look after her and she and her father kept a warm fire burning constantly in the bedroom fireplace. When Eliza went to the local shops for groceries, their neighbour Mrs Pollard came round to sit with her mother. She was a kindly soul, who had known Mrs Bell since they were little girls. Seating herself on a chair by the bed, she would talk to her about the old times and try to comfort her.

After five days, it was clear to everyone that Mrs

Bell was slowly becoming weaker. On the Friday night, George came over to spend the weekend. He ran upstairs to see his mother as soon as he got in, but, by now, she was slipping in and out of consciousness and barely acknowledged his presence. He spent half an hour at her bedside, then came downstairs again and stood in the hallway, looking lost and bewildered.

'Is she going to die our Eliza?' he asked.

'I think she is, George,' Eliza responded. 'The doctor's tried everything he can but she hasn't got any better.'

They went together into the sitting room, where their father was bending down to stoke the fire. As soon as he heard them come in, he straightened up and turned round. 'Hallo, my lad,' he cried, giving his son a hug. Eliza caught his eye as he did so and suspected he had been crying.

At three o'clock that morning, Mrs Bell passed away, with her husband, son and daughter by her side. Soon afterwards, the doctor arrived to issue the death certificate and Eliza then washed her and laid her out. The undertaker removed her body later that day and a short service took place the following Wednesday in the

Saltaire church she had attended all her life. She was buried in Nab Wood cemetery, a short distance from her home.

The week after the funeral, at her father's request, Eliza sorted through her mother's clothes and belongings. In the bottom drawer of her dressing table, she found two envelopes, one addressed to George and one to her. She later discovered that George's contained a pair of silver cuff-links that had belonged to his maternal grandfather. Her own envelope had inside it a large silver hatpin and brooch, together with a neatly folded letter in her mother's faltering handwriting, dated a year before her death:

Dear Eliza,

When you read this I shan't be here no longer but you mustn't cry, or not for long anyway. You have been a very good daughter and I pray that, in the future, your children will be as good to you as you have been to me.

I'm leaving you this hatpin and brooch. They belonged to my mother. You never met her but she had a very happy life, like me. I want you to wear them, not shut them away in a drawer. I hope they will always bring you good luck and that one day you will pass them on to a daughter of your own.

I know you will take care of your pa and George when I am gone.

Your loving ma.

On the eleventh of November 1918, Armistice was declared and the long war was over. The following Sunday evening, Alice came round to see Eliza, brimming over with excitement.

'Eliza, Eliza,' she spluttered, 'Jack has just asked me to marry him, and believe it or not I've said *yes*!'

'You never have Alice!' chuckled Eliza, 'Not after all you've said about men!'

'I know,' Alice replied. 'It caps everything, doesn't it?'

Eliza had known about Jack Halliwell for the best part of a year. He was the nephew of Mary Ellen Emmett, Alice's next-door neighbour, whose husband had been killed in the third year of the war. Since then, Jack had visited his widowed aunt most weekends to help with any heavy work in the house and to check if she needed anything. Alice had started talking to him one Saturday morning when he was putting a new lock on the front door and things had gone on from there.

Although of conscription age, Jack had been declared medically unfit to serve in the war on account of the fact that two fingers on his right hand were missing. At the age of thirteen, he had started work with Stephenson Brothers, a large soap manufacturer off Manningham Lane, but within a week, had caught his hand in the blades of the huge machine that sliced the hardened soap into long bars. He still worked at the factory, on the packing and delivery section, where he had recently been promoted to foreman.

Jack could not be described as in any way handsome. He was very short, with dark curly hair and a tiny moustache and he had a strange sort of waddling walk that amused Eliza. He usually wore his flat cap pulled down over one eye, so you only got a proper look at his face when he tossed his head back to laugh. Eliza liked him, though, because he was kind and funny.

'I'm that pleased for you, Alice, I am that,' continued Eliza. 'You've got a damn good 'un there, even if he does look a bit like Charlie Chaplin!'

The wedding was planned for early in the new year and Eliza was to be the only bridesmaid. On old year's night, Alice had a party for all her friends to celebrate her forthcoming marriage and also the end of the war. Jack knocked on the door at midnight with a piece of coal in his hand for good luck and all the girls kissed him as soon as he stepped over the threshold. Eliza's father played the piano and they danced and sang all the war songs that had become so popular. Alice sang a solo, *Keep The Home Fires Burning*, and everyone joined in at the end:

> *There's a silver lining*
> *Through the dark clouds shining*
> *Turn the dark clouds inside out*
> *Till the boys come home.*

At about one o'clock, Eliza and her father left to go back to the empty house. They walked steadily down the street, the steam from their warm breath rising up towards a clear night sky crammed with stars. They didn't say anything, but each knew what the other was thinking. It was their first new year alone together, their first harsh reminder that parties, however jolly, would never be the same again.

'I'll bring you a hot drink up to bed, pa,' she called after him as he climbed the stairs.

Eliza put the kettle on the stove and went into the sitting-room to wait for it to boil. The room was still full of all the things she had known since childhood – her father's piano in the far corner, the large oval gateleg table that took up so much space in the middle of the room, her parents' wooden armchairs on either side of the fireplace, and on the mantelpiece, a large brass key next to the black marble clock that, according to her mother, always wanted winding. She went to the front window and slowly drew the curtains, closing them on four long years of war and suffering and turmoil.

She thought of Laurie on the train and of all the other young men on countless other trains frantically waving farewell with the light of excitement flickering in their eyes, young men whose lives had been snuffed out in some terrible place she couldn't begin to imagine, and didn't dare let her thoughts dwell on, but which, in her mind's eye, she always saw as a muddy windswept field where no birds sang.

Chapter 5

Alice's wedding took place on Valentine's Day, 1919. That morning, Eliza donned her new dark blue dress and navy hat. For the first time, she fixed her hat in place with the silver hatpin given her by her mother and pinned its matching brooch onto the lapel of her winter coat.

'Happen it'll bring Alice a bit o' luck,' she thought to herself, standing in front of the long mirror in her dressing table. She adjusted her coat, then stared at herself. Her reflection stared back, revealing an older, more sober-looking Eliza, the fire in her eyes less passionate now and tempered by a certain sadness.

There had been a light snowfall during the night, so all the guests were waiting outside the church in heavy overcoats and gloves. The service went smoothly and everyone gathered in the nearby hall that had been hired for the reception. Alice's father made an amusing speech but Jack, looking ill at ease, struggled to get to the end of his. He thought he'd learned it off by heart. However, in front of such a crowd of people, he got nervous and kept forgetting what came next, so there were one or two embarrassing pauses. The more he panicked, the less he could remember. In the end he got through it, though, and all the guests gave him a sympathetic round of applause.

'I hope tha' does better than that tonight Jack,' called out one of his friends and everyone laughed.

Jack's workmates tossed confetti over the happy couple as they descended the steps of the hall. Then, before the pair boarded the train back to Bradford, Alice threw her bouquet to Eliza and the two friends kissed each other farewell.

Alice was planning to live with Jack and his mother in the centre of Bradford till they could save up enough money to rent a place of their own but she and Eliza had agreed before the wedding that they would meet each other once a month and go shopping together, both determined that marriage and a distance of a few miles would not destroy a friendship cemented over so many years.

'It's not goodbye really,' said Alice, fighting back the tears. 'I'm not going that far away and we're going to keep in touch.'

'Aye, that's true,' smiled Eliza. 'Write to me soon,

Alice, and let me know how you're getting on.'

Another year passed and Eliza got into the habit of going into Bradford shopping every Saturday afternoon. Sometimes she would meet Alice, whose marriage was turning out to be a very happy one. Often, she would just wander round the shops. Her favourite was Brown Muff and Co Ltd, the large department store known by locals as 'Brown and Muff's'. She never felt very comfortable looking round because everything was such high class and usually way beyond her price range. Nevertheless, she sometimes forced herself to walk through the great swing doors and down the aisle to take the lift to the second floor.

'Ladies' dresses, coats and evening wear,' the uniformed lift boy would cry, sliding open the heavy metal gates with grilles. Cautiously, Eliza would emerge and creep along each aisle, marvelling at the exquisitely cut dresses and gowns and praying that none of the formidable-looking shop assistants would ask if they could help her.

She would always arrive in Bradford at about a quarter past two, having caught the two o'clock train from Shipley, the small town about half a mile walk from her home, where she used to go to the pictures with Laurie. There was a market there every Saturday and she loved to hunt round for cheap sewing materials or silk ribbons for her hair. At precisely five minutes to two, she would leave the market and stand at the end of the platform on Shipley station, listening for a distant chugging sound, or craning her neck to see the first faint puff of steam on the horizon.

After a while, she began to notice that many of the same people regularly inhabited the platform with her. There was always the woman in the headscarf who loved to fiddle with the metal clasp on her handbag, the old man in the drab raincoat and worn shoes who looked as if he didn't have two halfpennies to rub together and the middle-aged gent with a briefcase who had the air of someone going somewhere very important. And then there was the shy, awkward young man hunched on the bench with his head in a book. She gazed across at him. He seemed gentle, sensitive.

Realising he was being stared at by a young woman, the man put his book down beside him and somewhat self-consciously removed a packet of Player's cigarettes from his inside pocket. While he was lighting one, Eliza glanced down at the book. It was called *David Copperfield*.

'What a thick book!' she thought to herself. 'I'm damn sure I could never read a book as long as that!'

One Saturday in early September, the young man sat opposite her on the train. It was raining and they were the only ones in the carriage together. She was curious to know where he was going to or from every week, so she plucked up the courage to speak to him.

'What a terrible day!' she ventured.

'Aye, aye it is that,' he stammered back, hardly daring to raise his eyes.

'I've noticed how you and me travel into Bradford every Saturday so I hope you don't mind me introducing myself.' She hesitated a moment, then added, 'My name's Eliza.'

'Mine's Arthur,' he said. 'Arthur Pendlestone. Pleased to meet you Eliza.'

From then on, they sat together every Saturday and Arthur began to talk to her more and more. She discovered he had only recently recovered from a leg wound and from shell shock. He had spent three years in St Luke's, which at that time was a war hospital specially designated to take care of soldiers from the Bradford district wounded in battle. The medical staff there had performed numerous operations and had helped his shattered leg to heal but both he and they knew well enough that the mental scars would take longer. While in hospital, he told her, he had passed the time by reading Dickens and she was amazed to hear that he had read every single one of Dickens' books. His favourite was *David Copperfield*, which he had read three times.

Eliza found their conversations fascinating. He was so different from her and from Laurie, much quieter with a strange kind of detachment from the world. Where she would rush in and speak her mind, he would hold back, and he never seemed to lose his temper, not even when he accidentally ripped his coat on the door of the train one day. She would have sworn and been angry, but he just frowned for a moment and sat down as if nothing had happened.

Over time, she learned that, when he boarded the train with her in Shipley, he was actually on his way back to Bradford from Burley in Wharfedale, where his mother had been in a mental institution for several months. In fact, his mother was his only living relative and had struggled to bring him up alone after his father had left them when Arthur was only two years old. It was only right, therefore, that Arthur should continue to see her regularly now, even though she no longer remembered his name when he visited and apparently spent most of her time staring vacantly out of the window.

Eliza gathered that Arthur had lived in Bradford all his life, apart from his time in the army. His mother rented a tiny back-to-back house near the centre of the city, in which he now lived alone. It appeared that, when he left the army, he studied at night school and passed some exams, which helped him to get his present job as a junior clerk in the corporation offices. He earned a reasonable wage there, but didn't seem to her to be at all ambitious or interested in promotion.

'It's as if the war has knocked all the stuffing out of him,' Eliza thought, and she wondered how he coped, living on his own.

One Saturday at the end of October, he invited her to have tea with him in Brown and Muff's restaurant. Her reaction was one of terror mixed with extreme pleasure. She was scared that she might show him up in such a high-class place but was also secretly delighted that he thought enough of her to invite her out for an expensive treat like this.

Brown and Muff's lift boy looked her up and down quizzically as she got out on the top floor and Arthur ushered her to a seat near the restaurant's large window, from which they could see right across the city. Waitresses fussed around them in their black dresses with white aprons and white frilly caps. One of them brought a menu to their table, then hovered in the background, waiting for them to make up their minds what to have. Like Eliza, Arthur seemed somewhat out of place in this grand setting but he overcame his nerves and ordered tea for two.

'I don't rightly know how to say this, Eliza,' he spluttered as he poured out a second cup of tea, 'but how do you feel about going out with me, on a date, like? I've got two tickets for Vesta Tilley at the Alhambra on the nineteenth of November. It's her final tour before she retires.'

Eliza thought he'd never ask her out on a date, but now he had, she was happy. She felt he needed someone with her drive, someone to stand up for him and push him onward and upward. She wasn't in love with him in the way she had been with Laurie, but the war had taught her that love wasn't just about passion, it was about putting others first, about counting your blessings and getting on with things.

'Oh, Arthur,' she sighed, 'I'd like nowt better!'

The Alhambra, Bradford's main theatre, was built in 1913 in the Moorish style, with a lavish, richly-carpeted interior. Lighting was partly gas, partly electricity and the theatre was snug, even in winter, thanks to the latest electric heating system and specially designed hot water pipes. The stage was clearly visible even from the seats high up in the balcony which, at ninepence, were the only ones Arthur could afford.

On the evening of the performance, Eliza brushed and brushed her long brown hair before tying it up at the back with a blue silk ribbon. She put on her best white blouse with the lace collar and her best grey skirt, selected a small hat which would not block the view of anyone sitting behind her, then went downstairs to wait for Arthur to collect her at six o'clock.

'Do I look all right, pa?' she asked, donning her shawl.

'You look lovely, lass,' he replied. 'just like your

mother did before we got wed.'

It was the first time Eliza had ever been to a theatre, so she was understandably filled with excitement. Vesta Tilley was one of the greatest entertainers of her day and Eliza loved all of her songs, many of which her father used to play on the piano.

'I do hope she sings *After The Ball,* pa,' she said as she hurried out with Arthur. 'It was ma's favourite.'

'I expect she will, love,' he called after her. 'Don't forget to give her a wave from me.'

They arrived at the theatre just after seven and Arthur showed his tickets to the doorman. A friendly usherette directed them up several flights of stairs to the balcony. The place was already buzzing with anticipation and Eliza sensed a magic in the air.

At exactly half past seven, the band struck up, and a few minutes later the red and gold plush curtain rose, transporting Eliza to a world of bright lights, gaiety and music that she was to remember for the rest of her life.

There were a variety of acts, including tumblers, comedians and the famous Sunbeams, a children's dancing troupe that were destined to enchant Bradford theatregoers for many years to come. Vesta Tilley, as top of the bill, came on just before the interval and again at the end of the show, taking the stage for a good half hour each time, firstly in top hat and tails and later in her famous soldier boy uniform. At the end, she sang her most well-known numbers, including *After The Ball*, and invited the audience to join in. Eliza sang her heart out, even though she didn't remember all the words. Her face flushed with happiness, she looked across at Arthur.

'Come on, Arthur, you must know this one. Why don't you join in?'

Arthur remained silent, however, content to watch and enjoy the performance, but far too self-conscious to sing. When Eliza pressed him to, he just looked down, seeming ill at ease and somewhat flummoxed, so she stopped bothering him and carried on singing at the top of her voice.

That evening marked the beginning of their courtship. Through the subsequent winter months, they met three or four times a week and went either to a dance or to the pictures. Occasionally, when the weather was better, they ventured on outings, bouncing up and down the Dales on the solid tyres of one of the latest motor charabancs, their bodies crammed between fellow day trippers on the small wooden seats.

Eliza's father got used to Arthur coming regularly to his house. He liked him a lot, though sometimes he thought he lacked a bit of spirit, or 'gusto' as he put it. Although he never mentioned it to Eliza, he couldn't help thinking how different he was to Laurie and wondering what it was that attracted her to him.

Arthur loved the countryside, and with the arrival of spring, he began to take Eliza on long walks to some of his favourite haunts, one of which was Bolton Abbey, a monastic ruin near Skipton, in Wharfedale. A renowned beauty spot known to both locals and those who lived farther afield, the area was especially pretty in spring, when kingcups and wild primroses scattered their bright yellow across the valley and newborn lambs roamed its gently rolling hills. The river Wharfe flowed behind the ancient ruins of the abbey through a wooded stretch of land known as The Strid. Here, the river was particularly fast-flowing, having to force its way through a narrow cleavage in the rocks, then gush through a series of huge stones before widening out two miles downstream.

When they arrived, it was a bright afternoon. Heavy showers in the morning had lent extra force to the river that roared along beside them and water still dripped from rain-soaked leaves on the trees that arched above. The Strid was strangely deserted and Arthur surmised that the morning downpours had deterred the locals from venturing out on their customary Sunday walk.

Hand in hand, Arthur and Eliza picked their way along the riverbank footpath, careful to avoid slipping on its wet stones. Arthur had been even quieter than usual all day, so when he signalled to her to come and stand beside him on a large rock overlooking the stream, she sensed he was probably building up to something.

She had been thinking for some weeks now about what she would say if and when he finally summoned up enough courage to ask her the inevitable question and had made up her mind to accept him. He was kind and thoughtful and dependable and she was sure that he would never desert her, come what may. Most women would jump at the chance to marry someone like Arthur, she thought, with a steady job and a good honest heart. She knew she was not likely to do much better. Given time, maybe she could push him to be more ambitious, give him a bit more zest for life.

'Eliza,' he said as she stood beside him on the

rock, 'I've been wondering if there's any chance that, in the future like, you might see yourself marrying me. You don't have to answer me straight away, of course, and I'll understand if you decide to say no.' His words tumbled forth in a great torrent, accompanied by the sound of running water lisping through stone.

Her reply made his eyes fill with tears and he held her close to him, daring to kiss her properly for the first time.

'I never thought I could ever feel as happy as this,' said Arthur. He put one arm around Eliza's waist and they gazed down at the fast-flowing river.

'Some day, Eliza,' he said, 'we'll come back here with our children. When we're old, maybe, and they're grown up, I'd like to bring them to this rock so they could see how it was, once, for us, before they were even born. I'll tell them that this is the spot where I proposed to you and where you smiled as you said 'yes' to me, and we'll stand here and listen to the sound of the water rushing off in all directions. That's how I want our children to be, Eliza, like that river, strong enough to find their own way through rocks and stones, strong enough to be themselves.'

Eliza smiled, pleased to hear him speak with a passion in his voice that she hadn't heard before. 'He'll do,' she thought to herself. 'Maybe he's not going to set the world on fire, but he'll do.'

Later that day, anxious to do everything right, Arthur formally asked Mr Bell's permission to marry his daughter. Eliza's father gladly gave them his blessing and it was decided the wedding would take place in late September.

When they next met, Eliza told Alice the news.

'By gum!' she chortled. 'It must have been that bouquet I threw that did the trick!'

Eliza's friends at the mill all told her how lucky she was to get a catch like Arthur, reminding her that, soon, she would be leaving the tough mill life she had known to become a wife and mother. They were pleased for her, but they couldn't help being a bit envious, too.

One Friday, three weeks after Arthur's proposal, Eliza returned home a bit later than usual, at eight o'clock. She'd been round at Alice's old house, having a drink with Alice's sister, Nellie.

Outside the front door, she took the key from her handbag and turned it in the lock, but the door wouldn't open. She tried again, pushing it hard, then realised that something was holding it shut. Worried, she called Frank, Mrs Pollard's son, to come and help her. His brute strength succeeded where she had failed and they practically fell in the hallway together. The hall table had toppled over and was still partly jammed behind the now open door. Beyond it lay her father, stretched out on the carpet, unmoving.

For two nights, Mr Bell lay unconscious on a makeshift bed in the sitting room. He had suffered a stroke, the doctor said, and must not be moved. On the third night, he passed away peacefully in his sleep, having never recovered consciousness.

Chapter 6

Despite Mr Bell's recent death, Eliza and Arthur went ahead with their wedding plans for September. They considered having the service in Saltaire, but Eliza couldn't face the thought of getting married in the church that held so many memories of her father. Besides, after Laurie's death, she had stopped going there regularly. Arthur hadn't attended any particular church for years, so they agreed to get married in Bradford Registry Office.

During August, Arthur approached the council about renting one of the new 'Homes fit for Heroes' the government had given grants to local councils to build after the war, in response to growing public pressure. It was scandalous, people said, that men who had fought for their country were forced to return from the war to cramped, insanitary living conditions in Britain's large industrial cities. In 1919, therefore, Bradford began to build many new council houses. As a war veteran, Arthur was told he would be given priority and was offered a house on a brand new estate in Bowling, a small suburb only about a mile from the council offices where he worked.

As soon as he set eyes on the property, he knew it would be perfect. It had three bedrooms, and although there was an outside toilet, its greatest advantage was that it had an inside bathroom upstairs. There was a front room, a small living room, a kitchen and pantry at the rear and a long back garden. At the front, there was another smaller garden behind a privet hedge.

The fact that it was close to a direct tram into the centre of Bradford made it easy for Arthur to get to work, and although the area around it was less picturesque than Saltaire, it had all the basic facilities, including a pleasant park.

Arthur took Eliza to see it before he confirmed his acceptance.

'Oh, Arthur,' she cried, her voice quivering with excitement as he gave her a tour of the ground floor, 'it's a lot grander than I ever imagined. Just think! Our own brand new place, even bigger than Albert Road and complete with a new gas oven installed. My ma would never have believed it!'

He took her upstairs to show her the bedrooms, deliberately leaving the bathroom till last.

Delighted with the size of the three spacious

bedrooms, Eliza was about to go back downstairs when she spotted the fourth door.

'Where does that lead? Is it a cupboard?' she asked.

Arthur smiled quietly to himself. 'Why don't you go and have a look, love.'

He heard a gasp of astonishment as she opened the door on the rather grand cast iron white enamelled bath with hot and cold taps, its four feet resting ceremoniously on the wooden floorboards. Next to it stood a white pedestal washbasin, also with hot and cold taps and a mirror fitted above.

'By hell Arthur, it's like a palace is this,' exclaimed a delighted Eliza. 'If we're not happy here, we never will be.'

They kissed then, both thrilled and excited that they had managed to find such a wonderful house so quickly.

Eliza couldn't wait to start her new life there. She gave in her notice at the mill, and on her last Friday, the girls in her section gathered round her at lunchtime to say goodbye. They had all clubbed together to buy her a present that they insisted she open there and then.

Surprised and delighted, Eliza tore off the brown paper as fast as she could. Inside was a red velvet box that snapped open to reveal a gold wrist watch with an inscription on the back: *To our good friend, Eliza, burler and mender, 1910 –1921.*

Eliza was astonished by their kindness and generosity. 'I can't believe it!' she exclaimed. 'How the hell did you afford this?'

'We got it from yon pawnshop,' laughed Polly, winking.

'Nay, I thought our overlooker got it for us when he robbed that jeweller's in Leeds,' called out Matilda.

Even the overlooker himself joined in the fun. 'Aye, I'm a dab hand at thieving. I learnt it from the wife,' he grinned.

'Stop it! Stop it!' shrieked Eliza. 'I won't ask you no more questions. I'll always treasure this watch, though, and I'll wear it a lot, I promise. Whenever I put it on, I'll think about every single one of you standing here today. I'm going to miss you all, I am that.'

The wedding was a small unfussy affair. Most of Arthur's friends had been killed in the war, so Jack was best man. Alice was a bridesmaid and the two witnesses were George and Alice's sister, Nellie. The only other guests were George's wife and a couple of Eliza's friends from the mill.

They gathered outside the registry office on a blustery September afternoon, the frilly skirt of Eliza's pretty white dress blowing in the wind. In line with the latest fashion, it was calf-length, her ankles at last visible to the world and made even prettier, Arthur thought, by the new low-heeled white leather shoes he had bought her specially for the wedding. Alice wore a smart light grey two-piece with shoes to match and both Arthur and Jack put on their best suits and sported a white carnation as a button hole.

Arthur had booked a table at Brown and Muff's for the reception and they were duly ushered to their seats by a cheerful waitress who, no doubt hoping for a large tip, kept commenting on how Eliza looked 'a proper picture, just like one of them models' and how Arthur was 'the handsomest groom we've had in here for a long time.'

The table was beautifully laid out with plates of dainty sandwiches and various three-tiered cake stands full of fruit scones and fancies. In the middle of everything, perched somewhat precariously on a tall silver stand, lay a modest wedding cake with crisp white icing and two small figures of a bride and groom resting on top. This was all that Arthur had been able to afford, but in the eyes of Eliza, it seemed the most wonderful wedding cake in the world.

Alice was overjoyed to see her friend radiant with happiness after all she had been through, although couldn't stop herself wondering how different things would be if Laurie, not Arthur, were now by her side. She missed her brother terribly and occasions like this always brought home to her the poignancy of his loss. Still, today was a joyous occasion, she mustn't allow herself to think of her own grief but must concentrate on celebrating with Eliza, as she was sure Laurie would want her to do.

The tea proved to be delicious, the waitress scurrying to and fro with extra cakes as required. Everyone chatted happily for what seemed like hours and there were no formal wedding speeches, much to Jack's relief.

That night, after a few more drinks with their friends, Eliza and Arthur went back to Albert Road to pack everything up in preparation for the move to

Bowling. Eliza had offered George first choice of anything he wanted but he said he didn't need any new furniture, she was welcome to it all.

'Do you think we should sell pa's piano?' she asked Arthur. 'It might be a bit too big for the front room.'

'No, no, let's keep it,' he replied. 'Happen one of our children might learn to play it some day. And besides, it'll be a nice reminder of your father.'

'We won't need the tin bath though,' she said, going into the scullery. She lifted it down for the last time and thought of all the Friday night baths her family had taken in it, all the water she'd heated for it in the copper, and how frustrated she used to get with the number of times she had to carry this water from the scullery to the kitchen in a big enamel jug until the bath was finally almost full.

'What shall we do with it Arthur?'

'Why don't you leave it here? It'll come in handy for the next family I shouldn't wonder.'

So leave it there she did, hanging it back on the rusty old nail where it had resided ever since her father and mother had moved in almost forty years before.

A removal firm had been booked for the Saturday morning so, on the Friday night, Arthur and Eliza packed everything in boxes and then slept upstairs in her parents' double bed. They had both secretly been longing for the moment when they could cuddle up together as man and wife, completely alone and safe from any form of disturbance. Now the moment had come, however, they were awkward and self-conscious.

Arthur undressed with his back to Eliza and pulled on his pyjamas as fast as he possibly could. Eliza sat nervously on the edge of the bed, her new nightgown laid out beside her, ready to be slotted over her head. Trembling with a mixture of fear and excitement, she undid the hooks on her corset and removed her various undergarments, dropping them on the rug she had carefully placed beside the bed for this purpose. Then, lifting her nightgown as if it were a delicate piece of china that might come apart in her hands, she carefully placed it on her knee and dipped her head down, thrusting her arms forward and into the sleeves. At the appropriate moment she stood up, letting the folds of the voluminous garment fall down quickly over her hips and knees and the upper part of her ankles.

Arthur was oblivious of the whole of this intricate procedure. Once in bed, he had politely turned his back on his wife, anxious not to embarrass her and thinking it indiscreet to watch her undress. He had even pulled the sheets over his head so as not to hear the rustling of her garments, feeling that this kind of eavesdropping was the sort of aural equivalent of a peeping Tom. Lying on his side in this somewhat unnatural position, he remained completely still and waited, listening to the sound of his own breathing beneath the bedclothes.

Eliza extinguished the old oil lamp, jumped hastily into bed, and feeling less self-conscious now that she could no longer be seen, put one arm around his waist.

'Well Arthur, here I am then. Do you still love me?' she laughed.

Turning round, he pulled her close.

'I'll always love you Eliza Pendlestone.' (He almost said 'Bell' but stopped himself just in time.) I don't deserve you, I know, but I'll always love you, no matter what.'

'It's for better or for worse then,' she giggled, rubbing her face against his stubbled cheek.

Safe under cover of darkness, they made love for

the first time. It was a rather quick, fumbled affair, both of them feeling a little uneasy to be in the same bedroom where Eliza's parents had no doubt often performed the same act. Though neither dared to admit it to the other, they each felt a certain degree of relief when it was finished and they could settle down to sleep, exhausted by the long and eventful day.

The removal men arrived early the next morning and loaded everything onto the back of their cart. Arthur went with them so he could direct them to the right house and Eliza stayed behind to sweep up and give all the rooms a final clean before another mill family moved in.

The house looked so much smaller now it was empty. Memories drifted on the air, sounds and scents that used to give shape to her week – smells of soap and damp washing on a Monday, of fresh bread and biscuits on a Tuesday, the sound of her mother winding up the marble clock every Wednesday and Saturday night, the sound of her father vamping songs on his piano every Sunday afternoon.

She went upstairs to her parents' bedroom. A shaft of sunlight slanted through the window, making visible the particles of dust still floating in the air after Eliza's recent sweeping. Here, in this room, she had spent her wedding night with Arthur. Here, she was conceived and born. Here, she had heard her mother weeping after what she now understood must have been a miscarriage. Here, many years afterwards, her mother had died. She went over to the window one last time and gazed down on the street below, recalling her childhood and all the games she had played on its cobbles. She pictured Laurie as a little boy standing on a shoe box and shouting for all he was worth. Then she thought of Alice asking her questions as they sat next to each other on the glen, looking across at the vast expanse of the moors.

'Will I ever be as happy again?' she wondered.

After locking the door for the last time, Eliza left the key with Mrs Pollard, as arranged, and took the tram to Bradford. It was then only another short tram ride to Bowling. She walked briskly down the steep slope to the new house and saw Arthur waiting for her on the front doorstep. A few curtains twitched in the houses opposite as neighbours peered to catch a glimpse of who was moving in. Eliza felt offended and annoyed. She was not accustomed to being stared at by neighbours.

'Take no notice, Eliza,' said Arthur, 'they'll soon get used to us.'

They had a cup of tea, then got down to the tiring job of unpacking all the boxes and deciding what should go where.

The layout of the house was not dissimilar to her old house in Albert Road. The narrow hallway had a door to a slightly bigger front room on the right, and the living room and kitchen at the back were also a bit larger, but the overall plan was much the same. Outside, there was a brick outhouse containing a toilet, and beside it, a small coal bunker, just as there had been in her old back yard. The difference here, of course, was the garden. On one side, a low fence divided it from her neighbours' garden, and on the other, a high wall screened it from the road beyond. At the end was another high wall, which Arthur said would be perfect for growing rambling roses.

Eliza arranged the front room just the same as it had been in Albert Road, with her father's piano in one corner, the gateleg table in the middle of the room and the two armchairs at either side of the fireplace. Although he thought it looked a bit cluttered like this, Arthur didn't mind. As far as he was concerned, the house was hers to arrange as she wished. He had very few possessions – two suitcases full of his clothes, a bookcase that had belonged to his father and his own sizeable collection of books. These included a large Bible, two dictionaries, various encyclopaedias, a few biographies, and of course, several books by Dickens.

Tired from her exertions of the day, Eliza went up to bed early that night.

'I'll be up in a few minutes, love,' called Arthur, wanting a bit of time on his own to savour his new standing as a married man. He sat down in one of the armchairs and let his thoughts wander.

Happiness was a strangely novel feeling, something he had become convinced would always be denied him. He *had* been happy once, as a small boy. He could recall his mother telling him stories as he fell asleep by the warmth of a blazing fire and had a vague memory of his father bouncing him up and down on his knee. That was before his father left, of course, and everything became a struggle and his mother changed.

At school, too, he remembered, he had been ecstatically happy one morning when his teacher said that he was very bright and should do well. How he had skipped home that day, bursting to tell his mother and wondering if she might be able to afford to send him to the trade and grammar school if he succeeded in winning a scholarship, but as was beginning to happen increasingly around that time, she simply gazed into the distance when he spoke to her, almost as if he were invisible.

Throughout his boyhood, she would spend hours in her bedroom lying down or staring blankly out of the window and Arthur usually had to fend for himself when he came back from school. He didn't mind doing the cooking, recognising that his mother must be tired after a day's work cleaning other people's houses and feeling he ought to take some responsibility as the only man of the house. But he missed the mother of his babyhood and wished he could somehow find a way to communicate with the remote and distant figure she had become.

From the age of eleven, Arthur went out to work half time in a nearby mill. He started as a doffer, scurrying about in his bare feet removing the filled bobbins and replacing them with empties. Later he progressed to working with a spinner, who taught him how to twist together the broken threads of yarn. He was then known as a doffer and piecer.

Although the work was hard, Arthur made lots of friends at the mill and enjoyed the social contact. He used to meet up with friends on Sundays and go for long walks across the moors or have a game of football in the field behind his home. These recollections, so long buried and forgotten, now came as something of a shock to Arthur, causing him to stir in his armchair. He tried hard to picture this other younger self, free from the experience of war and all that it entailed, a far livelier, more impulsive, less introverted boy who seemed a world away from the person he was now.

At eighteen, he had joined the Duke of Wellington's West Yorkshire regiment and had spent over two years at the front, a time of relentless, unimaginable horror, the memories of which had taken him almost another three years to learn how to keep sufficiently at bay so as not to destroy him completely. He knew now that this earlier more carefree self was lost forever, as much a casualty of war as his shattered leg or the many blood-soaked comrades he had cradled, twitching, in his arms.

It was still a daily struggle to blot out the terrors that haunted him and he succeeded in doing so only with great vigilance and effort. In the hospital, supported by a sympathetic doctor, he had discovered two lifelines which he used to protect himself whenever the unspeakable scenes he had witnessed threatened to rise to the surface and destroy him.

The first was an image of his mother, which he now considered to be his very first memory of life. She was smiling and he imagined she must have been tucking him into bed because he was lying on his back with a starched white linen sheet pulled tight across his chest. As she lowered her face over his, he raised his hands to tug at a soft brown curl of hair on her forehead and saw that her eyes were sparkling with love and laughter. It was these shining almond eyes that he held in his mind whenever he needed to, these eyes alone that could save him from a descent into uncontrollable trembling.

The second was Charles Dickens, in particular *David Copperfield*. Arthur had first come across Dickens at school. He had loved *A Christmas Carol* and this was the one book he could afford to buy from his wages at the mill. In the hospital library, however, there were rows of books by Dickens and Arthur devoured all of them during his stay. It was *David Copperfield*, though, which made the greatest impression. He identified with the lonely boy of its title whose unhappy childhood strangely resembled his own, and whenever the pressures of the world threatened to overwhelm him, this was the book he always took down from the shelf.

But tonight was not the time for brooding over old memories. The last few weeks had been the happiest he had ever known and he was grateful for the unbelievable good fortune that a chance meeting on a train had brought him. He must look forward now to a different future, a new and different world. As he loosened his braces on the way upstairs up to bed, he counted his blessings, promising himself that he would always cherish Eliza, as he had sworn to do at their wedding, and would take care of her through thick and thin.

And so Eliza and Arthur began to settle into the routine of married life, adjusting to each other's ways, learning what would or wouldn't please the other.

The first few months felt strange to them both. Eliza had been used to looking after her father, had waited on him hand and foot after her mother died and had grown accustomed to his likes and dislikes at home. Her new husband was proving to be very different from her father in every way – the food he enjoyed, the papers he read, the things he found amusing or interesting, the way he preferred to do various things for himself rather than let her do them.

Arthur, in turn, was unfamiliar with a life where he was 'looked after' and initially felt ill at ease with what appeared to be a loss of independence. He found it unsettling that the moment he came home from work, Eliza started chattering, wanting to hear about his day and tell him about hers. In fact, all Arthur wanted to do was sit down and read for an hour, just as he had done when he lived alone.

Eliza, sensing his frustration with her, confronted him, believing that a full scale row would clear the air between them and restore harmony.

'Why the hell don't you answer me when I'm talking to you!' she cried one night, exasperated by his silence. 'I'm sick of the way you just sit there when you come in of a night and never say a bloomin' word.'

Alarmed by this sudden vehement outburst,

Arthur sat upright and looked concerned. He felt flustered, unsure of what to do or how best to handle this. As a result, he said nothing. This aggravated Eliza even more, so she gave full vent to her feelings – 'Answer me, Arthur!' she screamed. 'Answer me this minute or I'll walk out of that door and not come back. Don't you see how angry you're making me, sitting there like a dummy every bloody night. I can't stand it any longer. I just can't stand it!'

Sensing that his hands were beginning to tremble, Arthur struggled to regain some composure before he spoke. He knew he wasn't capable of shouting back, which was perhaps what she wanted him to do, knew too that he had obviously hurt her terribly without realising he was doing anything wrong.

'I'm sorry, love,' he said, standing up now and moving closer to her. 'I just didn't think.'

'Didn't think!' she shrieked, still furious with him. 'All you bloody *do* is think Arthur Pendlestone. You need to frame yourself and liven up a bit at nights. It's not as if you do a physical job, so you can't be that tired.'

Arthur smiled back at her, searching for a way to calm her down and restore relations between them. He approached her tentatively, daring to reach out his hand and slowly turn her face to his. Her cheeks were flushed with rage and there was a spark of fire in her eyes.

'By gum, you're beautiful when you get angry, Eliza. Are you going to stay mad at me all night or are you going to let me say I'm sorry and make it up to you?'

Her heart was beginning to melt, he knew, though Eliza was determined not to show it yet. He wanted to kiss her, but she turned her back on him and busied herself in the kitchen for several minutes. Before long, however, she popped her head round the door and spoke the magic words that made him realise everything was back to normal again.

'Come on, Arthur. Your tea's on the table and it's going cold.'

Such disagreements happened regularly for a while until Eliza finally gave up trying to pick a fight with him, realising that he would never play the game and fight back. Laurie, she was certain, would have taken her on and given as good as he got until, having cleared the air and made sure they'd got everything off their chest, they would have thrown themselves into the passionate process of making up and no doubt would have made love.

But Arthur was not Laurie and never could be. 'I must put Laurie completely out of my mind now,' she told herself. 'I'm married to Arthur and that's all there is to it.'

While Arthur was at work during the week, Eliza followed all the usual washing and cleaning routines she had learned from her mother. These took up quite a lot of time but still left her with a number of hours to herself, a freedom she was unused to, but which was very welcome. Much of this spare time was spent chatting to her new neighbours or going shopping.

Alice was living only about two miles away now, so she and Eliza saw each other regularly, meeting twice a week in the centre of town. On Friday nights, they also went out together with Jack and Arthur to a new local pub not far from Manningham.

Less than a year after Arthur and Eliza had moved into their new home, in the middle of a visit to Brown and Muff's one afternoon, Alice said casually to her friend, 'By the way, Eliza, I've got summat to tell you. I'm pregnant and they think there's a fair chance it might be twins.'

'Well I never!' gasped Eliza. 'When are they due?'

'Round about the start of January,' said Alice. 'Happen I'll have them on your birthday.'

'Ay, maybe so,' replied her friend.

At the pub that Friday night, Arthur decided they should celebrate. He bought the first of many rounds of drinks. 'Here's to the safe arrival of the two bairns and to your future happiness, Jack and Alice,' he said, raising a glass of Guinness to his lips.

Eliza picked up her half of frothy milk stout and let it chink against Jack's pint of mild.

'May all your troubles be little ones, Jack!' she joked.

'You'd better watch out Eliza,' laughed Jack. 'It'll be your turn soon!'

Chapter 7

And so it was. Eliza discovered she was pregnant in September, to the delight and amazement of Arthur, who was speechless with happiness when his wife told him the news. He set to work clearing out and then decorating the smallest bedroom and they started saving for a cot and a second-hand pram.

In early January, Alice's twins arrived as predicted, missing Eliza's birthday by two days. Eliza went to see her friend soon after their birth. Nellie was there helping out and it was she who answered the door.

'Come on up Eliza,' she said warmly. 'Alice'll be delighted to see you.'

Eliza heard the twins crying even before she began to mount the stairs. She entered the bedroom to find Alice sprawled out in the middle of the bed with a screaming baby in each arm.

'By gum, you've got a pair o' rum 'uns there, Alice,' said Eliza, leaning over to kiss her friend. 'How are you feeling?'

'Not so bad now, but it hurt like hell at the time.'

Eliza sat down on the bed beside her. 'Have they

got names yet?' she asked, stroking each baby's head in turn.

'Aye, this 'ere bald one's called Amy and t'other one with a bit of dark fuzz on her head we're going to call Dorothy.'

'They've got two good pairs of lungs, Alice, I'll say that for them,' grinned Eliza. 'Are you getting any sleep, or do they carry on like this all day?'

'They don't sleep much and they're always wanting feeding,' moaned Alice. 'They're taking after Jack already!'

From the moment she discovered she was pregnant, Eliza did all the right things. Women could die in childbirth, she knew, and many babies also died before they reached their first year. Because of her mother's experiences, Eliza was determined to be as careful as possible. Every week, she attended a little clinic run by the Maternity and Child Welfare Committee, which was held in the cavernous room of a former corn mill. She went to all their lectures and learned about breast and artificial feeding, preparing baby food, cots, clothing, weaning, ventilation and cleanliness. At Arthur's insistence, she let the Home Visitor come and advise her and agreed to have the midwife attend her when her time came.

After what seemed to be a straightforward pregnancy, Eliza finally went into labour on the nineteenth of February. Arthur came home from work to find the midwife already there. She advised him to stay downstairs and keep well out of the way until called for.

It was a slow, difficult birth and the labour continued for eighteen hours. The midwife kept mopping her patient's brow and continued to offer words of encouragement but Eliza had bouts of excruciating pain when she couldn't stop herself from calling out. As the night wore on, she felt increasingly exhausted, and above all, lonely. She wished her mother could comfort her, just as she always had done in the past whenever she had been unwell. It would have been nice to have had Arthur beside her, too, holding her hand, but this could not be countenanced, she knew. As the contractions grew more frequent, an uncontrollable fear began to seize her, an awareness that this prolonged and difficult process was fast moving to some sort of climax, the end of which was impossible to predict. In the midst of now agonising pain, all she could do was pray that if she herself didn't survive, at least her child would be safe.

Meanwhile, Arthur paced around downstairs boiling kettles when asked and anxiously waiting for news. He found the whole mysterious process frightening. He knew he was expected to remain on the sidelines and he had no wish to intrude on Eliza's privacy, but it was hard not knowing what was going on and he, like his wife, felt very alone. He took down *David Copperfield* and turned to the first chapter, locating the page where Miss Betsy Trotwood waits downstairs for the doctor to deliver Mrs Copperfield's baby, convinced that it is bound to be a girl. He had just got to the part where the sex of the infant is about to be revealed, when a real baby's cry interrupted him.

The midwife shouted down, 'You've got a beautiful baby girl, Mr Pendlestone.'

Dropping his book, Arthur stood up and went into the hallway where, unable to hold back the tears of joy and relief that welled up inside him, he leaned for a moment against the banister, waiting to be called up to the bedroom. He noticed that his hands were trembling with joy and couldn't help thinking back to his time in the trenches. How different his life seemed now, how unimaginably different. Once, he had despaired of ever feeling hope or happiness again. Now, he had them both in overwhelming measure.

Half an hour later, he was finally invited upstairs to meet his new baby daughter, who was sleeping contentedly in Eliza's arms. Touched by how fragile, how vulnerable she looked, Arthur stretched out one finger and gently stroked her forehead.

'She looks just like you, love,' he said to his wife.

'She'll be a damn sight prettier than I am, I hope,' replied a tired Eliza.

They decided to call the baby Evelyn, after Arthur's mother.

Evelyn was a very happy, healthy, lively baby who slept well throughout the night and caused her parents little trouble. Eliza could hardly believe how lucky she was. She seemed to take naturally to being a mother and marvelled at the way this tiny infant lying contentedly in her cot was totally dependent on her, Eliza, for everything. All the new tasks involved in her daily life – heating bottles, feeding, changing nappies, pegging out tiny blankets and clothes, pushing the pram twice daily round the park – these were no real hardship and seemed as nothing compared to the rewards of motherhood.

Arthur was equally proud of his new daughter. He brought home a little office diary in which to record her progress, noting down when her eyes first seemed to focus on him and the first time she smiled or closed her hand around one of his fingers. Every week, he noticed changes in her and delighted in every small development.

Eliza felt closer to Arthur now than at any time in their marriage. They had something to focus on together, something which was theirs alone and which they both adored.

Twice a week, Eliza took her daughter over to Alice's house and helped Alice with the twins, who were proving to be very hard work. They often both cried at once or screamed for attention at the same time and poor Alice never knew which way to turn.

'I don't know how you manage, Alice,' said Eliza. 'I have an easy time of it, compared to you.'

'Aye, these two are a handful,' admitted her friend, 'but I wouldn't swap 'em for the world!'

Now Eliza had a family, she was keen to maintain contact with her brother, who was her closest living relative. She was conscious that Evelyn would have no grandparents to visit when she was a bit older but at least she would have an uncle.

She encouraged George to visit his new baby niece as often as he could and felt happy that Evelyn seemed to take to him, giggling as he dandled her on his knee. George was loyal and dependable, Eliza thought, and would always be there to take care of Evelyn should anything happen to her or Arthur. On one of these visits, however, George dropped something of a bombshell.

'I know you're not going to like this, our Eliza,' he said, shifting uneasily in his chair, 'but I'm thinking of emigrating to New Zealand.'

Eliza was speechless with astonishment. He had never mentioned anything about this before and the announcement took her completely by surprise.

'George, what on earth for?' she asked.

He explained that his wife had a relative in Auckland who was willing to give him a job on his sheep farm and provide him with a house. There would be more opportunities out there, he thought, and besides, the British government were offering a subsidised passage to anyone who had a guarantee of work on arrival.

'I know it's not easy for you, me going away like this,' he said, 'but I think it's the chance of a lifetime and I'd be a fool not to go.'

George sounded more animated and excited than he had done for a long time, so Eliza didn't argue. She would miss him terribly, of course, but if that's what he wanted, she was not going to object. For some while, she had had her suspicions that George and his wife might be unable to have children. They had been married a few years now, but so far, nothing had happened on the baby front. Eliza never mentioned anything to her brother, of course, but wondered if this 'new start' might be his way of putting the disappointment behind him.

The emigration plans went smoothly and George and his wife set sail for New Zealand about six months after the birth of Evelyn. 'Make sure you write to us often George,' said Eliza as she kissed him goodbye, 'and let us know how you're getting on.'

'I will, Eliza, I promise,' he replied.

She watched him stride off into the distance and stifled a tear, upset to think that the last close link with her family was now gone.

Soon after George's departure, Eliza realised she

had fallen pregnant again. Her second child, Eileen, was delivered by the same midwife at the end of the following March, and it was clear from the moment she was born that she was going to take after Arthur. She had his nose and his large dark eyes, even his expression when she gazed up at the world. Arthur adored her from the start, and as if she sensed the special bond between them, she would smile and coo at his approach.

The babies soon grew into toddlers and Eliza couldn't believe how different they were. Evelyn was boisterous, quick and agile and totally fearless, willing to try anything. Eileen was quiet, thoughtful and much more cautious.

Arthur loved to play with them when he came home from work. As soon as he reached the front door, he would hear cries or screams or the sound of noisy feet in the hall or on the stairs and know that Evelyn was around. It was always Evelyn who rushed to greet him first, Eileen being slower to leave whatever picture book or painting she was preoccupied with, and sometimes being so focussed on what she was doing that she didn't even hear him come in. The minute she saw him though, she flung her arms wide and waited for him to lift her up high in the air and then cuddle her close. His cheek felt rough against her hand and she loved to stroke it, fascinated by the strange sensation of its bristles on the ends of her fingers.

At the weekend, the girls would often follow their father around in his beloved back garden. He had dug flower beds on either side of the central lawn and had a small vegetable patch in the back left corner. The rambling roses were growing dutifully up the wall at the end and all that remained to be planted was a small rectangular patch of ground in front of them. Arthur had deliberately left this area, intending it to be land where his daughters could plant their own flowers when they were old enough.

One fine Sunday morning in April, he decided that the time had come to let them loose on it.

'Come on girls,' he called from the end of the garden. 'I've got something to show you.'

Eliza opened the back door and they rushed out together, Evelyn holding on to Eileen's hand and dragging her across the lawn almost faster than her little legs could go. Arthur explained that the patch of unplanted ground was theirs. He had carefully divided it in half and run a piece of string down the middle.

'This part on the left is yours Evelyn and the bit on the right is Eileen's,' he said, at the same time taking from his pocket several colourful packets of seeds containing easy to grow annuals. He spread them out carefully on the ground so the girls could see them.

'Look. These are all yours. Later on, you can choose which ones you want to plant but first you'll have to dig the soil over to let the air get to it.' He then produced two small trowels and stood back. 'Go on then girls,' he said. 'Get cracking. I'll only help you when you need me to.'

Evelyn, now just five years old, dived in at once, pushing her trowel into the earth with as much energy as she could muster. She loved to get her hands and knees dirty and was soon covered in soil.

'Come on Eileen,' she cried, seeing that her sister was hanging back. 'I'll show you what to do.'

Eileen duly tottered onto her patch of soil and let Evelyn dig some over for her, eventually managing to manipulate her own trowel sufficiently well to be able to turn over a surface layer of earth.

'That's it, Eileen,' said Arthur encouragingly, 'only

it needs to be a little bit deeper.'

He gently put his hand on top of hers and helped her to insert the trowel to the required level and they worked happily together until it was all done.

Next came the exciting part – choosing which annuals to plant. They could choose two each. Evelyn kept grabbing the packets, looking at all the pictures and trying to decide. Eileen stood back, wanting to consider everything before she made her decision.

'What are their names, dad?' she asked. 'I want to hear their names.'

Arthur held up each packet and slowly pronounced the name of the flower seeds it contained – lupins, geraniums, sunflowers, poppies, sweet peas, chrysanthemums, cosmos, stocks, nasturtiums, marigolds, snapdragons, sweet williams.

Eileen chose the two whose names most attracted her – sweet peas and snapdragons. Evelyn went for the ones with the brightest colours – sunflowers and poppies.

'Well, that's lucky,' said Arthur, smiling. 'You've both chosen a tall one and a shorter one. Let's put the tall ones at the back, shall we?' He helped them to open the packets and they carefully dropped the seeds one by one into the holes he made. Evelyn covered hers over with soil and Arthur held onto Eileen's trowel, guiding her to do the same. Finally, he gave each of them in turn his smallest watering can and they watered them in.

Eliza came out to admire their handiwork, bringing Arthur a cup of tea. She couldn't believe how quickly the girls were growing up and felt a little sad that, soon, Evelyn would be leaving her during the day in order to go to school. She would miss their baking sessions and their walks round the local area.

The sisters got on well together despite their very different characters. Evelyn, though nowhere near as bright as Eileen, was a natural leader and gave her sister the confidence to try new things and explore the world around her.

'Look, Eileen,' she said one afternoon running towards an old oak tree as Eliza was taking them through the park. 'Let's go inside it!'

There was a deep hollow in the base of its trunk and Evelyn had no doubt that it would be fun to crawl into the heart of it. Eileen, normally afraid of the dark, would never have gone near such a place on her own, but, believing her older sister wouldn't let her come to any harm, she crept in after her. Their mother stood and watched, amused, as Evelyn, now deep in the centre of the tree, stretched out her hand and pulled Eileen inside with her. They played happily there for half an hour, imagining they were in a goblin house or a dark cave by the sea.

Eliza took them round the park at least twice a week and let them go for a ride on the swings or feed the ducks on the lake. On Sunday afternoons, they would sometimes meet up with Jack and Alice and the four girls would play there together.

Occasionally, for a treat, they would all take the train to Ilkley and walk up to the famous Cow and Calf rocks. The girls loved clambering across the stones near the top and Eileen was fascinated by the messages and initials that previous generations had carved in the huge gritstone boulders.

'What do they say, dad?' she kept asking every time they passed another inscription, until Arthur grew tired of reading them all aloud.

Meanwhile, Evelyn would leap from rock to rock, picking up stones to put in the twins' coat pockets or search round for a muddy puddle to jump in, always closely followed by her mother, who knew that it would not be long before she got up to some other kind of mischief.

If the weather was good, they sometimes walked down into Ilkley and went for a stroll by the river. There was a wooded area about a mile to the north. Usually, they never went that far because Eileen was still quite small and easily grew tired. One particularly beautiful Sunday in early May, however, Eileen still seemed to have plenty of energy left by the time they reached their usual stopping point, so they decided to continue up the hill until they reached the edge of the wood.

It was filled with bluebells, a great carpet of them that stretched for miles. Only the woodland path and the exposed roots of ancient trees remained uncovered, beyond the reach of their spread. The flowers' unique, delicate scent pervaded the whole area and everyone paused for a moment, stunned by the endless expanse of blue that seemed to be swaying gracefully in the wind as if it were a part of an elegant dance to some secret unheard music.

With a shriek of delight, Evelyn rushed forward along the central path and disappeared into the heart of the wood, desperate to explore the full extent of it all.

'Come and see, mam, come and see!' she called out moments later, running back to take her mother by the hand. Eliza, laughing, allowed herself to be dragged off at high speed while the others followed at a more leisurely pace, enjoying the warmth of the bright sunlight filtering through the trees. A few minutes later, Alice and Jack caught up with her and the three of them sat down together on a flat stone situated conveniently in the shade of an ancient sycamore, from where they could keep an eye on the girls.

'I see what you mean about bluebells,' said Alice, giving Eliza a knowing look and a warm smile. 'Do you still want to pick one or is there no need now?'

Eliza's wistful expression told Alice that she still remembered their conversation of long ago.

'No, no need,' she murmured softly. 'I think we can leave all the picking to our girls now.'

The girls loved it. Amy and Dorothy found the felled trunk of a tree they could run along while Evelyn and Eileen picked some flowers to take home. Arthur was struck by the utter silence of the place, a silence punctuated only by occasional birdsong or a rustle of leaves in the late spring breeze. He withdrew from the others for a while and went to sit by himself to appreciate this rare stillness. If only he could freeze the moment, stop the flow of time and stay here like this forever, with the sun streaming through the branches that intertwined above him and the laughter of his wife and children echoing in the distance. Even if he were destined never to experience happiness again, he reflected, he would still have the memory of today, would always know that, suddenly, on a spring afternoon, he had been touched by the overpowering beauty and mystery of life.

Eileen, tiring at last, came over and sat down beside him on a large tree stump, giving him an armful of bluebells to hold. She remained completely still and thoughtful for almost a minute, as if sensing something of the mystery too. Then she looked up at him, her eyes full of wonder.

'Dad,' she said. 'Is heaven all blue like this?'

'I think it might be, my love. I think it might well be.'

As soon as they got home, Evelyn and Eileen put their bluebells in jam jars full of water, a long row of them, all lined up on the kitchen window-sill. When they went up to bed, the flowers were still fresh and smelling of the wood, but by morning, they were already beginning to droop. Eileen now felt guilty that she had picked them and wished that she could somehow return them to the shady, secluded spot where they had flourished. The feeling of sadness at their passing haunted her for a few days afterwards, but by the following Saturday, she had forgotten all about them.

Saturday morning was the highlight of the week for both girls. Immediately after breakfast, Eliza would give each of them a threepenny bit for pocket money and their father would take them to Butterworth's, the sweetshop and tobacconist's at the top of their road.

The sweetshop door would creak open and a half-hearted bell would announce their arrival. Both girls would run down the three steps and disappear to explore what seemed to them an Aladdin's cave of treasure. Evelyn delved immediately into the array of sweets and chose something different each week. Eileen paused halfway down the aisle as if to savour the heady mix of smells – peppermint and ginger, snuff and pipe tobacco, liquorice and sherbet – then always made for her favourite brand of chocolate, Fry's Five Boys. She was attracted to it, not so much by its flavour, as by the faces of the five boys depicted on its wrapping, and by the long words written under each face. Her father had read them out to her time and time again, so she knew them off by heart and loved to recite them: 'desperation, pacification, expectation, acclamation, realisation.' She had no idea of their meanings, of course, but she loved their sound.

Arthur would wait patiently for the girls to make their choice and would then buy twenty Player's cigarettes for himself. A walk through the park followed, where the girls would eat their sweets and feed the ducks, before returning home for lunch.

This was the happiest time of Arthur's life. He loved talking to the girls and listening to their strange, endless questions about the world, many of which he found impossible to answer.

'Can smells be green?' asked Eileen one day. 'And do birds yawn when they're tired?'

'And if the world is spinning all the time, why don't we feel dizzy when we run around?' said Evelyn.

'Well, you've stumped me there girls,' said Arthur. 'I've got a lot of books at home though. Maybe I'll have a look and see if I can find the answers for you.'

And so they would chatter on together until they got back to their house.

Chapter 8

Later that summer, the girls watched anxiously to see if the flowers they had planted would finally bloom. They had seen them slowly sprouting tender stems and shoots throughout May and early June and couldn't wait to see whose flowers would appear first. One Saturday in the middle of June, they were at last rewarded when Eileen's multi-coloured snapdragons appeared, their delicate pastel shades bringing a touch of life and colour to the end of the garden. Eileen spotted them before anyone else.

'Mine are first! Mine are first!' she called, running inside to announce the news. Evelyn didn't answer her and Eliza, catching the look of disappointment on her older daughter's face, decided to come to her rescue.

'Well, first isn't always best, is it? I reckon your sunflower, Evelyn, will take a lot of beating when it finally comes out,' she said, glancing at Arthur for some support.

'That's right,' said Arthur, taking his cue. 'Nature often leaves the best till last. Let's wait and see.'

Fortunately, Evelyn's poppies were next to flower. Then came the sweet peas, each one tied carefully to the row of canes Arthur had erected to support them. Eileen loved their variegated colours, and of course, their scent, which suffused the garden on warm summer evenings. They had to wait until late August for the sunflowers, but when they finally raised their enormous yellow heads, the whole family agreed that these were indeed the best of all. Evelyn stood beside one, delighted to discover that it was actually taller than her.

'Stay there love, don't move,' called Arthur. 'I'll go and get my camera and take your picture.'

Arthur emerged two minutes later with his Box Brownie, bought second-hand from a friend at work a few months before. He lined up the image carefully and Evelyn smiled at exactly the right time.

'Take us all Arthur,' said Eliza, beckoning her daughters to join her in front of the sweet peas.

He wound on the film with the handle and prepared once again to push the shutter button, hoping to capture the look of pride on his wife's face as she held their daughters close and trying hard, for Eileen's sake, to make sure the sweet peas were visible in the background.

Several days later, when the film was developed, he collected the pictures on his way home from work. He showed them to Eliza and the girls as soon as he got in.

'There you are, what do you think?' He placed them on the table in the front room and they gathered round to look.

The one of Eliza and the girls was a little hazy but Eileen was delighted with it because her sweet peas were easily recognisable. The one of Evelyn standing with the sunflower, though, was perfect.

'Can we plant seeds every year, dad?' asked Evelyn.

'Yes, can we?' echoed Eileen.

'We'll have to see,' Eliza responded. 'Remember, Evelyn, you're starting school next week and you won't have so much free time then.'

She was right. Evelyn made lots of new friends at school and soon forgot about planting seeds. Eileen, never as keen as her sister on getting her hands dirty, didn't mention gardening again.

Eventually, with both girls at school, Eliza's life settled into a routine. Like her own mother, and so many other women of the time, she continued to do the week's washing on a Monday, the week's baking on a Tuesday. On Wednesdays, she cleaned the windows and on

Thursdays swept and tidied the garden. The rest of the week was spent sweeping and washing floors, washing and scouring the outside steps, dusting, making beds, clearing out the ashes from the hearth and laying new fires. In addition to these daily chores, she also had to do the darning and mending and make sure there was a cooked tea on the table every evening for Arthur and the girls.

Every Saturday afternoon, Eliza would take her daughters into Bradford to do some shopping. While they were there, Arthur paid his weekly visit to his mother in the mental institution in Burley in Wharfedale. Mrs Pendlestone senior was now in the final stages of dementia and was deteriorating physically as well as mentally. Arthur had been told by the nursing staff that she was not expected to live much longer.

Each week, he sat close beside her, holding her hand, while she stared vacantly into the distance. Sometimes, as he waited for a respectable amount of time to elapse before he left her, Arthur would reflect on how the world had changed since she was first admitted to the hospital in 1919. She had missed so much – the wireless, talking movies, the virtual replacement of the horse-drawn cab by cars and trams and trolley buses, women's suffrage, the first trans-Atlantic flight... he wondered what her reaction might have been to the shorter skirts and new fashions, the gaiety of the dance bands playing the Charleston and the Black Bottom. And what would she have made of Eliza and the girls? Ah well, there was no point in speculating now.

He kissed her goodbye, following, as he did so, the line of her gaze through the window and into the garden. She seemed to be staring intently at something but all he could see was a slow snail clambering aimlessly up a wall.

Almost two years after Eileen started school, Arthur's mother died. Neither the girls nor Eliza had ever met her, so only Arthur attended her funeral. She was buried in Bowling Cemetery, not that far from where she had been born and where Arthur could easily visit and look after her grave. Arthur inherited sixty pounds, money that his mother had herself inherited after her father's death and which she had immediately invested in the Yorkshire Penny Bank. Her illness had meant that it remained there, forgotten, earning a small amount of annual interest for a period of many years. The money easily paid for the funeral and there was quite a tidy sum left over. Arthur and Eliza both agreed that this should be left in the bank and should be spent on their daughters, as and when the need arose.

Evelyn and Eileen both attended the local elementary school, which was a short walk from where they lived. Evelyn quickly made friends and soon knew lots of boys and girls in the neighbourhood, with whom she would go out to play every evening. She was something of a tomboy and loved to join in games of football with the boys or go off with them on bike rides round the estate.

Eileen remained shy and quiet and much less sociable. She spent her free time at home, reading or drawing or doing jigsaw puzzles and couldn't wait for her father to arrive back from work so she could tell him all the things she had done at school. After tea, he would sit her on his knee and help her to read the stories in an illustrated book of fairy tales by Hans Christian Anderson, which he had bought for her birthday. *The Little Match Girl* was the one she loved best. She imagined herself as the tiny frozen girl looking in through the window of the gorgeous house with its blazing fire and glorious Christmas tree, imagined herself striking the third match, and then tried in vain to imagine herself dying of cold, separated from warmth and life and safety by only a thin pane of glass.

While Eileen and her father were reading, Evelyn and her mother were often in the kitchen washing up or doing some baking together. Eliza would hear her husband and second daughter chattering away over some book or other, and convinced they were wasting time, would pop her head round the door and call out, 'Arthur, stop filling the child's head with a load of nonsense. I don't know what you see in them daft stories, I don't really.'

Arthur and Eileen just laughed, knowing she didn't really expect them to change and that she loved them both dearly, despite not understanding what they saw in 'all them books'.

When Eileen had gone up to bed, Arthur would turn his attention to Evelyn, who, being older, was allowed to stay up one hour later than her sister.

'Now then, Evelyn,' he'd say, 'what have you been up to today, then?'

'I scored a goal tonight, dad,' she said one

evening, 'and our team won three-nil. When I grow up, I want to play for Bradford City. Do you think they'll be taking on girls by then?'

'Well, I don't see why not, love,' replied Arthur, 'Happen they'd do a lot better with a few girls playing for them.'

'And happen they wouldn't, Arthur,' snapped Eliza.

When Evelyn had gone to bed, Eliza tackled Arthur about his attitude towards their daughters. 'I wish you wouldn't encourage our girls to dream so,' she said. 'This world's hard enough as it is, without you making them both think they can do owt they want. I'll thank you to help me keep their feet on the ground, in future, not fill their minds with false notions of how wonderful they are.'

Arthur didn't reply, merely took out a cigarette from his pocket and sat down by the fire with his Telegraph and Argus. They didn't speak for an hour, the gap between the two of them beginning to be made more apparent now by their different approaches to the children.

Before bedtime, Eliza swallowed her pride and

gently kissed Arthur on the forehead. She knew deep down how much he loved his daughters, even if he did annoy her at times. She was also realistic enough to accept that they would just have to live with their differences. The marriage, as she had now come to realise, was not ideal, but how many marriages were?

The winter of 1931 was particularly harsh. Snow fell in early December and covered the streets for a week. Evelyn, now almost nine years old, spent the end of every school day sledging with her friends down the steep slope that led to the playing fields behind her school, while Eileen built snowmen and snow castles in the back garden.

Straight after lunch that Sunday, Arthur offered to take the girls out to Ilkley so they could see the moor all its winter glory before the snow melted away. 'It'll look beautiful with the hills all covered in white,' he said, 'and we can walk up to the Cow and Calf rocks if it's not too slippery.'

Excited by the prospect of going for a walk in the snow, Evelyn and Eileen rushed to put on their

Wellington boots and warm coats. Eliza wrapped scarves around their necks and insisted they wore their gloves. 'And don't you be falling over in that wet snow,' she warned them as they left, 'or you'll catch your death o' cold.'

Arthur held on to his daughters' hands as they walked from the station up to the moors. The pavements had been cleared of snow, but once they began to ascend the steep path that led to the famous rocks, the going became more difficult, with patches of ice threatening to make them lose their footing. They manoeuvred past them though, successfully managing to remain on their feet.

At the foot of the Cow and Calf, Arthur looked above him to check that the pathways leading up to the top were still negotiable, as in fact they were, many of them having been well trodden earlier in the day. He gripped Eileen's hand and let Evelyn run on ahead of them, the steam from their frosted breath blowing back in their faces as they trudged onward. Finally, they scrambled over the last few rocks and onto the very top.

The view was breathtaking. Arthur gazed across at the distant hills, their contours softened by the heavy weight of snow. Dry stone walls and hedgerows had merged, roads had vanished, the river had turned to ice. Across the fields the sheep were huddling close, seeking warmth in the setting sun's diagonals. He felt so proud to be a part of this place. Although the Yorkshire moors were rugged, uncompromising, he had always felt there was a strange eternal beauty in their bleakness. Here, over the centuries, wind and weather had etched themselves on people and on landscape, chiselling them into one. Here, you touched bedrock.

Eileen and Evelyn gripped his hands tightly in the icy wind. 'Look,' said Eileen, pointing to the initials scratched in the rock beneath their feet. 'We're standing on people's lives!'

'So we are, love,' said Arthur. 'I hadn't thought of it like that before.'

'Dad,' cried Evelyn, impatient now with standing still. 'I want to go and throw snowballs. You said we could have a snowball fight.'

'Aye,' laughed Arthur, 'I know I did. Come on, then, let's be having you.'

He jumped down and led them through the rocks onto a flatter part of the moor. Evelyn screamed with delight as they played together, her whoops and cries muffled by the thick snow. Arthur suddenly noticed how much taller she had become. Unlike Eileen, whose dark wavy hair resembled his, Evelyn was brown-haired like her mother, with sparkling eyes and a pretty face.

'She's going to be quite a stunner in another four or five years,' Arthur thought to himself as they neared the station.

They got home late for tea but Eliza stopped herself being angry, realising from the glow on their faces what a good time they must have had. 'Come on, girls,' she said smiling. 'Your tea's on the table.'

That night they all sat round the fire together. Eileen loved watching the flames and the bright red sparks that would collect together sometimes, clinging to the back of the chimney breast for a few seconds, before disappearing. They often made distinct shapes that she could recognise.

'I can see a horse with wings, dad. Look!' she said.

'It must be Pegasus,' said Arthur. 'Maybe he's come to visit us.'

'Who's Pegasus?' asked Evelyn, prompting Arthur to launch into the magical tale of the flying horse.

At bedtime, Arthur went upstairs, as usual, to read them both a story. When they had been very small, he had sung them a lullaby as well, but this had stopped now they were getting older. Once they were both sound asleep, he came downstairs again and sat with Eliza.

'They're starting to grow up, Eliza,' he said, 'and I think we should give them a special Christmas this year, one they'll always remember, before they're too old to get excited about Christmas any more. Why don't we spend a bit of my mother's money and get them each a big present, something they'd really like?'

Eliza allowed herself to be persuaded. They decided to buy Evelyn a brand new bicycle. She'd always had to make do with a second-hand one up to now but she so loved cycling around with her friends that they both knew how much she'd appreciate a present like this. Eileen was to be given the hand-carved chess set she had fallen in love with on a recent visit to the top floor of Busbys', another large department store in Bradford. Arthur had taught her to play chess six months before, and she had already improved so much that she was beginning to beat him occasionally.

The week before Christmas, the girls made paper

chains from coloured paper and hung them round the front room. Eliza unpacked the small table-top Christmas tree she had inherited from her parents and they all had great fun fastening decorations to its branches. Evelyn and Eileen loved this time of year. The school usually put up a large Christmas tree in the hall and there was a Christmas party for all the children at the end of term. The girls' excitement mounted as the great day drew near. On Christmas Eve, they left their stockings as usual at the foot of their beds and struggled to fall asleep, unable to stop wondering what the next morning might hold in store.

That night, Eliza and Arthur carefully wrapped the two big presents in brown paper and left them in the hearth. Then they crept upstairs to fill their daughters' stockings with the usual collection of chocolates, sugar mice, fruit, and of course, a new penny.

The girls woke at six on Christmas morning and immediately started to dive into the stockings to explore their contents. After a few loud cries of 'Look at this!' or 'Look what I've got!' they both raced down to the living room, knowing that this was where Father Christmas normally left their biggest gifts. There, propped against the fireplace, they found two presents they had hardly dared dream of. The brown paper was ripped off in no time, and for a few seconds, both girls stood completely still, each taken aback by the splendour of the objects that lay in front of them.

Then, finding her voice at last, Evelyn screamed and raced into the garden, anxious to try out her new bike as soon as possible. It was bright red with a smooth black leather saddle and a shining silver bell on the handlebars. Arthur adjusted the height of the saddle till it was just right for her and off she went along the road, waving and shouting and sounding the bell every few seconds in the hope that some of her friends would come out and see her.

Eileen, face pink with pleasure and eyes alight with wonder, carefully picked up each of the chess pieces and set them out on the board in preparation for their first game.

Arthur looked across the table at Eliza. As their eyes met, both knew that all the trouble and expense had been well worth it.

Chapter 9

The early 1930s were difficult for everyone. The Wall Street crash of 1929 was followed by a time of depression. Large numbers of men were on the dole, and many of Eliza's neighbours struggled to make ends meet. Some went through their modest savings and fell behind with the rent or slipped into debt. Others were forced to take family heirlooms to the pawn shop or tramp round seeking odd jobs like chopping firewood. Many unemployed ex-serviceman picked up coppers by busking in the streets or in public houses.

One of Arthur's old comrades, desperate for work and with time on his hands, had joined some other ex-servicemen and formed a comic band. Their 'instruments', apart from a few drums and concertinas, consisted of old kettles and teapots to which tommy-talkers had been ingeniously connected. They wore crazy costumes and called themselves the Wiffan-Waffan-Wuffan Comic Band, marching and doing knockabout sketches at every public gala or carnival. Evelyn and Eileen loved to watch them and fell about with laughter at their ridiculous antics.

'Can we go and see the Wuffan Band?' they used to beg whenever there was a local festival or parade.

'No, you can't,' snapped Eliza, determined that the girls shouldn't always be given what they asked for. 'Do you think your father's got nothing better to do than take you to parades all over the place?'

But Arthur found it hard to resist their pleading expressions and usually agreed to take them in the end, even if it meant giving up going to a football match with Jack.

'Keep hold of my hands,' he would say, 'or we'll get separated in the crowds.'

He loved to watch them both as the Wuffan Band performed. Evelyn would jump up and down, trying to copy some of their acrobatic feats and silly dances. Eileen would stand completely still, mesmerised by the way they seemed to produce music from old watering cans, rubbing boards and various pots and pans.

'It's a clever trick,' said Arthur. 'They tie a tommy-talker to these old tin things and then hum a tune through it and it makes their voice sound funny, like a real instrument.'

'What's a tommy-talker?' asked Eileen, puzzled.

152

'It's something you can hum or sing into and it changes your voice so it sounds like some sort of musical instrument.'

Eileen still looked sceptical so, when they got back, Arthur took out his comb, wrapped some tissue paper around it and asked her to hum through it.

'That's right. Now do you understand?' said Evelyn, sounding a little superior and pleased to know something that her sister didn't. 'It's easy really,' she continued. 'It's all caused by vibration.'

Evelyn had already come across the tissue paper and comb device at school and was eager to show off her knowledge, keenly aware that, though her sister was younger, she usually understood things much quicker than her.

At school, Evelyn was keenly aware of how many of her classmates had fathers who were now out of work and was often surprised to see the conditions some of her friends were forced to live in.

'Do you know what, mam?' she said one tea time. 'Eric's parents have to drink their tea out of jam jars 'cos they haven't got any cups and saucers.'

'Do they, love?' asked Eliza.

'Ay, and they don't have no tablecloths neither,' revealed Evelyn. 'They use old newspapers instead.'

'Well, that just goes to show how grateful you should be, Evelyn, to have such nice things and a dad who's got a steady job when so many other folk are out of work.'

'Is Uncle Jack out of work, too?' asked Eileen, who had heard how many factories were closing down.

'No, he'll be all right, love,' replied Eliza. 'I don't think soap manufacturers are likely to close down. It's the mills that are suffering most.'

Eileen was delighted to hear this. In the school holidays, she and Evelyn were sometimes allowed to spend a morning in the factory with Jack, when he wasn't too busy. As foreman, he had his own office and was virtually his own boss so he used to smuggle them in and take them to see the long slabs of industrial soap being sliced into bars before it was packed into boxes and taken to the huge warehouse, from which it was dispatched all over the country. They were fascinated by the enormous weights and pulleys used to lift and transport the soap, by the heavy iron trolleys that were always whizzing past them and by the strange smell that emanated from the great vats of boiling liquid.

Jack encouraged the girls to pretend they worked there. He gave them stacks of newly cut soap to pack into boxes, which kept them occupied for most of the morning and had the advantage of tiring them out. Eliza would usually give them some sandwiches to take with them, and at lunchtime, they would proudly eat them with Uncle Jack, just like real factory workers.

From a very early age, Evelyn and Eileen had been intrigued by the mystery of Jack's right hand with its missing fingers and were constantly surprised that he could still use the affected hand to hold a pen or manipulate objects with apparent ease. Over lunch, they would watch his every movement as he carefully unwrapped and then extracted his sandwiches from the brown paper that Alice had put them in, mesmerised by how he used his thumb and two remaining fingers to undo the string.

'Uncle Jack,' said Evelyn one lunchtime, suddenly fixing him with an intense stare in the middle of their meal. 'Can I touch the place where your fingers used to be?'

Jack seemed taken aback for a moment, then

laughed out loud. 'Of course you can,' he cried, holding out his hand obligingly.

Evelyn immediately reached out her own hand and carefully ran her fingers across the two stumps. 'They're so cold!' she exclaimed. 'Are they always like that?'

'I suppose they are, love,' Jack grinned, amused by her forthrightness. 'I'm not sure why.'

'Can I feel them, too?' asked Eileen, not wanting to be left out.

Jack smiled and nodded his assent. Eileen hesitated for a moment, then gently moved the tip of her forefinger over the smooth rounded ends of white flesh, trying hard to imagine what it must feel like to lose a part of yourself.

'Have you finished then, girls? Can we get on with our lunch now?' asked Jack, sensing that their curiosity had at last been satisfied.

They nodded happily and returned to their sandwiches.

After their full morning of activity, the girls usually began to look very tired, so Jack would spread some sacking on a few cushions on the floor of his office, where, in no time at all, they both fell fast asleep.

Despite their obvious differences in temperament, Evelyn and Eileen remained close as they were growing up. They looked forward to sharing the excitement of the annual events that lent a bit of colour to life – the summer gala in Peel Park, Bowling Tide, the parades at Easter, plot night on the fifth of November. Most of all, they looked forward to Manningham Fair every Whitsuntide. This was held in Manningham Park, not far from where Jack and Alice lived. Arthur and Eliza would take their daughters to have tea with Dorothy and Amy and then all four girls, accompanied by Jack and Arthur, would rush off to the nearby fair.

Like dogs straining on a leash, the girls pulled their fathers down the long grassy slope to the muddy pleasure ground, ablaze with a thousand brightly coloured lights. Accompanied by the cries of stallholders, the roar of engines and the cheerful blare of fairground organs, they jostled their way through crowds of people to a plethora of fun-filled attractions. Everywhere people were queuing. Some queued for toffee apples or candy floss; others queued for rides or sideshows, for the weird or the

157

wonderful. Bearded lady or hall of mirrors, ghost train or coconut shy, rifle range or roll-a-penny – the choice was overwhelming.

The girls normally went off in pairs to find the most interesting ways of spending their pocket money. Amy and Eileen opted for the stalls where you could win something. Evelyn and Dorothy always made straight for the thrilling rides, daring each other to go on the one they considered to be the most frightening.

Meanwhile, Alice and Eliza enjoyed an evening in together, having a drink and a chat.

'Yon lasses are growing up that fast,' said Alice. 'They'll be taller than us, soon.'

'They will that,' replied Eliza. 'Whether there'll be any work for them when they leave school, though, is another matter.'

'Nay, Eliza, this depression can't go on forever. Any road, your Eileen's that clever, I should think she'll have no trouble at all finding a job, and a good 'un at that.'

'Maybe so,' Eliza sighed, 'but our Evelyn's more of a worry. She's ten years old now, but all she thinks of is laikin' about with her friends and riding round as fast as she can on that bike of hers.'

'She'll be all right,' Alice reassured her. 'She's got plenty of time to sort herself out. I'm more worried about my two. They don't get very good reports from school, you know. Amy's not bad, but Dorothy's near the bottom of her class.'

'What's schooling Alice!' scoffed Eliza. 'It's life that matters. You've got two grand girls there and you should be damn proud of them, I'm sure of that.'

The long school holiday came round once more and Evelyn spent the summer days playing out with her friends. Naturally adventurous, she had begun to go slightly farther afield on her bike now, and unbeknown to her parents, sometimes cycled the mile and a half into Bradford with her friend, Gladys. They would have a look round the shops for an hour and then cycle back, pretending they had been riding round the estate or playing together in the park.

'Can I go out on my bike with Gladys, mam?' asked Evelyn one Monday afternoon after she and Eileen had helped their mother take in a second load of washing.

'It's nearly half past four already, Evelyn,' replied

Eliza. 'Can't you wait till dad comes home at six and we've all had our tea?'

'Please mam,' cajoled Evelyn, 'I'll be back in time for tea, I promise.'

'Go on then,' her mother agreed, 'but make sure you're back here to help me set that table at ten minutes to six, no later!'

Evelyn sped off on her bicycle, leaving Eileen to help Eliza fold and put away the newly washed clothes.

At ten minutes to six, there was no sign of Evelyn, so an angry Eliza began to lay the table herself, banging the pots down as she cursed her daughter under her breath. Arthur arrived just after six.

'Where's Evelyn?' he asked as he sat down at the table.

'On that bloody bike again!' exclaimed Eliza. 'I told her to be back here before six but it's in one ear and out the other with her these days.'

'She won't be long, I'm sure,' ventured Arthur, trying to pacify her.

They ate their tea in silence, Eileen sensing that now was not a good time to talk. She hoped her sister would remember to come back soon or the rest of the evening would be spoilt by arguments and recriminations.

At a quarter to seven, just as they were finishing tea, there was a loud knock on the front door. Eliza got up grudgingly, irritated by this further disruption to her routine and expecting to see some kind of salesman. But the door swung open on a tall policeman with a solemn face.

'Mrs Pendlestone?' he ventured hesitantly.

'Yes.'

'I'm sorry to trouble you, madam, but I'm afraid I have to tell you that your daughter has been involved in a road accident. May I come in?'

Eliza's hands dropped to her sides. In a daze, she stood back to let the policeman go past her into the front room. By this time, Arthur and Eileen were both standing at the table, already terrified of what they might be about to hear.

The policeman told them the facts of the case as he knew them. Evelyn had been cycling towards Bradford on Wakefield Road when she swerved to avoid a pothole, not realising that a car was coming up behind her. The car driver apparently braked, but was going too fast to stop in time, hence the little girl was crushed by his front left wheel and lapsed into unconsciousness almost immediately. Someone called the police and Gladys gave them her friend's name and home address. Evelyn was taken by ambulance to Bradford Royal Infirmary but was pronounced dead on arrival. It was now his sad duty to give them this terrible news and to ask if either Mr or Mrs Pendlestone could accompany him to the hospital to formally identify Evelyn's body and collect her personal belongings.

'I'll go,' murmured Arthur softly. 'Stay here with your mother, Eileen, and look after her.'

The funeral was held one week later. The minister from Bowling Church had visited them every day since the accident to offer his support and it was agreed that Evelyn's body would be taken there for a short service before the burial in Bowling cemetery.

Alice and Jack came, of course, and George sent a telegram expressing his sympathy. There were only a few mourners – a teacher from Evelyn's school, Gladys and her mother, and a couple of neighbours.

Arthur, Eliza and Eileen stood in silence at the open grave as Evelyn's coffin was lowered into the ground. Too stunned to weep, they watched the minister sprinkle earth into the grave, intoning as he did so:

Ashes to ashes, dust to dust,

From dust we came and to dust we shall return.

Then, together, the three of them slowly placed a wreath of white flowers on the lid of the coffin. Attached to it was a card, which bore a message from them all:

To Evelyn, beloved daughter and sister,

who knew how to live life to the full.

All our love – mam, dad and Eileen.

The fatal accident was reported by a campaigning journalist in the local paper, who noted that Evelyn was one of seven thousand cyclists or pedestrians killed every year, a victim of the growing number of cars with few rules or safety regulations to control them; a victim too, perhaps, of the 1930 road traffic act, which abolished the twenty miles per hour speed limit for all vehicles carrying fewer than seven people, thereby giving affluent young men a licence to kill. Since the passing of this act, argued the journalist, accidents had increased dramatically.

Evelyn's parents, though, didn't see the relevance

of statistics. To them, Evelyn would always be the victim of her own love of risk and irrepressible sense of adventure.

Chapter 10

After Evelyn's death, Arthur started going to church again. He liked the young minister who had conducted her funeral and found that church gave him the time and space he needed to begin to come to terms with what had happened. He took Eileen with him. She would spend an hour in Sunday School while he attended the morning service.

Eliza rarely accompanied them. Although she believed in God, she found the services too long and complicated and struggled to stay awake during the sermon.

'I can pray just as well at home,' she'd say, as Arthur and Eileen went off to matins together.

The following April, about eight months after Evelyn's death, Alice and Jack tried to persuade Eliza to go away with them on an Easter break to Skegness. One of Alice's cousins had a boarding house there and she could offer them cheap rates.

'You need a few days' holiday, all of you,' said Alice. 'Skegness'll be a change. It'll do you good.'

Eliza hesitated. 'I'm not sure, Alice. It's not the

money. We can afford it, but it might be a bit soon after...' She looked away, leaving her sentence unfinished.

Alice, of course, understood. 'Well, have a think about it at any rate,' she urged.

Eliza talked it over with Arthur that night. He thought it might not be such a bad idea. It would get them away from the house with all its memories and could be good for Eileen, who hadn't had much attention, or indeed much fun, since Evelyn's accident. She had been quieter than ever recently and although she rarely mentioned her dead sister, they both knew that she missed her terribly.

When they told Eileen where they were going, her eyes lit up. She had never been to the seaside before, only heard about it from a couple of school friends who had once been on a day trip to Scarborough. Her father showed her the exact location of Skegness on his map of Great Britain.

'It's in Lincolnshire,' he told her, 'a different county. It's very flat all round there so you'll be able to see for miles.'

They boarded the train at Bradford but had to change trains twice. Eileen sat between Amy and

Dorothy. Eliza kept smiling across at her, thinking how good it was to see her chattering away to her two friends, as if she didn't have a care in the world.

'Are we nearly there?' the girls repeatedly asked, long before they reached their destination.

'Wait until we've changed trains again,' said Jack. 'Then we'll be nearly there.'

They chugged through miles of flat farmland, past hedgerows and ditches and meadows filled with wild flowers. Eventually, their train pulled into Skegness station, and for the first of many times, Eileen saw the famous *Welcome to Skegness* poster, its jolly fisherman strutting across the sands with his beaming face and white beard, the words *Skegness Is So Bracing* written beneath him. She quickly grew to love this picture, which seemed to capture something of that rising excitement all children feel as they look over the brow of a hill and suddenly catch their first glimpse of the sea.

The small boarding house was just off the front. To their delight, the girls had their own three-bedded room adjoining one of the two doubles occupied by their parents. The place was clean and comfortable, with a washbasin in each bedroom and a toilet on a nearby landing. Eliza helped the girls unpack before they all went out for a walk by the sea.

On her first afternoon, Eileen explored the wide sandy beach with Dorothy and Amy. They took off their shoes and socks to go paddling, their feet sinking deeper and deeper into a smooth muddy softness as the cold waves broke against their calves. Then they walked back across the hard, ribbed area of wet sand and over the endless sand dunes, where sharp marsh grasses cut their legs and seaweed wound itself around their toes. They kept on for what felt like miles until they saw their parents waving to them in the distance. Jack and Arthur had spread two travelling rugs on a patch of sand sheltered by a high dune and Alice was about to open their sandwiches and a large flask of tea.

Eileen loved everything about the place – the donkeys with their jangling bells, the long pier full of slot machines and amusements, the huge funfair, the seaside shops with their sticks of brightly coloured rock laid out neatly in rows between the beach balls and buckets and spades. She loved the salt smell of the sea and all the other smells that drifted past her nostrils as she strolled along the promenade – the sweet smell of freshly cooked doughnuts, the strong fishy smell of crabs and lobsters, of cockles and mussels, the smoky appetising smell of sausages sizzling on open grills.

In contrast, Eliza didn't enjoy herself at all. The whole experience only served to highlight what was now missing. In her mind's eye, she saw Evelyn everywhere she looked – begging for a ride on the donkeys, racing along to be first to the end of the pier, queuing to have a go on the fastest ride.

'It's too early, Arthur, too early for us to have come away on holiday,' she said as they got into bed on the first night. 'I wish we'd stayed at home.'

'I know, lass, I know,' he replied.

After her daughter's death, time passed slowly to Eliza. She forced herself to do all her household chores as usual and made sure that Arthur and Eileen had a proper cooked tea, but everything seemed more of an effort now and the house just wasn't the same. This wasn't the first great loss that Eliza had encountered in her life and grief had begun to take its toll on her. Her face looked drawn at times and a few strands of grey hair were now visible amongst the brown. Arthur couldn't help noticing that she was generally much quieter, less inclined to see the funny side of things and laughed far less than she used to do.

Eliza knew only too well that she was not the only one to have lost a child. In the streets of Saltaire, many babies and children had died of scarlet fever, diphtheria or measles, and even since she had lived in Bowling, there had been of the death of a one year-old only a couple of streets away. But this didn't make her own daughter's death any easier.

Her main reason for living now became Eileen. All Eliza's energies were directed towards ensuring that her younger daughter, almost eleven years old and in her last year of elementary school, made the most of the new opportunities that were opening up for women. From the age of seven, she had always come top of her class and had often been given extra homework to keep her motivated, so Eliza knew she must be clever.

One day, when she was waiting to collect her daughter at the school gates, Eileen's form teacher came over to have a word. She told Eliza that the school wanted Eileen to take some exams to win a place at grammar school.

'She's one of the cleverest pupils we've ever had,' Miss Oldroyd said. 'The headmaster thinks she's definitely university material. I know it may be something of a financial strain on the family to let her go to grammar school, Mrs Pendlestone, but I'd be failing in my duty if I didn't ask you to at least consider it. I really don't think there's much doubt that she'd pass the scholarship exams.'

Eliza had a serious talk with Arthur about what they should do. Although winning a scholarship meant you didn't have to pay school fees, you had to be able to pay for the uniform throughout the time the child was there. Many families, unable to do this, didn't allow their child to enter for the exams, and a few had to let their child's free place go to someone else when, at the eleventh hour, they found they couldn't actually afford it.

'I'm sure my mother's money would cover the uniform,' said Arthur, looking anxious, 'but she'll need books and tram fares to and from school and there'll probably be a few unseen extras as well.'

'I don't care Arthur,' replied Eliza. 'This could be her big chance to make something of herself and I'm not going to let it go. If need be, I'll take a cleaning job to bring in a bit of extra cash.'

Next day, Eliza went up to the school to tell Miss Oldroyd they had made up their minds to let Eileen sit for the exams.

'I'm sure you won't regret it,' said Miss Oldroyd, overjoyed at the news. 'That girl of yours is going to make you so proud, one day, Mrs Pendlestone. She really is exceptionally bright.'

The morning of the first scholarship exam came round at the end of June. Eileen had been working harder than ever in the weeks leading up to the big day and Miss Oldroyd had done all she could to help her prepare. Before he left for work, Arthur popped his head round her bedroom door to wish her good luck and Eliza made sure that she had an extra slice of toast for breakfast, insisting this would help to keep her going and would stop her feeling hungry in the middle of the exam. As she left the house, Eileen looked back over her shoulder, smiling nervously.

'Good luck, my love,' cried Eliza, waving. 'You'll do it. I know you will.'

She watched her daughter walk away and imagined all the opportunities a place at a grammar school would bring. For the first time in many years, she felt the old fire stirring again in her bones, felt the heat of a flame she thought had long since gone out, and that strange unstoppable passion for life she had known so long ago, when Laurie had promised to take her with him to see the world.

Chapter 11

One Saturday morning in late July, an official-looking envelope dropped through the door. Neither Arthur nor Eliza dared pick it up.

'Go on Eileen,' said Arthur. 'It's what you've been waiting for, so you'd better open it.'

Trembling with fear and excitement, Eileen ran a knife along the top of the envelope and took out a letter typed on headed notepaper. She scanned it quickly, then beamed at her parents. 'I've passed!' she cried, 'I've got a scholarship to Bradford Girls' Grammar School.'

Arthur hugged his daughter tightly, hardly able to speak for joy. Eliza was so happy she did a little jig round the table before rushing out to tell the neighbours.

News of Eileen's success soon spread down the street and lots of people called in to congratulate her. Miss Oldroyd, thrilled to hear the news from the headmaster, came round to visit later that day.

'We're all so proud of you, Eileen,' she said. 'You're the first girl in the school to win a scholarship to Bradford Girls' Grammar. Come back and tell us how you're getting on, won't you?'

'Yes, yes I will,' murmured Eileen, looking slightly embarrassed by all the fuss.

'Don't worry, Miss Oldroyd,' said Eliza, showing her out, 'I'll make sure she does.'

The following Saturday, Jack and Alice had promised to take Eileen, Dorothy and Amy for a day out in Harrogate, the famous spa town about half an hour by train from Bradford. Arthur and Eliza now decided to come, too. They insisted on taking everyone for afternoon tea in Betty's cafe as a special treat to celebrate Eileen's success.

The fame of Betty's was already spreading around the whole of West Yorkshire and beyond. It was *the* place to go for tea. Built in 1919, the elegant, fashionable Harrogate tea rooms had already been patronised by royalty, prompting the owner, a Swiss confectioner by the name of Frederick Belmont, to inscribe the words *Royal and Distinguished Patronage* on its letterhead.

At precisely four o'clock, both families gingerly edged their way through the glass-panelled doors and into a world of luxurious elegance, the like of which they had never seen before. Large glittering chandeliers hung from the ornate ceiling, tall potted palms leaned decorously between pillars, and waitresses in starched white aprons and frilly caps weaved their way in and out of tables, vanishing or reappearing through the double doors that led to the kitchen at the back. Above the delicate chink of teaspoon on cup, of cup on saucer, above the constant buzz of polite conversation, the melodies of George Gershwin and Cole Porter floated unobtrusively, played with great panache by Gerald, the resident pianist.

A gushing waitress showed them to a table and they gazed at the vast assortment of china and silverware spread out before them. Eileen's eyes lighted on a silver dish full of sugar cubes with what looked like a pair of tweezers in them.

'What are those?' she whispered.

'I think they're called sugar-tongs,' said Alice, who remembered her own mother talk of how she used to polish them when she was in service.

Eliza ordered tea, with scones and jam, trying as hard as she could to disguise her broad Yorkshire accent but failing dismally. The waitress returned quickly, bearing a silver tray with two teapots, which she placed in the middle of the table. These were soon accompanied by a three-tiered solid silver cake-stand containing a variety of scones, delicately arranged on white doilies. Finally, four large bone china dishes arrived, two filled with clotted cream and two with strawberry jam.

In virtual silence, the families ate their tea, overawed by the splendour of the place. At one point, Jack was tempted to joke with one of the passing waitresses, but before he had time to open his mouth, Alice whispered loudly, 'Shhh, Jack! Don't! You'll show us all up!'

The scones were truly delicious and everyone made sure they did them justice, eating every last crumb. Arthur asked for the bill, which duly arrived, and then they rose as one, taking care that their chairs didn't scrape too loudly on the polished wooden floor. They headed for the cash desk at the front.

While Arthur was paying, Eileen watched the sophisticated ladies with their long cigarette holders, all leaning back in their chairs, nonchalantly sipping tea, and wondered if grammar school would ever make her feel at home in such company. Would she ever be able to mix with people like them?

Once they were safely outside and could talk normally again, Alice proclaimed loudly, so that all the world could hear, 'By hell, they know what to charge in that place!'

At the end of August, Eliza took Eileen to the designated outfitters in Bradford to buy her new school uniform. They went into a cubicle together for Eileen to try on the various items of clothing listed on her letter of acceptance from the school.

'They're a bit big,' Eileen said, looking down at the blazer sleeves that fell below her knuckles and the long grey gymslip that came almost to her ankles.

'I know, but we've got to give you a chance to grow into them,' said Eliza, meaning they couldn't afford the right sizes because they would be too small within a year or two. 'I can always turn up the sleeves and shorten the skirt on the gymslip and then alter them again when you get a bit bigger.'

With the addition of two white blouses, a regulation tie, navy blue knickers, a velour hat and a pair of hockey boots, the total cost was much higher than either Arthur or Eliza had expected. Yet these outfits were only for the first two terms. In the summer, Eileen would need a regulation summer dress and a panama hat.

Eliza knew she had no alternative. She had to find a job.

Since Evelyn's death, Eliza had got to know her neighbours much better. Many of them had called round to offer help and support after they heard of the accident. She was particularly friendly with Mrs Newbury, next door, and with Mrs Braithwaite, three doors down. They often popped in for a cup of tea and a chat and Eliza told them both about how she'd have to get some work to help pay for Eileen's education.

One afternoon in early September, Mrs Braithwaite called round to tell Eliza that she'd heard there was a cleaning job going at some solicitors' offices about half a mile away in Manchester Road. She said a friend who worked there happened to know that their evening cleaner had just handed in her notice. Eliza took down some details and paid the firm a visit the next day.

After a brief interview, she was taken on to clean five nights a week from seven to half past nine. She was to be paid ten shillings a week and was expected to start the following month. Although she knew it would make life hard and meant that she wouldn't get much of a chance to see Eileen during the week, Eliza was pleased, thinking it worth any sacrifice to get her through grammar school.

On the first day of term, Eliza straightened Eileen's tie before waving her off. Her little girl looked so small in her oversized blazer, so vulnerable, that Eliza wanted to put her arms around her. She knew instinctively, though, that her daughter would shy away from such an open show of affection on the front doorstep, so she gave her a quick peck on the cheek and a whispered, 'Good luck, love.'

Tram fare in hand, Eileen slung her schoolbag on her shoulder and strode off into her new life. She got off at a stop very near to the school gates and walked down the steep slope of Hallfield Road to the old building which, in early Victorian times, had been a school for boys. It had been refurbished in 1875, when the girls' grammar school was founded, a school now renowned for its excellent academic record.

Eileen stood outside for a moment, gazing up at the soot-blackened three-storey building with its high pointed gables and long narrow windows. It looked dark, forbidding. Yet this was to be her second home for the foreseeable future.

The butterflies fluttered in her stomach as she

made her way through the front entrance and into the playground at the back, where scores of girls were congregating, all busily exchanging news following their extended summer holiday. She was struck by how refined they all sounded, how self-confident they all seemed.

'Mummy took me to London in August,' said a tall girl to her friend. 'It was so hot and crowded I could hardly breathe. How about you?'

'Oh, we went to one of those big hotels in Scarborough. It was all pretty boring really, apart from the horse riding.'

Eileen was daunted by the strange way they spoke, pronouncing the 'h' at the beginning of words and sort of elongating all their vowels, just like people did on the radio. And how could anyone possibly think a seaside holiday in a grand hotel in Scarborough was boring?

At the sound of the bell, she went inside and tried to follow directions to classroom 1A, her footsteps echoing down the gloomy stone corridors. The place was huge and every corridor looked alike. After several minutes she panicked, realising she was lost. Desperate now, she forced herself to stop one of the older girls walking past.

'Excuse me,' she faltered, 'I'm looking for classroom 1A.'

The older girl was pleasant enough, directing her left and right down further long corridors. Eventually, she discovered the room she wanted and joined twenty-five other first year girls, all about to be addressed by their form teacher, Miss Lucas.

Eileen took a seat at a wooden desk with a white china inkwell in the corner. She placed her pen in the long narrow ridge running along the top of the desk, then opened the desk lid to check how much space there was inside. At this point, Miss Lucas tapped on the board for silence and formally welcomed them to the school. First of all, she gave them a copy of their weekly timetable and Eileen was amazed to learn that she was to have different teachers for different subjects. She was equally amazed to discover that they would sometimes have lessons in different rooms. Such things were unheard of in her previous school.

After checking their names, Miss Lucas took them to the great assembly hall where the rest of the school had now gathered to be addressed by the headmistress, Miss Browning, a tall grey-haired woman with a pinched face, who swept imperiously down the central aisle and up the steps onto the stage.

'Ladies, welcome back,' she began, scanning the rows of girls for any sign of fidgeting or lack of attention. 'May I remind you all, especially the new girls, that you are extremely privileged to be here and that the highest academic standards will be expected of you throughout your stay.'

Not daring to move a muscle, Eileen sat bolt upright, absorbing every single word until the announcement of a hymn, when she followed the lead of those in front of her and rose to her feet. After a short prayer, they were dismissed, filing out one row at a time.

Later that morning Miss Lucas took them on a tour of the building, pointing out the library, the domestic science room, the gym with its adjoining changing facilities, and finally, the art room. They were told that there were no playing fields attached to the school. They would use the grounds in the nearby preparatory school, where tennis courts and hockey pitches were available. Netball lessons, however, would take place in the school playground.

'I realise, girls,' said Miss Lucas, 'that our sports

facilities are far from ideal at the moment, but you'll be pleased to hear that you won't have to endure them for long. In just over a year from now, we shall all be moving to a brand new building in another part of town, with excellent hockey pitches and brand new tennis and netball courts available on site.'

A polite murmur of approval from the class greeted this announcement, at which point a bell rang for the first lesson and Eileen trooped out after the others. Terrified of losing sight of them and getting lost again, she increased her stride to make sure she kept up and soon found herself in another classroom with long lines of desks, hardly distinguishable from the first.

The lesson passed quickly, and at break time, Eileen discovered two other girls in her class who, like herself, had won a scholarship. They huddled together in a corner of the playground, chatting, all three somewhat overwhelmed by the brave new world they had just entered. One girl came from Bierley, not far from Bowling, the other lived on the other side of Bradford. Conscious of how different they sounded, how much more awkward they looked compared with their more affluent classmates, they vowed to stick together and give each other moral support.

At the end of her first day, Eileen caught the tram back home with her new friend, Bertha, who got off two stops after her. Relieved to be back, Eileen had something of a spring in her step as she walked down the hill to her house.

'Well, come on then,' said Eliza, standing anxiously at the front door as her daughter came up the path. 'What was it like?'

'It was just as if I'd stepped into another world, mam,' said Eileen, 'but I think I'm going to like it.'

At the end of her very first week at grammar school, Eileen persuaded her parents to go blackberrying. This was something they had done together each September since Evelyn's death. A colleague of Arthur had told him of an excellent place to go, which very few other people knew about. It was near the village of Spofforth, about two miles from Harrogate.

The three of them caught the train to Harrogate early on Saturday morning and walked for about half an hour along a winding country lane before cutting through a gap in the dry stone wall and crossing a field to the bramble hedges laden with blackberries. They each carried a large metal dish. Eileen loved the soft thud the first blackberries made as she dropped them into it. Once she had picked enough to line the bottom of the dish, of course, they made no sound at all. The satisfaction then lay in watching the small pile grow steadily bigger until the container was full to the brim.

'Why the hell are the best ones always just out of reach?' moaned Eliza, trying to pull down a high branch that was holding a tantalising cluster of large blackberries about three feet above her head.

As her mother was struggling to get them, Eileen turned and suddenly caught sight of a strange creature climbing one of the oak trees beyond the hedge. It settled on a high branch, stretching itself out in the sunshine, its shiny black coat glistening in the light. With both of its pointed ears twitching, it stared at them warily through bright green eyes.

'Look!' said Eileen to Arthur. 'What on earth is it, dad?'

'It's a wild cat, love,' he replied. 'I haven't seen one for years.'

Eileen was fascinated by it. As soon as she arrived home, she looked in one of Arthur's encyclopaedias, trying to discover more about this wonderful creature. Meanwhile, Eliza baked four blackberry and apple pies, intending to give two of them to Alice.

At school on the Monday, Eileen was delighted when Miss Lucas asked if anyone had been anywhere or seen anything unusual at the weekend. She put up her hand at once.

'Me and dad saw a wild cat while we were blackberrying,' she said, excitedly.

But Miss Lucas was not impressed. 'Eileen,' she said in a somewhat reproving tone, 'just think about what you're saying before you speak. You meant *my father and I,* I'm sure.'

'Yes, miss,' replied Eileen, covered in embarrassment and blushing to her roots.

She was crestfallen. For the first time, she realised that it was not just the content of what you said that mattered, but the way you said it. From then on, she resolved to develop a school way of speaking which would be entirely separate from the way she spoke at home. Never again would one form of speech encroach on the territory of the other.

Chapter 12

Eileen's first year at grammar school was happy and successful. She thrived in the academic atmosphere, excited by the challenge of new subjects and the stimulation of new ideas. Before long, she was proving to be the cleverest girl in her class, coming top in the end of year exams.

In her second year, the whole school moved to a new building on the outskirts of the city. Its location was farther from Eileen's home and meant that she had to take two trams to get there, but Eileen felt it was well worth it. The classrooms and corridors were so spacious, light and airy, and as Miss Lucas had promised, there were large grounds and playing fields, including tennis courts. She soon settled into the new travelling routine and took full advantage of the extensive facilities on offer. The girls all felt that they now inhabited an establishment worthy to compete with the prestigious Bradford Grammar, a school for boys that dated back to the sixteenth century.

Around this time, Arthur became a sidesman at the local Anglican church and Eileen, having grown too old for Sunday School, accompanied him to the morning service every week. Together, they would join in the songs of praise that reflected the passing of the seasons – Epiphany, Lent, Easter, Pentecost, Harvest, Advent – each season clearly defined by its particular cluster of hymns that marked life's eternal rhythms.

Eileen loved them all, especially *O Love That Wilt Not Let Me Go*. Its tune was slow and solemn and the words had enormous emotional power. She sometimes felt the hairs on the back of her neck bristle in the last verse, especially the last line, where a long high note is held for what seems like an eternity before the dying fall of the final two notes:

> *I lay in dust life's glory dead,*
> *And from the ground there blossoms red*
> *Life that shall endless be.*

After the service, Eileen would stroll home with her father, both always avoiding the short cut through the park where they had walked with Evelyn only a few years before.

It was on one of these walks that Eileen mentioned to him that she now felt ready to take holy communion and asked if she could attend confirmation classes. Arthur assented, of course, and it was arranged that she should go to classes in the autumn with a view to being confirmed just before Christmas. Her faith was growing and developing now, moving away from the simple 'picture book' theology of her childhood days. She had always been drawn to the figure of Christ, and as far back as she could remember, had prayed. It seemed right, therefore, that she should prepare herself to take the next step in her spiritual life and start to participate in the sacrament of holy communion.

She was duly confirmed that December and Arthur and Eliza attended the ceremony, both of them filled with pride as she took her vows. Eileen herself was nervous, hoping she would remember the responses she had learnt off by heart. Kneeling at the altar with four others, she waited for the bishop to pass along the line and place his hands upon her head, confirming that she had now accepted for herself the vows taken on her behalf at baptism and had become a full member of the church. The moment soon came. She felt the bishop's palms resting on her hair and heard his deep, gentle voice intone the words from the Book of Common Prayer, which, as always, were beautiful and filled her with a deep sense of wonder: *Defend O Lord, this thy child with thy heavenly grace, that she may continue thine for ever and daily increase in thy Holy Spirit more and more, until she come to thy everlasting kingdom.*

The following Sunday morning, Arthur proudly accompanied Eileen down the aisle and knelt beside her as she took communion. His relationship with his daughter remained incredibly close, and sometimes, watching her as she walked back from church, her delicate features and dark hair streaked with sunlight, her face alight with happiness, he felt his heart was about to burst with love.

He saw more of her in the week now than Eliza, who went out to her cleaning job at half past six every weeknight, leaving Eileen to do the washing up. Arthur would often give her a hand with this and then they would sit down together to do Eileen's homework. At first, Arthur encouraged his daughter to explain to him all that she had learned in school that day, thinking that this might help her to consolidate and better understand new ideas. He found it fascinating to listen to the way she explained difficult concepts so clearly and loved to share with her the little knowledge he had.

Their evening routine worked well for a time, but before long, Arthur began to struggle to keep pace and Eileen found the whole process slow and frustrating. Arthur sensed this and gradually withdrew, contributing to his daughter's homework only when she asked for help. He would pretend to read the paper but would secretly watch her working on the sitting room table, her tiny face screwed up in concentration, her pen scraping across the blank pages in her exercise books as she filled them with ideas, perceptions, judgments that were way beyond his understanding. Then, his heart would swell with pride and he would think of his words to Eliza as they stood together beside The Strid. Eileen would find her way in the world, all right, she would be her own woman.

Eileen's relationship with Eliza was very different from the one she had with Arthur. She was close to her mother, too, but in a less intellectual, more practical way. Eliza never attempted to understand what Eileen was reading or what she was doing at school or how her mind worked. These things never mattered to her. She would just enjoy chatting to her or going shopping or doing some baking with her on a Saturday afternoon.

If she was ever ill, it was always to Eliza that Eileen would turn for comfort and emotional support. Eliza would sit for hours beside her sick bed, anxiously turning over the pages of her red 'Doctor Book' that outlined the symptoms of common ailments and prescribed ways of treating them. It was filled with rather gruesome-looking photographs of goitres and bunions and such like and Eliza was always panic-stricken when Eileen's symptoms corresponded in any way with some of the more serious illnesses listed. Usually, Eileen would recover from whatever ailed her in a day or two, and then Eliza would return the red book to its place in the bookcase until the next illness came along.

One evening, while they were having tea, Eliza turned to Eileen and asked about how her friend, Bertha, was getting on.

'Oh, she's fine,' replied Eileen. 'I didn't come home with her today, though, because she's learning to play the piano. She's got lessons every Tuesday afternoon.'

Eliza and Arthur exchanged a knowing look.

'Is that something you'd like to do, lass?' he asked his daughter.

Eileen paused for a moment. 'Yes, but only if you can really afford, it, dad,' she answered.

'We'll see what we can do, love,' smiled her father.

More scrimping and saving followed. With some of the money she had saved from her cleaning job, Eliza paid for her father's old piano to be tuned. Arthur's recent small wage rise paid for the lessons.

Eileen made quick progress. Before long, strains of *The Carnival Of Venice* could be heard as Arthur came in from work. Various classical pieces came next, regularly prefaced by half an hour of scales.

Knowing it was her mother's favourite, Eileen got the music for *Onward Christian Soldiers* and played it for her one Sunday afternoon. Eliza's face lit up with joy, but there was a tinge of sadness in her voice as she said, 'Ee, I wish my pa could hear you play this. He'd be that proud of you.'

'Do you still have any of his music?' asked Eileen.

'Oh no, love, no, he never had any music. He played by ear,' Eliza said. 'I think they call it vamping. He used to play all the music hall songs, especially the ones that Vesta Tilley sang. His favourite one was *After The*

Ball.'

Eileen returned to her piano practice, amazed that anyone could have such an extraordinary gift and wishing that she had it, too.

That summer, Eileen was chosen to play for the school's junior tennis team. The six girls in the team had already won a number of fixtures, when one Friday in late May, they travelled to Keighley Girls' Grammar School.

Eileen's partner, Margaret, was better than her. She had an excellent backhand, so usually played on the left side of the court. Although they had won all their previous games, the pair struggled hard to defeat their Keighley opponents and their match went to three long sets. Eventually, they were victorious, but by the time they had eaten tea, it was almost seven o'clock. As they were walking back to the school bus, Margaret suddenly called out, 'Look! What's that up there in the sky?'

Everyone stopped to stare at the strange object hovering above them. Eileen thought it looked like a huge fat floating cigar. It obviously had engines inside because you could hear them droning in the distance, like a motorcycle ticking over. The mysterious craft continued sailing towards them, its left side lit up by the rays of the setting sun.

Awestruck, Eileen gazed at the craft for a full five minutes as it passed slowly overhead, almost blocking out the sky. It seemed to be flying so low that it could touch the treetops, and from its windows, she could see the faces of people staring down at her. There was some writing on the side and Eileen made out the name, *Hindenburg*. She looked along the huge main body towards the tail fins, on each of which she saw a great black symbol, like a diagonal back to front 'z' with another back to front 'z' going across it. The strange image resembled a dark maze or the sign of a cross with projections jutting out at right angles from each end.

'What on earth is that?' she said to Margaret, who was standing open-mouthed beside her.

'I haven't got the faintest idea,' she replied, neither of them realising that they were actually gazing at the symbol which was to dominate Europe over the next decade and strike fear into so many hearts.

Later, Eileen discovered that the object she had seen was, in fact, Germany's Hindenburg Zeppelin, the largest airship in the world, on its way back from the

United States to Frankfurt and carrying hundreds of passengers. Scores of people in and around Keighley had left their chores or their wireless sets and rushed out into their gardens with box cameras to take a picture of the strange flying machine. The unprecedented event was already the talk of the entire neighbourhood by the time she got home.

The following Tuesday night, after tea, Arthur suddenly tossed the local paper across to Eileen while she was doing her homework on the living room table. 'Here, you want to read that article, love,' he said. 'It's all about what you saw on Friday.'

Eileen scanned it quickly. The report said that one of the passengers on the Hindenburg had dropped a parcel from the ship directly onto Keighley High Street. It was opened by a local resident and found to contain a bunch of carnations, a small silver and jet crucifix, a picture of an airship, some postage stamps and a sheet of Hindenburg notepaper, on which was written the following:

To the finder of this message.
Please deposit these flowers and cross on the grave of my dear

brother, Lieutenant Franz Schulte, Prisoner of War, who was buried in Skipton Cemetery in Keighley, near Leeds.

Many thanks for your kindness.

John P Schulte, the first flying priest.

NB. Please accept the stamps and picture as a small souvenir from me. God bless you!

The newspaper article went on to confirm that Franz Schulte was indeed a prisoner of the First World War, who had died of influenza and had subsequently been buried in Skipton cemetery. As requested, the flowers had been duly deposited on his grave.

For weeks afterwards, the Hindenburg story was the talk of Bradford. It was discovered from the various photographs taken that the airship had flown over most of the town, lingering especially above factories, foundries, railway lines and engineering works. This gave rise to grave suspicions, many local people believing that the airship, far from being an innocent passenger craft, was actually flying low for a purpose, probably because it was on some kind of reconnaissance mission.

The next two years ushered in momentous events

both at home and abroad – Hitler's invasion of Austria, the Spanish Civil War, the death of King George V, the abdication of his older son, Edward, and the crowning of his second son, George. It was the last of these events that had the most immediate impact on Eileen.

On the day of the coronation, all the girls assembled in the school hall to listen to the ceremony broadcast on the wireless, the tension of the occasion increased by everyone's fears that the new king's stammer might let him down at the crucial moment. Everything went smoothly, though, and despite persistent rain washing out the afternoon pageant in Peel Park, which Eileen's class had hoped to attend, there was still the evening firework display to look forward to. In celebration of the momentous day, all the children in the school were given a commemorative coronation mug. Eileen carried hers home very carefully and Eliza made sure it was given pride of place next to the marble clock on the mantelpiece.

One day in November 1938, the pupils were addressed by the headmistress at a special assembly and told that, just as a precaution, every girl in the school was to be issued with a gas mask. They were not to worry about this, it was simply a precaution, she reassured them. Mr Chamberlain, she was sure, would protect the country from harm and successfully negotiate a lasting peace with Hitler.

She was, of course, proved wrong. Less than a year later, on the third of September, the solemn voice of Neville Chamberlain, far from proclaiming a lasting peace, announced that the country was now at war with Germany. Soon afterwards, the sound of the first air-raid siren was heard. A nationwide blackout had already been ordered by the government, so Arthur had recently put special tape around all their windows to stop flying glass and Eliza had made blackout curtains. At night, the city was plunged into darkness; street lamps remained unlit, all road signs were removed and air-raid wardens patrolled the streets to ensure not a chink of light was visible from people's homes.

Mrs Braithwaite's husband built an Anderson shelter in his back garden, which was reinforced with concrete bricks. Eliza and the family, together with other neighbours, were invited to share it. Everybody would squeeze in there as soon as the sirens went off. Eileen found it claustrophobic and frightening. She hated being squashed between other people's bodies, hated the stench of damp earth and sweat and musty blankets. The shelter was prone to flooding, however, and was sometimes unusable, greatly to Eileen's relief. She much preferred the alternative way of taking cover – sitting under the stairs with her mother.

A few months after the declaration of war, a very large, extremely long white van drew up beside the school. Lessons were suddenly interrupted as pupils in every class were told to go outside, carrying their gas masks, and line up in front of it. Every girl was then forced to walk through the gas-filled vehicle wearing her mask. Many were terrified and Eileen never forgot the sensation of panic as she staggered from one end to the other, struggling to breathe, the uncomfortable mask clasped tightly to her face. As soon as she made it through the exit door, she quickly wrenched off the repulsive object, but the smell of rubber mixed with disinfectant lingered in her nostrils for hours afterwards.

Against the somewhat surreal backdrop of gas masks, blackout curtains, darkened streets and roads with no signs, amidst the constant drone of enemy aircraft flying overhead towards Liverpool and Manchester, much of life went on as normal. The clip-clop of the coal man's horse continued to wake them all on Tuesday, the sound of the hurdy-gurdy man's barrel organ blasted forth, as always, every Saturday morning and the cries of 'rag and bone, rag and bone' still echoed down the streets on Friday nights.

Apart from rationing and food shortages, which everyone found hard, the war brought with it an air of danger and excitement. Life was less humdrum, routines were more easily broken, new friendships more easily formed.

Arthur felt he should do something to help the war effort and volunteered to be a fire watcher at his offices. The job involved watching for incendiary bombs outside of working hours and he volunteered to be part of a rota, usually working two nights from around half past ten until the early hours of the morning. Each fire watcher was issued with a bucket of sand, a bucket of water and a stirrup pump and was expected to extinguish the incendiaries before a fire could take hold. Eliza was back from her cleaning job before Arthur had to go out on fire duty, so there was always someone in to take care of Eileen.

In July 1940, however, the cleaning job came to an end. Many of the young solicitors had been called up and the firm, inevitably a much smaller operation, was looking to make cuts. Eliza wasn't too worried, since there was now no shortage of jobs for women. Within a fortnight, she had found part-time morning work as a cleaner in another small company on nearby Rooley Lane. Although this meant she had to spend time on household chores in the evening, Eliza didn't mind at all, since she saw more of Eileen and could also meet Alice on a more regular basis.

Dorothy and Amy were both working now, Dorothy in Lister's mill and Amy as a filing clerk in the gas board. Eliza hadn't seen much of any of them for a while and was eager to catch up on their news. During her first week in the new job, she arranged to meet Alice in Collinson's cafe in the centre of town. A waitress ushered them to a table not far from where a string trio were playing the latest dance hits, and they ordered two toasted teacakes and a pot of tea.

'Come on, Alice, I'm dying to hear all your news,' Eliza said. 'How are those girls of yours getting on?'

'Oh, not so bad, not so bad. They bring in a fair

bit of money between them so they're managing all right. They miss seeing you and Eileen, though. Maybe now you've got a bit more time, Eliza, we can all meet up one Saturday.'

'Ay, that'd be grand,' replied Eliza. 'We could go round Rawson Market and have something to eat at Pie Tom's like we used to. And maybe we can go to a film at the new Odeon in the evening. I'm dying to see what it's like inside.'

They arranged to meet up at three o'clock on the last Saturday in August. The three girls went off shopping together while Alice and Eliza trawled the market, looking for bargains. They met up later at Pie Tom's for a meat pie and some mushy peas covered in mint sauce, which, despite being more expensive than when they last had them, still tasted wonderful. Then, soon after seven, they walked excitedly down Manchester Road for their first visit to the new Odeon.

The cinema had opened just over eighteen months earlier and was the largest Odeon in the country at that time, even bigger than the one in Leicester Square. It could seat almost three thousand people and was said to have cost more than seventy-five thousand pounds to build, its interior being described as 'a study in silver and gold.' The all glass top of its tower was radiant, its red and green neon lights making it a landmark visible across the city, until the outbreak of the war, of course, when all its outside lights had to be turned off.

Eileen had heard of its magnificence from school friends and had been longing to see a film there. Eliza and Alice paid for the girls. They were charged ninepence for the cheapest seats in the stalls, being assured by the woman on the cash desk that all the seats were identical and offered the same level of comfort, regardless of price.

The long stalls foyer with its bright lights led down to a wide staircase curving to the left and into the rear of the auditorium. Their first impression was of the sheer vastness of the place. Suspended chandeliers provided a soft amber light which, combined with the graduated colours of silver at the back, down to gold at the front, gave the place a restful atmosphere. Alice and Eliza were surprised to see there was no organ, unlike other cinemas they had visited, but Eileen pointed out that it was the quality of the film that mattered, not organ music in the interval.

For a little more than two and a half hours, they

reclined in the luxurious gold plush seats, carried away by the wonderful acting of Walter Pidgeon and Deanna Durbin, and like all the rest of the enraptured audience, forgetting totally the hardships of war.

When the lights went up at the end, there was an audible sigh of disappointment from the audience, signalling their realisation that they would now have to return to the gloomy real world of shortages and ration books and the constant struggle to make ends meet.

'What would we do without pictures like this?' exclaimed Alice.

'I know, I feel a hell of a lot better after seeing that. Don't you girls?' asked Eliza.

They all agreed and Amy, whose crush on Walter Pidgeon was well known, made her sister giggle by whispering how much she'd like to have him all to herself on a desert island.

Eileen and Eliza led the way to the exit, and arm in arm, stepped out into the street, blinking several times in an attempt to encourage their eyes to adjust to the pitch black all around them. Alice and her daughters followed and they stood together for a moment, trying to work out the way to the nearest tram stop.

'I think it's this way,' said Alice. She was about to say more but was suddenly interrupted by the loud, ominous wail of an air-raid siren. The sound pitch rose and fell, rose and fell, spreading panic amongst the crowds that were leaving the packed cinema and sending them rushing in all directions in search of the nearest air-raid shelter.

'Where shall we go?' screamed Dorothy, straining to make herself heard above the racket all around them.

'I think there's a public shelter in the old recreation ground about half a mile behind the cinema,' Alice cried. 'Let's go up there.'

They ran together hand in hand up the steep street that led away from the town towards the moors high above. Others followed and soon a great crowd of people were making their way to one of the many temporary refuges the council had built on the outskirts of the city. They were larger and stronger than the Anderson shelters and consisted of trenches dug deep into the ground and lined with concrete. It was vital to camouflage them, so they were usually grassed over or capped with earth or sometimes tarmac. People knew they offered no protection against a direct hit but they did give excellent protection against a near miss and against flying debris such as roof slates, masonry and glass.

Eliza reached the shelter first and pulled Eileen close to her. They squeezed their way in through a tiny entrance and down into the heart of the earth, carried along by a surging mass of bodies, everyone anxious to find a place inside. Alice and the twins caught up with them, picking their way through to the long damp tunnel lined with wooden benches and lit dimly by a couple of electric lights attached to the ceiling.

It was the first time any of them had been in such a shelter and they found it scary and uncomfortable. Here they would have to stay until the all-clear sounded, but no one knew when that would be, possibly not for many hours. Although lots of people were standing, they managed to find a seat together on one of the benches at the side and settled themselves for what might be a long wait.

Eileen gazed around, anxious to take in every detail of these new surroundings. There were various notices – 'No Smoking' and 'Pets Not Allowed'. She was amused to see that the concrete walls had been used by some people as a canvas or sketch-pad on which to draw or scribble their thoughts. Above the head of the man opposite she could see a portrait of Hitler with two breasts, and next to it, a pencil drawing of him naked with one testicle. Beneath it were the words, 'Hitler's only got one ball, the other's in the Albert Hall'. Farther along, there were 'Victory V' signs followed by a dot-dot-dot-dash and then lots of the usual love messages you saw regularly behind the door of every public convenience.

The thought of public conveniences made her aware that she badly needed a toilet. Peering down the tunnel to her left, she spotted a large 'WC' sign in black capital letters with arrows pointing to left and right, one for ladies, the other gents. Eliza assured her she would keep her place, so Eileen jostled her way through the crowd and then entered the narrow passage to the lavatories. There were three of them, all situated behind rickety wooden doors with no locks. The toilet itself was a large rectangular concrete bucket with a wooden seat and smelt dreadful. Eileen did what was necessary as fast as she possibly could, being careful not to sit down, then returned to her mother, relieved to be away from the stench.

Above them they could hear the low buzz of

209

aircraft and intermittent explosions, followed by various crashes and bangs. Eliza took hold of Eileen's hand and held it tightly, sensing her unease. The noises were scary enough, but not being certain of exactly what was happening outside seemed worse.

'Was dad on fire watch duty tonight?' Eileen asked her mother, suddenly remembering it might have been his turn on the rota.

'My God, I think he was!'

Eliza's voice had a note of panic in it and Eileen was worried. They sat in silence, each thinking about Arthur and praying that he might be safe.

At about a quarter to ten, Arthur went upstairs to the bathroom. He always liked to have a wash and shave to freshen himself up before going out for his fire watching duties. Shaving brush in hand, he covered his face with lather. Then, picking up his razor and contorting his face to tighten the skin on his left cheek, he slowly drew the blade down in a straight line from ear to chin.

The thought of fire watching didn't bother him at all now, although, when he had first been asked about volunteering, he had hesitated, afraid that the noise of warplanes going over and the occasional incendiary bomb might once again trigger the memories that had continually haunted him and that, at last, he seemed to have under some sort of control. There were occasional times when he felt the need to read Dickens or summon up the image of his mother's face, but these were becoming rarer and rarer.

He had moved his razor to the other cheek now and was listening to the slight scraping sound the blade made as it removed the stubble. He remembered how Evelyn and Eileen had both loved to run their hands across his bristles when they were tiny. It was strange how quickly they had disappeared, his little girls. He could see them still in his mind's eye, still hear their giggles as he lay beside them on the hearthrug, one sitting on his head and pulling his hair, the other astride his chest and running her fingers over the prickles on his cheeks.

His shave complete, he dabbed his face dry, rinsed the washbasin and went down to the hallway. He removed his jacket and tin hat from one of the coat pegs below the stairs and left to catch the tram to the centre of Bradford.

The offices were four storeys high and Arthur had to pick up his bucket of sand, water bucket and stirrup pump from his locker on the third floor before climbing the final set of stairs onto the roof. It was now exactly twenty minutes past ten, and just as Arthur emerged through the trap door that opened onto the top of the building, the keening of an air-raid siren pierced the silence.

Initially unconcerned, he eased himself up onto the concrete roof and gazed around. The siren often sounded, but the planes usually just flew over, having more important targets than Bradford to concentrate upon. Tonight, though, was different. Very soon, the sound of low flying aircraft was accompanied by loud explosions and fires started to break out all over the place. It was the worst night of bombing the city had seen so far and Arthur feared that Eliza and Eileen were caught up in it somewhere. The raid must have begun a few minutes after they left the cinema and he was terrified that they would not have had time to get to a shelter.

Suddenly, an incendiary bomb landed on the roof about thirty yards away and another fire watcher arrived to help Arthur put it out. Still frantic with worry about his wife and daughter, Arthur put the end of his pump in one of his buckets of water, and with his foot firmly lodged in the stirrup, pumped away, his colleague holding the other end of the hose and directing the water jet onto the bomb before it had time to do any damage. It was soon extinguished, but there were fires everywhere now, and enemy planes continued droning high above on their way back from raids on Liverpool and Manchester.

Arthur kept checking his watch. It had been hours since the warning siren had first sounded and he was desperate for the raid to end so that he could go in search of his family. 'Jack,' he thought, 'must be worried. Perhaps he's braved the blackout and is on the streets hunting for them.'

It was approaching two in the morning before the world fell silent again and the all-clear siren was heard, a long continuous high-pitched cry that carried across the city like the wail of a banshee. Half an hour later, his shift completed, Arthur took out his torch and raced down the stairs of the building he had been guarding. He ran through the battered, darkened streets across the centre of town until he reached the top of Manchester Road. There, he stopped, unable to believe his eyes. The new

Odeon cinema had been flattened, razed completely to the ground. A heap of smoking rubble was all that remained.

Seized by uncontrollable panic, he scrambled over the stones, desperate to know if anyone was trapped or injured beneath them. His face felt clammy and sweat began to run down his forehead as he sensed the old memories threatening to surface again, threatening to paralyse him. His hands were trembling just as they used to do. Clambering frantically across the heaps of rubble, he told himself to fight, keep the memories at bay, push them down, deep down out of his mind. Desperate now and fearing he was about to lose all control, he forced himself to summon the image of his mother's face, his mother's eyes. They were oval, he remembered, oval and brown like her hair. He reached up to touch the wispy curl on her forehead, but his hand struck only the smouldering remains of the huge screen his family had been gazing on a few hours before.

'Arthur, Arthur, is that you?'

A familiar voice broke on his consciousness. He turned round at once and saw Jack standing behind him.

'Don't worry, no one was killed here,' Jack

continued, anxious to reassure him. 'Eliza and Alice are all right and so are the girls. They were damned lucky, though. They left the cinema about ten minutes before the bomb was dropped.'

'Thank God,' Arthur gasped, struggling to hold back his tears. 'But where are they now, Jack?'

'Safe and sound back at home,' smiled his friend. 'I found them coming out of the shelter on the playing field up there and I've just put them in a taxi. They asked me to stay on here by the wreckage and see if I could see you – they were sure you'd come looking for them.'

Unable to speak, Arthur hugged his friend warmly by way of thanks and they walked their separate ways back home.

Eliza and Eileen had waited up, still worried about Arthur. Eileen flung her arms around him as soon as he came in, just as she had done as a little girl. Eliza just grinned and feigned annoyance.

'Where the hell have you been Arthur?' she said, recovering her talent for dry humour. 'We had to take a taxi you were that long in coming.'

Chapter 13

During the first half of the war, Eileen's education continued as normally as possible at Bradford Girls' Grammar. In 1939, half of the school had been evacuated to Settle High School, including some of the teachers, but Eileen was one of the lucky ones who remained behind. Her friend Margaret used to write to her occasionally from Settle, trying to sound cheerful. Reading between the lines, though, Eileen could see that she was finding country life pretty boring.

Eileen wrote back, trying to cheer her friend up. She told her how the classroom windows had all been taped crosswise to prevent glass from shattering in the event of an air-raid and how the cloakrooms had been bricked up to make air-raid shelters. 'The most interesting bit of news, though,' she wrote, 'is that the teachers take it in turns to sleep in the school overnight, on fire watching duty. Can you imagine Miss Lucas walking the corridors with a torch and a winter coat pulled over her nightdress?'

Throughout her time at grammar school, Eileen continued to meet Dorothy and Amy, often going for walks in one of Bradford's many parks or looking round the shops with them. She was sixteen now and they were both seventeen. Dorothy had a boyfriend in the fire service. She had met him at one of the regular dances in the local hall and they had been going out for a while.

One Sunday, as the three of them were walking through Lister Park, Amy began to chuckle, and elbowing her sister in the ribs, whispered, 'Go on, tell her!'

'Tell me what?' Eileen feigned a look of surprise, already half guessing what she was about to be told.

'I've got a bit of good news. Bob's asked me to marry him and I've said *yes*.' Dorothy positively glowed with happiness, her face flushed with pleasure, her eyes alight with excitement.

'You look as if you've just won the pools!' laughed Eileen. 'I'm really excited for you, though. When's the wedding going to be and can I come?'

'We've set a date for next March. It's a Saturday, so you won't have to miss school.'

'I bet your mam and dad are delighted.'

'They are that,' said Amy, still giggling. 'They can't wait to get her off their hands.'

The big day soon came round and Eileen and

Eliza spent the night before pressing and brushing their best clothes. Eliza had saved up their clothing coupons, and although they were unable to afford completely new outfits, they had gone out together the previous weekend hunting for bargains. Eileen had fallen in love with a wide-brimmed Fedora style hat. It was dark grey and she knew it would go perfectly with her best coat. Eliza had bought herself a pair of navy blue leather shoes. The assistant had eased her feet into them with a shoehorn and then had waited very patiently as she dithered about whether or not she could really afford them.

On the morning of the wedding, Arthur got ready first, Eliza wanting him downstairs out of the way so that she and Eileen could take their time. He put on a freshly ironed white shirt, a red tie and his best grey suit, complete with waistcoat. The button hole, a white carnation, was in a glass of water in the kitchen, waiting to be pinned in place on his way out.

Eileen was excited. She had never been to a wedding before and wanted to look her best. The door of her wardrobe creaked open to reveal her limited collection of clothes. She took out her best dress, the red V-neck with three quarter sleeves that her parents had bought her for her sixteenth birthday. It was simple but elegant, with buttons down to the waist, a narrow belt and a slightly flared knee-length skirt. She fastened it, then quickly turned round, admiring the swirl of the skirt as she did so. The mirror confirmed that the belt was not twisted and that the seams on her stockings were straight. Her dark grey coat was already hanging behind the door, so all she had to do now was remove her hat from its box on top of the wardrobe and fix it in position. She opened the lid and lifted it out from beneath the protective layer of tissue paper. Moving back to the mirror, she manoeuvred it into position, adjusting it so it tilted at exactly the right angle to show off the way her hair fell down across her forehead and waved its way almost to her shoulders. Satisfied at last, she donned her coat and stood on the landing.

'I'm ready mam.'

Eliza stuck her head round the door of her bedroom, then emerged in her dressing gown to admire her daughter. 'You look a proper picture!' she cried. 'A real young lady you are now. Go down and show your dad.'

Arthur was waiting for her in the living room and

Eliza heard them chattering away together as she sat down at the dressing table and put on her make-up. She had decided to wear her best suit (navy blue with pin stripes) and a little pillbox hat she'd had for a few years but rarely worn. She pulled open the top left-hand drawer and rummaged around for her hatpin box but her eyes fell on her keepsake bag. Somewhat worn now, it was made of black velvet with drawstrings at the top and had once been her mother's. Feeling an urge to look inside, Eliza undid the drawstrings and removed the contents one by one.

There was a rabbit's foot that her mother was convinced would one day bring her good luck, a gold pocket watch that had belonged to Mrs Bell's father, and a Bible containing some pressed white flowers, a memento of her parents' wedding day. Also, there was the photograph of Martha that Eliza had seen long ago in the wardrobe and beneath it, wrapped up tightly in a white cotton handkerchief, a lock of Martha's hair, clipped by her mother from her dead child's head on the day before she was buried.

Into this motley collection of keepsakes, Eliza had inserted a few more of her own – first, the photograph of herself and Laurie, taken just before he went off to war, and then the photograph of five-year-old Evelyn standing beside her sunflower. She would have been taller than her flower by now, Eliza thought, imagining how beautiful her oldest daughter might have become and how she would have loved dressing up for Dorothy's wedding. Lastly, there was the tiny box containing the silver hatpin and brooch her mother had left her when she died. She opened the box and removed both items, placing them in the palm of her hand. Should she wear them today, as she had for Alice's wedding? It was a special occasion and the brooch would look splendid on the lapel of her suit. But in the end she decided against it. She wanted to save them for something even more special – her own daughter's wedding, which really would be a day to remember.

Its contents still intact, the velvet bag was carefully returned to its familiar place at the back of the drawer, nestling between lipsticks and powder compacts, sewing kits and old cough sweet tins full of buttons.

Hurrying now, Eliza selected a different hatpin and brooch, eased her new rayon stockings to the top of her legs and fastened them to the suspenders dangling from her corset. She stepped into her skirt, careful not to let the zip catch in her white blouse, then slipped her arms into the navy jacket and sat down on the bed to wriggle her feet into the brand new shoes. Finally, she pinned her hat in place, trying hard to make it cover the grey hairs that were now beginning to multiply at the front of her head.

At last, they were all ready and set off together for the church in Manningham where the service was to be held. They were ushered to a seat near the front not far from Alice who, looking very grand in a beige straw hat with a feather, turned round to give them a friendly wink and a 'fingers crossed' sign.

The moment the organ struck up *Here Comes The Bride*, they all stood, waiting eagerly to catch their first glimpse of Dorothy on her father's arm. Despite not being able to afford a traditional white wedding gown, she looked every inch the bride in a pale cream silk dress with lace on the collar and the edge of the sleeves. Her hat was also cream with a wide brim and hatband of pink silk. Jack wore a pale pink carnation in his buttonhole to match, and Amy, the only bridesmaid, had chosen to wear a pretty rose pink dress.

The service was everything Eileen had imagined it

would be and she enjoyed every moment. During the various pauses, she thought of what it must be like to be married, to promise to give yourself wholeheartedly to another person for the rest of your life, to have babies and bring them up. Was it something she would want for herself soon? She wasn't sure, finding it difficult to imagine a life of set routines. There was a whole world to explore and she couldn't see herself marrying until she had at least seen some of it. Perhaps, if she fell in love, she would feel differently, but for the moment, she was happy as she was.

The reception was held in the church hall. Here, despite the more severe rationing that had now been introduced, Jack and Alice had managed to put on a good spread.

Eileen chatted to Dorothy for a while and was introduced to her new husband, Bob.

'You're in the fire service, aren't you?' said Eileen politely. 'Tell me all about it.'

Bob proceeded to do so, becoming quite animated at times. He loved the variety of the job, the camaraderie, and assured her that, despite its dangers, he wouldn't swap it for the world.

Eileen liked him, impressed by his enthusiasm and his ability to make her forget her shyness and feel at ease. Eliza and Arthur also took to him and were pleased for Dorothy.

'She's got a good 'un there,' Eliza pronounced on the way home. 'I shouldn't think it'll be long before Alice is a grandmother.'

Academically, Eileen continued to shine. She passed her School Certificate with flying colours and began to study for the Higher School Certificate examinations.

In the second term of her final year, there was a parents' evening at the school. Arthur and Eliza had never been to any of these, fearing they would feel out of place or say something that might embarrass their daughter. This time, though, Eileen asked them to go.

'Miss Bottomley says she really wants to meet you, so please, please go. She says to tell you that she won't bite.'

Looking ill at ease in the great school hall, Arthur and Eliza sidled past the other parents and the rows of fearsome teachers in their long black gowns. They hesitated in front of Miss Bottomley's table, trying to summon up enough courage to approach her.

'It's Mr and Mrs Pendlestone, isn't it?' called Miss Bottomley in a warm voice. 'Come and have a seat.'

They drew up two chairs and listened attentively as Miss Bottomley sang the praises of their daughter for fully two minutes, announcing that she and the headmistress had decided they would like to put Eileen forward for an Oxbridge scholarship. However, this would involve her staying on at school for another year, she explained, as the exams would be in December.

'Is this something you think you will be able to afford?' asked Miss Bottomley, rather tentatively. 'If not, it may be possible for us to apply for a special grant from the school's emergency fund...'

'No, there'll be no need for that,' said Eliza, determined not to accept any form of charity.
'We've managed so far. I'm sure we can manage a bit longer. What do you think, Arthur?'

Arthur nodded in agreement. 'Of course we can manage,' he replied. 'We want Eileen to make the most of every opportunity that's offered to her, Miss Bottomley. She can stay on at school for as long as you think you can help her.'

Miss Bottomley was delighted, explaining that, after passing Higher School Certificate, a number of girls went into the Third Year Sixth Form to prepare for scholarship and other advanced exams required by universities. Eileen would need to stay on for at least two more terms, ideally three if she succeeded in getting an Oxbridge place. This would give the school plenty of time to prepare her for the rigorous demands of academic life.

When they got home, Eileen was waiting up for them, eager to hear how things had gone. 'Well, did she tell you about the Oxbridge exams?' she asked, as soon as they had taken off their coats and joined her in the living room.

'She did love, she did,' replied Arthur.

'And what do you think?'

'We think it's champion, love,' her mother responded. 'But where *is* Oxbridge, Eileen? Is it near Leeds?'

'Oh, mam,' laughed her daughter, 'let's make a cup of tea and I'll tell you all about it.'

When she discovered the truth, Eliza gasped in astonishment. 'By hell, you're never going there!' she exclaimed. 'You'll be that posh, you'll never speak to us again.'

'It's not like that, mam,' Eileen reassured her, 'it's not like that at all.'

She did understand how her mother felt, though. When her teachers had first mentioned the idea of her applying for Oxford or Cambridge, Eileen, too, had shied away from such a suggestion, certain that such famous places were only for the rich, not for working class girls like her. She would be out of place and unhappy, she was sure. But Miss Bottomley was persistent and spent hours talking to her, trying to persuade her that her fears were unfounded. She made college life sound exciting and challenging, stressed how many new opportunities it would open up for her and eventually succeeded in giving her the confidence at least to try.

Over the next six months, therefore, Eileen studied hard until late every night, spreading her library books all over the table. Arthur and Eliza would sit in the back room and listen to the radio so she could have the front room to herself.

After she'd gone up to bed, Arthur would sometimes have a look at the practice exam papers she'd been doing. Once, to his surprise, he saw a question on *David Copperfield.*

Next time he brought her in a cup of tea, Arthur sat down with her at the table.

'I see you're studying *David Copperfield* lass.'

'Yes, that's right dad,' she said.

'Well, you might not realise, but I've read that book five times, and I can help you with it, if you want. You can ask me anything you like about the characters or the story – I know it inside out.'

But Arthur had chosen the wrong moment to approach her. Eileen was grappling with a particularly frustrating set question that Miss Bottomley thought might come up in the forthcoming exams.

'No, you can't help me, dad,' she snapped at him. 'You don't know anything at all about Dickens' narrative technique or the way he achieves his effects. That's what I have to write about, not characters, not what happens.'

Surprised and hurt, Arthur withdrew to the kitchen. After that, he never interrupted her again.

Chapter 14

As expected, Eileen passed her Higher School Certificate with flying colours, and from the beginning of the autumn term, began to prepare for the Oxbridge entrance exams. After much thought, she selected Girton College in Cambridge as her first choice, applying for a scholarship to read English. She knew very little about the ladies' colleges at either Oxford or Cambridge but had selected this one because Miss Bottomley had been there and had told her quite a lot about it. Apparently, it had an excellent reputation for English.

Having completed the necessary written examination, Eileen was subsequently invited to attend for interview at her chosen college on the tenth of December. In view of the fact that this interview was scheduled for ten o'clock in the morning, it was decided that she should travel down to Cambridge the day before and stay overnight at the college, at a cost of nine shillings. The school offered to pay for this accommodation from their emergency fund but Arthur and Eliza had to pay the rail fare.

Aware of the importance of making a good

impression, Eliza insisted that Eileen should have a new winter coat so that she would look smart for the interview. Despite Eileen's protestations, she took her daughter into town and used up all the money she had saved from her cleaning job to buy her a dark grey woollen overcoat.

On the day of the interview, Eliza brushed the coat proudly. 'There,' she said to Eileen, 'you'll look a proper lady, now.'

Having checked her overnight bag to make sure all the essentials were packed, Eliza waved her daughter off on yet another adventure into an alien academic world which she didn't understand but nevertheless recognised as the passport to privilege and success.

Eileen had to change trains twice, arriving in Cambridge at half past one. The college itself was located about a mile and a half from the centre, so she decided to have a look around the city and explore some of the other colleges first. It was bitterly cold as she walked across the large green in front of her, trying to follow the map she had been sent. During the train journey, she had circled all the places she wanted to see. It was now a matter of getting her bearings and finding them.

Over the next couple of hours, she feasted her eyes on the architectural splendours of the ancient city – the Medieval colleges with their echoing cloisters and winding stairwells, the secluded courtyards and stone bridges, the narrow streets and alleyways filled with unexpected treasures, such as the tiny Romanesque Round Church.

The setting sun was already beginning to turn the sky deep orange as she approached the final building on her list – King's College Chapel. Each year, from the age of seven or eight, Eileen had listened with her father to the service of nine lessons and carols broadcast at three o'clock on Christmas Eve. Each year, without fail, she had waited eagerly for the chosen chorister to sing the first trembling notes of *Once In Royal David's City,* which, for her, marked the start of Christmas. Now, she could hardly believe she was here, standing beside the choir stalls she had so often imagined. She put out her hand and touched them. She loved their warm dark woodwork, the delicate carvings on their seats, the canopies and panelling that enclosed them. Three steps led up to the simple altar with its timber reredos in the classical style. Eileen paused on the first of these, then turned back to look up at the glorious fan-vaulted ceiling.

People were now beginning to file in for evensong, so Eileen walked back to the nave and found a seat near the great Medieval choir screen on which Henry VIII and Anne Boleyn had carved their initials. She decided to stay for the service, knowing that she didn't need to be at Girton until six o'clock.

As the lights dimmed, a procession of choirboys took their places in the candlelit stalls. It was exactly fifteen days to Christmas Eve, and to the music of Tallis and Gibbons, Eileen dreamed of what the chapel would actually look like when the annual carol service was broadcast. This year, she would be able to tell her father how she had sat only a few yards from the choir they were listening to, although she doubted she could ever convey to him her sense of the building's awesome splendour and mystery. She recalled how Wordsworth must have sat here, too, remembering some lines of the sonnet in which he had described the chapel as a place

Where light and shade repose, where music dwells
Lingering – and wandering on as loth to die:
Like thoughts whose very sweetness yieldeth proof
That they were born for immortality.

The service came to an end all too soon, the choir's solemn *Amen* rising and echoing for several seconds before it subsided. Eileen waited for the other worshippers to file out before she rose to her feet and slowly made her way to the exit. Here, she paused, turning back for one last look before stepping forth into the cold.

Outside, the world was already turning white, lawns and gardens shivering in the frosty air. The roads, of course, were in darkness, but there was a full moon and the early evening sky was dotted with stars. Following the route she had memorised from the map the college had sent her, Eileen made her way along the blanched country lanes, arriving at Girton just before six.

She was greeted by one of the mistresses and introduced to the second year student who was appointed to be her guide. It was explained that, after breakfast, she should go to the far end of the building, where the interviews for prospective English students were being held. Eileen was then shown to her small study bedroom and told that dinner was at seven o'clock. For this, she was informed, she would have to wear the short black gown hanging up behind the bedroom door.

After unpacking her things, Eileen duly donned the strange new item of clothing and went downstairs for something to eat. The dining hall was daunting, a huge room lined with wooden panels and portraits of important-looking people, none of whom she recognised. A few of the mistresses were seated at the raised table at the top, each in a long black robe. Feeling conspicuous, Eileen quietly ate her food, speaking to no one. She spent the rest of the evening reading and trying to predict some of the questions she might be asked the next day.

That night, she hardly slept at all. It was her first night away from home, and quite apart from being nervous about the next day, she couldn't help missing her parents. She knew they would be missing her, too, and worrying. Her father was on fire duty that night, so her mother would be all alone in the house, no doubt itching to know how things were going in Cambridge. She wished there was some way of speaking to her but they were not on the phone, and even if they had been, she doubted there was a phone box anywhere near the college. Her watch told her it was three o'clock and her thoughts turned to the writers she had studied in preparation for what was now today. She began to go over the quotations she had learned, reciting them in a whisper as if she were counting sheep, their rhythms rising and falling in her mind until she drifted into a fitful sleep.

The time for interview came round at last and she was relieved to be one of the first ones to be called. Dr Melrose, a kindly middle-aged woman in a long gown, emerged from her study, bid Eileen good morning and invited her in. She smiled encouragingly, waving her towards an ancient chair opposite her imposing desk, which was full of neatly arranged files and papers. The study was huge, with a marble fireplace at one end and an armchair beside it. Three of the four walls were lined with books – more books, Eileen thought, than in the whole library at school. She hardly had time to be overawed though, before the interview began.

To her surprise, the questions were not too taxing and she was given plenty of opportunity to talk about the writers she admired. She had been well prepared by her teachers for the kind of questions to expect and was thus lucky enough not to be thrown off her guard by anything that arose. Once she had got into her stride, she forgot her nervousness and even quite enjoyed discussing some of the allusions in *The Waste Land* or the use of the grotesque in Dickens' Christmas books.

The long-anticipated interrogation was over far quicker than she had imagined and she soon found herself walking back across the country lanes and into the centre of Cambridge, proud and relieved to have come through the ordeal without making a fool of herself.

She had two hours before her train was due, plenty of time to explore the city further and to have a browse round the shops. There were some wonderful bookshops and a large music shop she had noticed on the way in, but having left her map of Cambridge in her room at Girton, she was a bit worried about getting lost and missing her train. On a board near King's College she saw a guide to the city and studied it carefully, working out how far it was to the station and exactly which direction to follow when she was ready to go.

The narrow streets and alleyways crammed with ancient buildings were a delight to wander through, and she tried to imagine how wondrous it must be to study here. She probably wouldn't get in, she knew, but it was exciting to imagine herself here all the same.

A particularly large and well-stocked bookshop

across the street suddenly caught her eye and she stepped inside. There were signs pointing in all directions to the different departments, arranged over three floors. She headed immediately for the Literature section, where she enjoyed a full half hour scanning the tremendous range of books, occasionally opening one that took her fancy and skimming its pages. Her father had secretly slipped her five shillings before she left home and she couldn't wait to spend it.

On a high shelf to her left she noticed a complete set of Dickens, each novel beautifully bound in a dark green cover. Standing on tiptoe, she took one down to examine it more closely. The print was clear and attractive and there were wonderful illustrations by Boz interspersed throughout the story, each of them covered with a delicate piece of thin semi-transparent paper to keep them clean. The only time she had seen such a thing before was in the Hans Anderson book of fairy stories her father had bought her when she was a child.

She knew immediately what she must do. Reaching up again, she returned the book she had just removed and took down *David Copperfield*. What better could she spend some of her money on than a present for her father? This had always been his favourite and his own copy was very worn and dog-eared. She opened the front cover to check the price – two and sixpence. It was expensive but she would still have plenty left to spend on herself. The assistant wrapped it for her carefully and tied it with a piece of string. Then off she went again, in search of more treasures.

Her next stop was the music store. She rarely had the chance to buy new piano music and poured over the endless array of stands, each clearly labelled and either sorted by composer or style. Many pieces were also sorted into grades from beginner to advanced.

Not knowing where to start, she began by flicking through the Baroque sections. She had enjoyed playing some dances from this era when she was in her second year of lessons. A dance suite by Handel attracted her. It was called *Keyboard Suite in D Minor* and was originally written for solo harpsichord. The dances looked relatively easy to play and offered a variety of tempos. One of the dances, the sarabande, she already knew, having heard it many times at school. She looked at the price – one and sixpence. This would leave her one shilling for something else.

She held on to the suite, deciding to explore the popular music at the back of the shop before finally making her purchase. This ranged from tunes by the big bands of the thirties to popular wartime hits, from ragtime and blues to songs by Gershwin and Cole Porter. In the farthest corner was a section labelled *Music Hall*.

'I wonder if they have that song my mother mentioned, the one her father used to love,' Eliza mused. She started to finger through the titles, and sure enough, there was Vesta Tilley's *After The Ball*. The front cover was adorned with violets and red hearts entwined together, and above the large italics of the title, there was a drawing of a lady in Victorian dress gazing into the eyes of a soldier. Eliza knew at once that her mother would love it and was prepared to give up her dance suites in order to buy it for her. However, to Eileen's delight, the price scrawled on the back in pencil indicated it was only one shilling, so she had exactly enough money for both purchases.

As she left the shop, Eileen checked her watch and was pleased to see that she had half an hour to reach the station. Excited by her new acquisitions, she held them protectively against her breast, not wanting them to get creased or damaged as she hurried through the narrow lanes. At the market square, she turned round for one final glimpse of the glories of this city, then strode purposefully across its spacious green and onto platform four in good time for her train.

After what seemed a very long journey, Eileen at last boarded a train bound for Bradford, which was due to arrive at a quarter past seven. Too tired to read any more, she settled back in her seat to reflect on her first adventure away from home. Her emotions veered from relief and pride in her achievement to fear and disappointment at the thought of being turned down.

'Surely they won't want somebody as ordinary and working class as me,' she kept telling herself, but part of her said that the interview had gone well, so she tried not to completely rule out the possibility.

Tired but happy, she disembarked at Bradford and caught the tram to the top of her road. As she walked down the hill she could see her mother standing at the front gate, looking out for her.

'Come on in love,' cried Eliza, overjoyed to see her daughter again. 'You must be starving. I've made a shepherd's pie for tea and your dad's set the table so we're all ready to eat.'

They sat down together, Arthur and Eliza longing to hear everything about Cambridge and what had happened there. 'Go on, Eileen,' said an eager Eliza as soon as she had served the meal, 'tell us all about it.'

Eileen obliged, giving them as graphic an account as she could of the architectural marvels and long history of the place, her stay at Girton, the amazing study where she'd had her interview and the various shops that she thought would be of interest to them.

'By the way,' she said when they had finished eating, 'I've got you both a present.'

At this, she got up and brought in one of the gifts she had secretly left under the hall table.

'This is for you, dad.'

'You shouldn't have, love.' He undid the string and removed the wrapping.

What he found inside almost took his breath away. His own copy of *David Copperfield* was rather grubby now and had several loose pages. It had never had any illustrations. This was in pristine condition and the illustrations were better than anything he could have imagined, bringing to life in vivid detail so many of the scenes he loved.

'Where on earth did you find this, Eileen? It's wonderful, wonderful. But it must have cost a fortune!'

'Not really,' she lied. 'I couldn't resist getting it for you dad. I knew you'd appreciate it, being a bit of an expert on Dickens.'

He remembered their last conversation about Dickens and knew this was Eileen's subtle way of apologising.

'It's the best present I've ever had love,' he said. 'I shall treasure it to my dying day.'

This was all that Eileen wanted to hear. She kissed him gently on the cheek and then went to get her mother's gift.

'Here you are mam. This is for you.'

Eliza excitedly took the sheet of music out of its paper bag and gazed at the colourful front cover. 'Arthur, just look at this,' she exclaimed. 'It's my father's song!'

He took it from her, pleased to see Eliza with something of the old fire in her eyes.

'Why don't you play it for us, love?' he said, handing it back to his daughter.

'Go on then, I'll try. But you'll have to forgive any

mistakes because I haven't heard it before.'

Eileen pulled out the stool and took her seat at the piano. Soon, the tuneful strains of *After The Ball* filled the room and Eliza began to waltz up and down, singing at the top of her voice. Even Arthur joined in a bit this time, his deep voice providing a steady bass to his wife's somewhat tremulous contralto. Eileen giggled as she was playing, tickled by their duet and by her mother's complete loss of all inhibitions, something she hadn't seen before.

'By, that took me back,' laughed Eliza as her daughter sounded the final chord. 'It's a pity Fred Astaire has never heard of me.'

'Nay, you're no match for Ginger Rogers, is she?' said Arthur, winking at Eileen. 'And there's no need to practise that piece any more, love. You played it perfectly first time round.'

'But didn't you buy anything for yourself?' interjected Eliza, suddenly conscious that her daughter had spent a lot of money on them but hadn't yet showed off anything of her own.

'Yes, I bought some new music. It's classical, though, so I'm not sure you'll like it.'

'It doesn't matter if we like it or not,' said her father, 'we want to hear you play it. Come on, give us a concert. It'll be as good as anything on that third programme, I'm sure.'

Eileen went in the hall to fetch her music while Arthur and Eliza settled themselves in the armchairs beside the fire.

She opened the keyboard suite at the fourth movement, the slow sarabande with two variations which she had heard in music lessons and had always loved.

'I don't know what you'll make of this but it's one of my favourite pieces. It's very slow, so you can sit back and relax.'

The stately opening chords signalled the beginning of a melody of great beauty but also great sadness, and as Eileen's fingers moved skilfully across the keys, faithful to the graceful triple time, her parents began to listen with rapt attention. This was a melody the heart of which they recognised – it was the ache of loss. Every cadence, every repeated phrase, every rich chord spoke to them both with greater and greater power, not just of the pain of losing, but of that mysterious intermingling of beauty and grief that lay at the heart of life. Their eyes met and the shadow of Evelyn flickered between them.

As the melody was repeated a second time, Eliza thought of her mother grieving over Martha, and of Laurie, his brief life cut short, like Evelyn's, almost before it had begun. Arthur, too, thought of a mother, one who was lost to him long before he became a man, long before she actually died.

No love without the risk of loss, the music seemed to say to them, rising steadily towards a crescendo before coming to rest on the final two exquisite chords, *no love without the risk of pain.*

The piece was not very long, no more than a few minutes, but Arthur and Eliza felt they had travelled far in this short space of time. Eileen sat in silence for a moment at the end, waiting for the last two chords to die away before she turned round to gauge her parents' response. Seeing the tears in their eyes was the greatest reward she could have hoped for.

'It's an amazing piece, isn't it?' she murmured softly.

'Oh Eileen,' said Eliza. 'We've never heard anything so beautiful in our lives. Is all classical music like that?'

'No, I don't think so, mam,' Eileen laughed. 'I'll play you the faster pieces in the suite, though. They should cheer us up a bit.'

Turning to the first page, Eileen played through the Prelude, then the Allemande, Courante and Gigue, explaining they were all seventeenth and eighteenth century courtly dances.

Arthur got up and stood beside her, wanting to get a closer look at the music.

Eliza sat back in her chair and listened, wondering where on earth all her daughter's cleverness came from. 'Certainly not from me,' she thought.

By the end of 1942, the effects of the war were felt more seriously in every household, 'make do and mend' being the order of the day. Arthur dug up half of the lawn in the back garden so they could grow their own vegetables. Food was scarce, rationing stricter than ever. Even coal was in short supply, making it difficult for many people to stay warm. Fortunately, Arthur knew about the remains of an open caste coal seam off Tong Street, not far from where they lived. Early on Saturday mornings, he and Eileen would walk there with a wheelbarrow and fill it up with any bits of coal they could find, taking care to cover the whole lot with an old blanket before they wheeled it home. Eileen loved sorting through it, finding the bright shiny bits of coal that she knew would burn well.

Every night, the three of them would gather round the fire and listen to the grim news on the wireless. Everyone was desperate to do whatever they could to help resist the German invasion, urged on by the stirring rhetoric of Winston Churchill. Eliza, Alice and the girls sometimes went to Bradford Town Hall on a Saturday afternoon, responding to Bradford's call for volunteers to assist the war effort. There, in the Banqueting Hall, huge frames had been set up with gigantic nets draped over them. Along with scores of other women, they would spend a couple of hours weaving hundreds of coloured rags into what was soon to become camouflage netting for tanks and gun installations.

Soon after Eileen's interview at Cambridge, Eliza met Alice for tea again in Collinson's. Alice couldn't wait to tell her that Dorothy had found out she was expecting a baby.

'So I'm going to be a grandmother at the

beginning of May, Eliza. What do you make o' that?'

'It doesn't seem two minutes since Dorothy was in her pram,' said Eliza, 'and now she's going to be pushing a pram about herself. Tell her I'm pleased for her, Alice, and say I'll be coming round to wet the baby's head when it's born.'

Eliza poured them a second cup of tea.

'And what about Amy? 'Has *she* found herself a man yet?' Eliza continued.

'Not yet,' said Alice. 'She's worried about being called up, though. It'll be her twentieth birthday next month, so it's very likely. At least Dorothy's safe now she's married and pregnant, too. Anyway, that's enough about us, tell me all about Eileen. Did she think them exams went well?'

'It's hard to tell. She doesn't say much about her school work.'

'And how about boyfriends, Eliza? Is there anything happening on that front?'

'Our Eileen? No, she hasn't so much as looked at a man yet,' Eliza confided, 'she's too wrapped up in her studies. She's not like us Alice, she's got her head in the clouds most of the time. She's like her dad. A born dreamer.'

One morning in January, a white envelope with a Cambridge postmark dropped onto the mat. This time, Eileen didn't hesitate to pick it up. She tore it open as fast as she could, her parents watching nervously, just as they had done almost eight years before. Eileen paused for a moment then slowly put the letter down on the table.

'I've got in.' She sounded stunned. 'I've got a scholarship to Girton College to read English.'

This time, Eliza was far too taken aback to contemplate doing a jig around the table. She simply sat down on the nearest chair, flabbergasted.

Arthur's eyes filled with tears.

'I knew you'd do it love,' he said. 'I knew you'd do it.'

Ten minutes later, fully recovered now from the initial shock, Eliza was running up the road to the telephone box to ring Alice.

'She's got in Alice, she's got in!' she bellowed down the phone, still out of breath from her exertions. 'She's going to Cambridge University in October!'

'By gum, Eliza, you've reared a right brainbox there. She'll be taking Ernest Bevin's place 'afore long!

Make a better job of running the country than him, too, I shouldn't wonder.'

As if aware of the possible future threat to his livelihood, Ernest Bevin made the first move. At the beginning of the year, he decided to reduce the conscription age for single women from twenty to nineteen, thereby ensuring that Eileen's degree course would be postponed until the end of the war. She received her call-up papers soon after her nineteenth birthday, towards the end of the Easter term.

Eliza was mortified. How dare they call her daughter up at such a crucial time? Didn't they realise how much she had sacrificed for a place at Cambridge? Both Arthur and the school wrote letters, pleading that Eileen be given special consideration, but to no avail. An official letter came back confirming that, after due deliberation, there was found to be no reason why she should be treated any differently from others of her age, especially in view of the fact that she could take up her place at Cambridge when the war was over. Whilst this was true, it was very hard to accept and Eliza deeply resented what had happened.

On Eileen's last day at school, there was a great

sadness in the air. As usual, all the girls came together for an afternoon assembly in the hall and Eileen found it hard to join in the traditional end of term hymn, *Lord Dismiss Us With Thy Blessing*, its final verse seeming more poignant than ever this year:

> *Let thy Father hand be shielding*
> *All who here shall meet no more;*
> *May their seed-time past be yielding*
> *Year by year a richer store,*
> *Those returning*
> *Make more faithful than before.*

She looked round at all the staff, at all the girls who were staying on and at the few who, like herself, were leaving and may soon be serving their country in some distant place. From the corner of her eye, she saw Miss Bottomley wipe away a tear as she closed her hymn book and realised, for the first time, that teachers could cry, too.

Eileen was given a choice regarding her immediate future. She could either work in one of the munitions factories, join the women's Land Army and be sent to a farm in one of England's rural areas, or sign up for one of the emergency services. Never having had the slightest interest in agriculture, she immediately ruled out the Land Army. The thought of working on one of the monotonous assembly lines in a factory filled her with dread. So that left the Ambulance or Fire Service. Eventually, she chose the Fire Service, partly because she'd already heard something about what it involved from Dorothy's husband, but also because the local paper had recently printed an article appealing for more women to join. There had been a photograph of six new recruits on a fire float holding the hoses and Eileen remembered thinking that their life was probably quite interesting.

After signing up, she was sent on a short training course in the centre of Bradford, where she was taught the names of the wide variety of appliances used in the service and given a brief introduction to what would be required of her as a firewoman. She was also taught some First Aid and underwent various drills and physical training exercises.

At the end of the course, she heard that she was to be posted to Margate. Arthur got out his map of Britain to work out exactly where this was.

'It's on the south east coast, love,' he said, showing her the map. 'Look, right on this corner. You'll be able to go for walks by the sea and get some fresh air in your lungs.'

'It's not far from Canterbury either,' said Eileen. 'I'd love to go there. I've studied Chaucer's *Canterbury Tales* in school.'

The week before Eileen's departure was tense. Her mother made sure all her clothes were ironed and everything was ready to be packed.

'I've bought you a new pair of pyjamas, Eileen,' she said, returning home from an afternoon shopping trip. 'They're those nice stripy ones we saw in Cheapside Market last week. He was selling them off for half price.'

She laid them carefully on top of the steadily growing pile of clothes on the chair in Eileen's bedroom, all neatly folded and waiting to be placed in her suitcase.

When the time came for her daughter to go, Eliza helped her to pack them. Together, they wrapped two old brown leather straps round the outside of the case and tightened them as much as they could, making sure that everything would stay firmly in place on the long journey.

'Don't forget your label,' said Arthur, joining them in the bedroom. He had written Eileen's name and address on a bit of cardboard and now tied this to the handle. Then he carried the suitcase downstairs.

They stood around awkwardly for a while, checking their watches and trying hard to make conversation, but each of them was edgy and apprehensive, dreading the moment when they had to say goodbye and wondering what dangers lay ahead.

'Well, I think it's time,' said Eileen, looking at her watch yet again.

Eliza was determined to accompany her on the tram and see her off at Bradford station. Arthur said goodbye on the doorstep.

'Look after yourself, love,' he muttered, kissing her gently on the forehead, 'and write to us soon.'

She hugged him tighter than usual.

'Bye, dad,' she called as, carrying her suitcase, she walked slowly up the slope towards the tram stop, holding on to her mother's arm. Arthur stood on the doorstep, waving until they were long out of sight.

An hour later, Eliza once again found herself saying goodbye to someone she loved on a hissing, steam-filled platform. 'I know you won't do anything daft,' she said, hugging her daughter one last time before she boarded the train, 'but don't forget to keep in touch.'

'I won't, mam, I won't, don't worry. I'll write as soon as I get there.'

Eliza watched Eileen slowly disappear, her face veiled by clouds of steam as the train puffed its way into the distance. She stood in silence for a moment, a lone figure on the platform, then turned and trudged out of the station to catch the tram home.

Feeling more and more unsettled as the tram rattled along, Eliza thought about what lay ahead. What on earth would she and Arthur talk about now they had lost the one thing they had in common? And how was Eileen going to cope, all on her own in a strange new place? She was still so young, so naive.

Unable to stop herself from worrying about the future, Eliza walked slowly down the hill towards her home and paused for a moment at the front door, her face bathed in the light of spring sunshine. Lost in thought, and with a heavy heart, she turned the key and entered the empty house.

That night, Arthur came home with a bunch of tulips in his hand. Knowing that it was almost impossible to buy flowers any more, for several days he had been asking colleagues at work where he might get some. He had been lucky enough to find an elderly man in accounts who was about to dig up the last of his flower beds and was only too happy to be given a shilling for his remaining blooms.

'Here you are love,' Arthur said, placing them gently on the table in the front room. 'I thought you might need cheering up a bit.

Chapter 15

Breathing heavily after its almost four-hour journey, Eileen's train heaved a long sigh as it hissed and screeched to a laboured halt.

'King's Cross,' called the guard. 'All change at King's Cross.'

Eileen stepped nervously off the train and an elderly porter came to her assistance, offering to carry her suitcase to the bus stop. He showed her where to catch a bus to Waterloo and raised his cap in appreciation of the small tip she gave him.

Her bus slowly made its way through a world of bustle and noise, past trams and double-deckers, bicycles and cars, past gigantic buildings and huge archways and then across Waterloo Bridge, where Eileen caught her first view of the Thames. In the distance, the Houses of Parliament, with Big Ben, were just about visible through the smog and her heart beat faster as she suddenly saw Westminster Bridge, already familiar to her through the immortal lines of another of Wordsworth's sonnets. On her left, she could make out the dome of St. Paul's rising majestically above the surrounding rooftops, while beneath her flowed the grey river, bringing to mind the words of a poem she had read: *Sweet Thames, run softly, till I end my song.*

Hundreds of people were walking across the bridge – bowler-hatted businessmen, secretaries rushing home from work, service men and women in khaki, labourers in overalls and tin hats. Young and old, rich and poor, the whole of humanity seemed to have collected here, the hub of the civilised world.

After half an hour, she struggled off the bus and dragged her case up the long flight of steps beneath Waterloo Station's famous clock. In the letter she had received exactly a week before, she had been told to make her way to Waterloo and catch the six o'clock train to Margate, where someone would be waiting to pick her up and give her a lift to the women's fire service residence, Victoria Homes. The station proved to be much bigger than she had imagined, however, and for a while, she stood on the concourse, wondering which direction to take. The place was full of people rushing in and out, all of them appearing to know exactly where they were going. Eventually, she plucked up the courage to accost another elderly porter, who kindly directed her to the right platform, then helped her lift her case into a carriage where there was a vacant seat between two rather expansive middle-aged women, both of whom were carrying large parcels. They glanced at her somewhat disapprovingly as she sat down, determined to allow her only the minimum of space.

The journey took over two hours and Eileen spent most of it wondering what lay ahead of her and how she would cope with a life that was bound to be so different from the one she was used to in Bradford. She gazed out of the window on farms and marshlands, surprised at how flat the landscape seemed compared to her native Yorkshire.

When the train eventually pulled into Margate station, she was exhausted, too tired even to be scared of what might await her. As instructed, the moment she got out, she put down her suitcase and held up the large piece of paper she had been sent, on which her name and the words *Victoria Homes* were printed in large letters. No sooner had she done this than she saw at the end of the platform a short, plump young woman in a fire service uniform, waving her forage cap and shouting at her: 'Come on Eileen, over 'ere, come over 'ere, love. They've sent me to pick you up. They thought you might like a cheery face and a broad Yorkshire accent. My name's Renée. It's easy to remember 'cos it rhymes with Martini. And I'm from Bradford, like you.'

Grabbing Eileen by the arm, she bundled her off in the direction of the fire service vehicle parked outside the station. 'Jump in,' she said, hardly pausing to draw breath, and before Eileen had a chance to get a word in, she had opened the door of the truck and started the engine. 'I've never driven this one before and I'm buggered if I know how to get it into third gear, but we'll get back, somehow, even if I have to push the damned thing.'

She laughed then, or rather cackled loudly in such a funny distinctive way that it made Eileen want to laugh, too. 'My surname's Pedley but you can call me 'Peddles' if you want to,' said Renée. 'That's what the rest of the girls call me.'

Eileen took to Peddles at once, as, in fact, everyone else always did. Relieved she didn't have to say much, she let her chatter on all the way to Victoria Homes, reassured by her incredible warmth and vitality.

They reached Victoria Homes at nine o'clock, by

which time it was already dark.

'This bloody blackout!' cursed Renée, shining a torch so they could see their way down the long drive to the entrance. 'Why the hell we've got to have all this carry-on every night I don't know. Them Nazis are hardly likely to bomb a bunch of daft women that don't know their arses from their elbows, are they?'

She muttered on like this all the way to the front door. They went in together and Eileen blinked, plunged suddenly from total darkness into a warm, bright hallway. A group of women had collected to greet her at the foot of the stairs.

'Let me take your case upstairs, ducks,' called Maude, Renée's best friend.

'And I'll put the kettle on,' cried Muriel, a slight young woman with brown wavy hair whose accent revealed her to be yet another Bradfordian.

'Welcome to Victoria Homes,' said Babs, smiling. 'I come from Margate so I'll be able to give you a guided tour of the place tomorrow.'

Eileen soon discovered that she was to share a room with seven others, her bed being between that of Muriel and a girl from Doncaster called Nancy Riley, who

261

was described by Renée as having 'a bit of a crooked shoulder but we don't say anything about it.'

After a cup of tea, Muriel showed Eileen to the dormitory, which was bright and cosy with plenty of space for her clothes.

'This is your part of the wardrobe, Eileen,' Muriel explained, 'and this is your own chest of drawers. It's lights out in half an hour so you'd better get undressed quite soon.'

Eileen unpacked quickly and got ready for bed, thinking, as she pulled on her new pair of striped pyjamas, how long ago it already seemed since her mother had folded them and placed them in her suitcase.

'Hey, look, Eileen. Look at me! Snap!' cried Muriel.

Eileen turned, only to discover Muriel standing on her bed wearing an identical pair of pyjamas.

'Half price in Cheapside Market!' they screamed together, both giggling hysterically.

They laughed and laughed until tears were streaming down their faces. After that, they became firm friends.

Next day, Eileen woke early and scribbled a letter

to her parents before the others got up, knowing they would be relieved to hear that she had arrived safely. She told them the story of the pyjamas, partly to amuse them but mainly to reassure them that she had already made a friend. There was a post box opposite the residence so she ran across the road to send it off, then made her way to the long dining hall, where the others were now assembling.

After a rather frugal breakfast, she was taken to meet Miss Hawkins, the commanding officer, a stern-looking woman with an abrupt manner but a soft centre which emerged occasionally and took them all by surprise. She gave Eileen a list of the house rules, a brief talk on what was expected of her and explained that she was to be assigned to red watch. Her duties would become clearer after a period of training. Initially, she would stay with the other members of her team and receive instruction from them. She would be expected to report for duty at eight o'clock on Monday morning but should first collect her uniform from a small office located at the back of the fire station.

Later that day, Babs and Renée took Eileen into Margate for a look around. Like Skegness, it had a sandy beach and a long pier that, before the war, had been filled with amusements. It also had a clock tower, which, in Renée's mind, was invested with great significance.

'This is the most important thing you should know about, Eileen' she said, affectionately patting the tower's stones. 'It's where we meet up before we go out boozing.'

'Do you go to pubs on your own then?' asked a wide-eyed Eileen.

'Course we bloody do!' cried Renée. 'You'll not survive long down here without being able to knock a few pints back.'

'Don't worry, Eileen,' said Babs. 'We're not all as bad as Peddles. We do enjoy a tipple, though. It's quite safe; we're always in a group.'

'We're meeting in The Old Kent pub tonight,' said Renée, 'that scruffy looking pub over there. It's not the best one, but it's handy for going on to Dreamland later.'

'What's Dreamland?' asked Eileen, puzzled.

'Well, it's two things really,' said Babs. 'It's the name of that big amusement park you can see in the distance but it's also the ballroom where we go dancing every Saturday night.'

At this point, oblivious of the strange looks received from passers-by, Renée began to do a waltz in the street with an imaginary partner, singing at the top of her voice:

> *Meet me tonight in Dreamland*
> *Under the silvery moon*
> *Meet me tonight in Dreamland*
> *Where love's sweet roses bloom*
> *Come with the love light gleaming*
> *In your dear eyes of blue*
> *Meet me in Dreamland,*
> *Sweet dreamy Dreamland*
> *There let my dreams come true.*

'That's our signature tune,' she proclaimed. 'Come with us tonight, Eileen. You'll love it.'

Eileen smiled. 'All right,' she said, 'I'll give it a try.'

That night, Eileen took the bus to the centre of Margate with Muriel and Nancy and they walked along the front to the clock tower. Renée and several of her friends were waiting for them and more joined them in The Old Kent pub. From then on, Eileen was introduced to a whole crowd of new characters, all full of life and determined to make the most of every minute, well aware that it could be their last.

'Come on, what are you drinking?' Renéc shouted in the crowded pub. She was always the first to buy a round and had developed the knack of getting served quickly by elbowing her way to the front of the bar and chatting up the barman.

'Hallo my beauty,' she'd say to him. 'Think on, you'd better serve me first if you want to see them tattoos again, later.'

'Go on with you,' he replied, grinning. 'What are you all having tonight then?'

Babs and Maude helped her carry the trays of drinks back to the tables where they were sitting, and so began the first of many riotous Saturday nights.

At ten o'clock, they all moved on to sample the delights of Dreamland. Eileen never forgot her first introduction to the place. It cost sixpence to go in and Renée, generous to a fault, insisted on paying her entrance fee. Eileen tried hard to give her the sixpence she owed, but Renée would have none of it.

'No, no it's my treat, Eileen. I invited you to

come. You can pay for me another time if you decide you want to risk joining us again.'

The dance hall was everything Renée had led her to believe it would be – a magical wonderland of coloured lights and music. She took a seat at a table near the band and gazed at the couples waltzing around the dance floor. Muriel got up to dance a foxtrot with an air force officer and Eileen was amazed to see what a wonderful dancer she was, so light-footed and sure of what to do next. One by one, the other girls took to the floor with their regular partners. Most, but not all, were dancing with men. It appeared there were sometimes not quite enough men to go round, so some women had to partner each other, one of them taking the lead just as the man would normally do.

Too shy to join in, Eileen offered to look after their handbags while they danced, content just to watch them and listen to the music. Eventually, Renée, having none of this, came over to the table with Muriel to persuade her to take to the floor.

'Come on, lass, come and have a dance with Muriel,' she cried. 'She'll be the man. You don't have to do much. Just follow her lead.' She held out her hand to

Eileen, determined to draw her out from behind the table. 'Don't worry,' she said, passing her across to Muriel. 'I'll sit down for a bit and look after the bags.'

Feeling exposed but unable to think of an excuse to avoid what she was sure would be a terrible ordeal, Eileen reluctantly allowed herself to be pulled forward. She had never danced publicly before, her only experience being occasional turns around the living room with her mother to the big band rhythms of Joe Loss or Roy Fox. Terrified of showing herself up or looking a fool in front of so many people, she clung desperately to Muriel, who led her unfailingly up and down the dance hall, manoeuvring her round tight corners and steering her through the mass of bodies that threatened to scupper their progress by treading on their toes or inadvertently knocking into them. By the end of this slow foxtrot, Eileen was beginning to relax a little, amused by Renée's constant comments from the sidelines on the ineptitude of the other dancers and amazed at how, with Muriel's help and encouragement, she soon began to get the idea of where to turn and what to do next.

'There. We weren't that bad, love, were we?' said Muriel, leading her back to her place. 'Next time, we'll do even better!'

Muriel and Renée soon got up to dance again and Eileen resumed her role as guardian of their bags. After a while, sitting alone at the table, she became aware of happiness creeping up on her, the way it does sometimes, slowly, casually, when you least expect it. Who would have imagined you could feel such joy in the middle of a war, she thought, but there it was, swirling in the air above her, in the soft white specks of light thrown on the ceiling by the revolving silver ball, in the faces of her friends, and in the slow unforgettable pulse of *A Nightingale Sang In Berkeley Square.*

Chapter 16

On Monday morning, as requested, Eileen reported for duty at the nearby fire station. She was issued with the regulation uniform – two white shirts, a navy tie, a navy blue jacket with red edging plus matching skirt and pair of trousers, a forage cap and a nebbed cap.

Her first day was spent observing what went on and learning lots of new terminology. The work mainly involved plotting the boards, which meant keeping a record of where all the fire appliances were. This was not easy, as, after a night or perhaps a day of bombing, the engines were called to a succession of fires in buildings all over the area. Another major task was the preparation and delivery of dispatches to a variety of fire stations throughout Kent, some as far afield as Maidstone.

The women from Victoria Homes were divided into three watches, red, blue and white. Eileen discovered that these watches worked different shifts, rotating at the end of every week. She would therefore spend one week working from nine to five o'clock, the next week from five to one in the morning and the final week from one to nine in the morning.

At the end of her first day, Eileen came off duty with the other members of red watch, which consisted of herself, her friends Muriel Mason and Nancy Riley, and also Gwen Tate, a quiet, mousy-haired girl from Canterbury. Renée was on blue watch, together with Babs, Lucy Parsons from Essex, and her best friend, the cockney, Maude Cooper. These eight girls all shared a dormitory together so Eileen was much closer to them than to the girls on white watch, whom she chatted to occasionally but rarely went out with.

It didn't take Eileen long to settle into the routine of work and life in the residence. She quickly discovered that Renée was the pivot around which all their lives turned, the force of her personality and sheer exuberance acting like a magnet to draw the girls together and give them a sense of belonging. She had been there the longest, having joined up in 1940 because she wanted 'a bit of adventure'. By the time Eileen appeared on the scene, Renée's adventures were already legendary. Eileen never tired of hearing the stories of her misdemeanours – how, bleary-eyed and hung-over, she had turned up for parade one morning with curlers protruding from under her cap, or how she had once arrived two hours late for duty, gesticulating wildly from the pillion of Maude's motorbike and shouting drunkenly at the furious commanding officer that she had been 'attending to a fire in Cobb's Brewery'.

It was on the parade ground, however, that Renée's propensity for causing chaos particularly came to the fore. To be fair, this was not entirely her fault but was due mainly to what she called her 'gammy leg'. As a small child, she had suffered from a tubercular knee, which had left her with some joint pain and an occasional slight stiffness in her left leg. This lack of flexibility could sometimes cause problems when she was marching, since the leg had a tendency to stick out at an awkward angle and trip up any unfortunate girl who was marching next to her.

'Keep in step, Pedley! Keep in step!' Miss Hawkins would shout at regular intervals, usually to no avail.

One Saturday morning, Renée's leg seemed to be having a particularly bad day, and Eileen, along with most of the others, was struggling desperately to stifle her giggles. She could see that Miss Hawkins, nicknamed OP (observation post) on account of her eagle eyes, was becoming increasingly angry.

'Firewoman Pedley!' she bellowed. 'For goodness sake march properly or I'll put you on a charge!'

'I'm trying my best, I'm trying my best,' retorted an equally irritated Renée, 'but it's not *my* fault if my leg's been shoved into my arse any road!'

Eileen soon picked up what was required of her on red watch and learned a lot from Muriel, who, like Renée, had been one of the first ones there. She was kind and supportive, and being that bit older than Eileen, became something of an older sister to her as well as a best friend. Eileen discovered that Muriel had had several boyfriends, 'but none of them serious'. She was now friendly with a Polish airman who was stationed at RAF Manston. He had fought in the Battle of Britain and was looking forward to returning home at the end of the war.

'We're not really in love or anything,' said Muriel. 'We're just keeping each other company and having a bit of a laugh till the time comes for him to go back to Poland. I don't see that much of him, really, but we enjoy a few dances in Dreamland on a Saturday night.'

'I don't know why you don't find yourself a more regular feller, Muriel,' said Maude. 'There's no shortage of good-looking blokes at the moment.'

'By gum, you're right, there,' chuckled Renée. 'We have to fight for our honour every night, here, Eileen. It's harder than fighting bloody Hitler!'

The 'good-looking blokes' referred to by Maude were in fact soldiers massing on the coast of Kent in the slow build-up to the invasion of France on D-Day. Most of them were stationed in the big hotels at Cliftonville, the more select end of Margate. They would often send towing trucks to collect groups of girls from Victoria Homes and bring them back for tea in their hotels. As she gazed at the trestle tables laden with sandwiches and delicious cakes, Eileen couldn't get over how well fed they were.

'How come we get such meagre rations when they get all this?' she said.

'Aye, well,' said Renée cynically, 'maybe it isn't a very good sign. I reckon the government are fattening them up for the kill.'

Over the next few weeks, Eileen began to love the new world that had opened up before her, glad now to have postponed Cambridge, which she was sure would have been nowhere near as much fun. She soon became firm friends with all the girls in the dormitory and felt flattered that they were willing to be so open with her, sharing their secrets and including her in all their exploits.

On Sundays, she went to Holy Trinity, a large Anglican church overlooking the harbour. She had been introduced to it by Renée and Muriel, who often went with her to the morning service. They would catch the bus to the clock tower and walk up the gentle slope beside the sea, their conversation punctuated by the loud cries of passing seagulls or the sound of waves crashing against the harbour wall.

Holy Trinity was an important landmark in Margate. It was an early Victorian building set in beautiful gardens and had a tall slim tower which could be seen for miles. The interior was lovely too, warm and inviting and always decorated with fresh flowers arranged by members of the Mothers' Union.

The church had served the town as a place of worship for more than a hundred years, but in June 1943, just two days after Eileen's last visit, it was bombed during a midday air-raid. Eileen heard the news from Renée later that afternoon, and together, they went to look at the extent of the damage.

As soon as they got off the bus, it was clear that a lot of the building had been flattened. They walked sadly up the steps to the gardens to examine the site. The tall tower was still standing, but that was all. The rest of the building was rubble. Several other people were there, gazing at the wreckage, and Renée recognised one of them.

'Was anybody hurt, love?' she called to her.

The woman came over to join them.

'No, thank goodness, no one at all. Tom, the gardener, had a lucky escape, though. He normally sits in the church garden to have his lunch, but today, by some miracle, he decided to go for a pint before the raid started. It's just as if something told him not to stay there.'

'By hell, it's a queer thing is fate,' said Renée. 'We can only go when our time's up, that's what I think.'

She and Eileen moved on, picking their way through the dust and rubble towards what had once been the front pews. Scattered amongst the stones and broken wood and glass were many poignant reminders of the church's life and history – a brass eagle that used to hold the huge Bible, a cracked font, the remains of a wooden rack that still contained one of Sunday's hymn numbers, and several green hand-embroidered hassocks. Renée suddenly stooped to pick up a prayer book which, though dusty, had survived the onslaught intact. Inside the front cover, the words *Holy Trinity Church* had been stamped.

'I'm going to keep this,' she said. 'They can bomb us all they like but there are some things that can't be destroyed.'

The months passed quickly and Eileen continued to be amazed at how easy it had been to adjust to her new surroundings and feel at home in such a different world.

Dreamland was a regular Saturday night event now, and Eileen's circle of girl friends had widened to include the men they were going out with.

Renée's boyfriend was called Maurice. He was an infantryman based at Cliftonville and Renée had fallen for his 'gorgeous blue eyes.' He was much taller than Renée with light brown hair and a boyish face that frequently broadened into a cheeky smile. They were an amazing sight when they were on the dance floor together, Maurice trying hard to shorten his stride so as not to pull Renée off balance and Renée occasionally struggling to keep her gammy leg out of the way of the other dancers. Like Renée, Maurice had a wonderful sense of humour and a knack of putting people at their ease. Eileen loved to be around them, knowing they would always be entertaining. She liked to listen to their completely different accents, Renée's broad Yorkshire mixing with Maurice's broad cockney to produce a wealth of amusing expressions.

Sometimes, they would each try to imitate the other's way of speaking, much to the amusement of all concerned. 'Are yer gonna go up them apples and pears for a kip later on, Maurice my old son?' Renée would joke.

'By gum, lass, I'm right glad you're not *my* trouble and strife, I am that,' retorted Maurice, giving as good as he got.

'Go and have a dance with him, love,' Renée said to Eileen one night, 'and get him out of my hair for a bit.'

It was with Maurice, therefore, that Eileen first took to the dance floor with a man. Although she was naturally musical, she had no idea of what steps were required in any particular type of dance, so struggled to follow Maurice's lead. He was very kind, though, and just laughed when they went wrong, putting it all down to too many beers on his part.

It wasn't only Renée who had a regular boyfriend. Maude was going out with Albert, a fireman from Ramsgate whom she had met on one of her regular motorbike trips to deliver dispatches, and Babs, whose long dark curly hair and strikingly pretty features were the envy of the dormitory, was about to become engaged to one of the sergeants in the fire station. The others all had boyfriends too, with the exception of herself and Nancy Riley, whose extreme self-consciousness about her mild scoliosis made her ill at ease in social situations.

When she had first arrived at Victoria Homes, Nancy had apparently been very old-fashioned in both dress and physical appearance. Muriel had taken her under her wing, though, showing her how to put on make-up and helping her to select clothes that either minimised or almost completely concealed the unevenness of her shoulders. As a result, Nancy had grown in confidence and had recently started to accompany them on their Saturday night trips to the dance hall.

One Saturday in early April, shortly before

Renée's birthday, they all made their way past the closed-down fairground rides and the once famous scenic railway to the doors of Dreamland, where, in contrast, everything was in full swing.

Eileen had a dance with Pavel, Muriel's Polish airman, and was pleased with how much her dancing had improved since, over six months earlier, she had taken her first few hesitant steps with Maurice. Muriel was mainly responsible for this improvement, having given Eileen hours of instruction on the floor of the dining room in Victoria Homes. Together they had waltzed and fox-trotted across the lino as the latest big band hits crackled from the large wireless on the sideboard near the door. As a result, Eileen was skilled in most dance forms now, although she found the quickstep, with its sudden bursts of fancy footwork, a little too flamboyant at times, regarding it as a dance perhaps more suited to an extrovert than to someone with her natural shyness.

The next dance, as it happened, was a quickstep, so Eileen decided to give it a miss and Pavel showed her back to her table. Happy to relax for a while and watch her friends enjoying themselves, Eileen remained seated for the following dance, too. It was a waltz. She waved as

Muriel and Pavel glided past her, with the far less proficient Renée and Maurice not far behind. What surprised her, though, was that Nancy Riley, previously unseen on the dance floor, had obviously been asked to dance by a friendly-looking corporal who was guiding her gently round the edge of the ballroom. Eileen thought how well suited they seemed and hoped, for Nancy's sake, that he might ask her out. The waltz soon ended, but Nancy and the corporal remained on the floor, obviously keen to try something else.

Just as the band were about to strike up again, a tall young man with wispy blond hair came across to Eileen, cutting quite a dash in his officer's uniform. 'May I have this dance?' he said, smiling and offering Eileen his outstretched hand.

They stepped onto the floor to the strains of the latest popular favourite, *Long Ago and Far Away*. Eileen hadn't heard the song before but was soon captivated by the beauty of Jerome Kern's melody. The young officer led her unerringly round the dance floor to its slow rhythm, and she relaxed, no longer having to think about where to put her feet or what step to do next. She looked up as the vocalist took the stage to sing, and as she listened, the words seemed to take on a life of their own, speaking to her with an unexpected power:

Long ago and far away
I dreamed a dream one day
And now that dream is here beside me,
Long the skies were overcast
But now the clouds have passed
You're here at last.

Chills run up and down my spine
Aladdin's lamp is mine
The dream I dreamed was not denied me
Just one look and then I knew
That all I longed for long ago was you.

Caught in its spell, Eileen wanted the music to go on and on, wishing that she could stay on the dance floor forever, with cigarette smoke swirling in the air above, and other couples brushing past, and the glitter ball casting its soft white specks of light, like tiny snowflakes, across the darkened walls and ceiling.

But the dance ended all too soon and she was ushered back to her table, the dream over, at least for the moment.

'I'm afraid I have to go now, Eileen,' said the young officer, 'but perhaps you'll be here next week? I'd love to dance with you again.'

'Yes, yes, of course,' she replied, blushing slightly.

'Who the hell was that?' called Renée after he had gone. 'He was like something out of one of them Hollywood films.'

'His name's Raymond,' said Eileen, feeling rather flustered. 'That's all I know.'

Chapter 17

Eliza and Arthur both felt very lost in the first few months after Eileen left. They tried to keep themselves busy, Arthur working hard digging up the rest of the lawn to extend the vegetable patch, Eliza spending more time in the kitchen trying out wartime recipes heard on the wireless or thinking of different ways of making their meagre food supply go further and taste less bland.

But nothing seemed the same any more. Their whole lives had centred around their daughter and every room had memories of her. Eliza often looked at the coronation mug still sitting on the mantelpiece and thought of Eileen rushing to school every morning and coming back to tell her about what teachers had said or what friends had done. She smiled to herself, remembering what a good mimic Eileen was and how she used to imitate the headmistress and make her laugh.

There was so much fun before this terrible war, she thought, a war which was fast becoming almost too difficult to bear. Rationing had continued to be extended and even the most basic foodstuffs were now in short supply.

'Is this damned war ever going to finish?' she said to Arthur one night in November as they sat in front of the fire, trying to eke out the few bits of coal they had left.

Arthur lit a cigarette with a rolled bit of paper (matches being impossible to find now) and sat back in his chair. 'I know love, it gets harder and harder to keep your spirits up,' he replied. 'But at least Eileen seems to be having a much better time than we thought she'd have down in Margate. That's the most important thing.'

Eileen's letters home were the high spot of every week and Eliza would persuade Arthur to read them aloud to her several times. On hearing some of the latest exploits of the girls in Margate, she'd say, 'That Muriel is really bringing our Eileen out of her shell.'

'Aye, she sounds a lot more grown up, now,' said Arthur.

They would always write back to her as soon as they could. Arthur would compose his own letter, then Eliza would dictate hers to him. She found it easier like this, so she didn't have to worry about punctuation or spelling. Her letters usually sounded as if she was just chatting, one subject following on from the next without any of the linking devices normally present in writing.

Dear Eileen,

We got your letter yesterday, love. I must tell you because I forgot in my last letter – Dorothy's going to have another baby at the end of May and if all goes well she wants me to be its godmother and I saw Alice again last week. She says that poor Amy's finding it hard going with the Land Army in Norfolk.

They're going to call the baby Hilda if it's a girl – they'd like a girl this time, I think.

By the way, Uncle George has written. He says him and his wife are planning to buy a house on the coast when he retires in a few years' time. I've sent him a photograph of you in your uniform – you know, one of those you put in your last letter to us, where you're standing at the clock tower with Renée and Muriel. He sends his love and says to take care of yourself.

Your dad's still digging for victory in the garden. He's determined to try and grow carrots behind the coal bunker next year. Don't know what Alice thinks about becoming a grandmother again, though. Makes her sound old, doesn't it?

I'm just going to put the kettle on so I'll carry on with this after a cup of tea. Oh yes, I wanted to ask about Muriel and

and so she would continue, Arthur struggling to keep pace but generally managing to write everything down exactly as she said it, knowing that Eileen would be amused.

Eliza continued to meet Alice every couple of weeks, although the cafes had little to offer now, so they had to settle for a pot of tea and whatever few tasteless biscuits were on offer. One Saturday morning in February, they met in Collinson's cafe and got chatting as usual. Alice talked a lot about her first grandchild, William, and how he was now crawling and trying to stand up.

'He's a grand little lad,' said Eliza. 'Dorothy must be that proud of him. Anyway, how is she? It won't be long now before her second bairn is due.'

'Aye, that's right, Eliza. She can't wait to get it over with, but it should be here by around the end of May. She'll have her hands full, then, with two of them to look after.'

'And how about Amy? Any letters of late?'

Eliza knew she had to be careful about Amy as,

the last time they had met, Alice had been in tears about her. Being in the Land Army was making her miserable, she thought.

Alice's eyes misted over again. 'I don't know what to think, Eliza. She doesn't write very often. When she does she tries to sound happy, but reading between the lines, I know she isn't. I'm not daft. She might think she can fool me, but she can't.'

'But is she really miserable or just fed up with this war like the rest of us?'

'Well, life might be hard and drab for us but we're in our own homes, aren't we? She's bloody miles away in Norfolk working long days in the fields. It's damned hard work as well, digging and such like. At least your Eileen gets to stay warm and dry in the fire station.'

Eliza had to accept this and realised she would have to be sensitive when mentioning Eileen's letters, not letting on how often she received them.

'Ah well,' she said, looking for a way to change the subject and perhaps cheer Alice up a bit before she had to leave, 'it can't go on like this forever. Hitler's no match for Churchill, we know that much, so we'll just have to pull together till the tide turns. Just think, Alice, what it'll be like to wear nylon stockings again instead of these damned lisle ones.'

'Aye, and what it'll be like to go into a shop and find what you want. I went into the grocer's this morning and all he had were shelves full of custard powder and mustard!'

They laughed and shook their heads in disbelief.

'Aren't we unlucky Eliza, to have two daughters caught up in all this?'

'I suppose so, Alice, but at least Dorothy's escaped conscription. Anyway, I reckon it could have been a lot worse. We might have had sons.'

They both knew of neighbours whose boys had recently been killed.

'You're right, Eliza, you're right. I'll stop moaning and be on my way.'

Later that morning, Eliza got home to find another letter from Eileen behind the door. She ripped it open at once and read it through several times. As always, she then asked Arthur to read it aloud to her when he came back from work. He stoked the fire, trying to get a few flames to appear, then sat back in his armchair opposite his wife. Such letters were like gold dust to them, the one flash of colour in their otherwise grim lives. Eileen always wrote so well, bringing her world to life for them.

'I'd love to meet that Renée,' said Eliza as Arthur finished reading and laid the letter on the table. 'She sounds a proper character!'

Chapter 18

Just before Renée's birthday, on the nineteenth of April, all leave was cancelled in the build-up to D-Day. This was particularly disappointing for Renée, who had been looking forward to spending a week with her mother back home in Bradford.

'My birthday's on Primrose Day,' she told them, 'and my mother always puts primroses on the table for me and bakes me a sponge cake.'

Renée was very close to her mother, who had struggled to bring her up alone after her father deserted them both at the end of the First World War. Every week, she would send home three pounds of her weekly wage in order to help pay the bills. This meant Renée had only six shillings and fourpence left for herself, just enough to buy basic essentials and a few rounds of drinks, plus her entrance fees at Dreamland.

Partly to make up for Renée's disappointment at not being allowed to go home, and partly out of gratitude for the years of entertainment she had given them, the girls in Victoria Homes decided to club together and do something special for her birthday. A surprise party was suggested. However, for this to work, they knew they would have to ensure that Peddles was off duty on the day in question and also gain OP's permission to hold the event in the dining room. Eileen, recognised as the most articulate member of the group, was chosen to represent them. The following morning she knocked hesitantly on the door of OP's office.

To her surprise and relief, Eileen found that, once she had explained their proposals, very little persuasion was necessary. OP had always had a soft spot for Renée, and when told of the plan, she just smiled wryly.

'If it's for Renée,' she said, 'I can hardly object, can I? Will I be invited, too?'

'Oh, yes, you will, ma'am, of course you will,' replied an astonished Eileen.

Plans were thus set in motion and excitement mounted as the big day approached. Renée's name was deliberately put on the duty roster for the five o'clock shift on her birthday, and a girl from white watch offered to stand in for her on the evening in question. Muriel was convinced that if Renée thought there was no time to celebrate her birthday at night, she would be anxious to go out in the afternoon of her big day. This would allow time for the dining room to be set up in her absence and ensure that everything remained a complete surprise.

Maude was designated as the liaison officer, whose job it was to ensure that Renée went out after lunch, returned at around four o'clock and was then encouraged to look her best before coming downstairs at half past four, ostensibly for a piece of birthday cake before she went on duty. Muriel and Eileen's job was to collect together as many of Renée's friends as they could to help them with the preparations for the party.

The great day finally arrived and Renée took little persuading to go on a pub crawl at lunchtime. She knew every pub in the area, from The Hussar just across the road all the way to The Five Bells in Birchington. Her favourite was The Queen's, near the sea front, mainly because her sense of humour appealed to Tom, the barman, so he often gave her free drinks.

After lunch, Maude revved up the motorbike and waited for Renée to scramble onto the back. Together, they sped off down the road, Renée's gammy leg sticking out at an acute angle, to the consternation of several passers-by. They stopped outside The Queen's and Renée clambered inelegantly off the bike, accompanied by the sound of whistles and hoots from some soldiers on the corner. Once inside the pub, she rushed up to the bar and waited for Tom, the barman, to come across.

'I hope this bloody town's going to give me a medal for saving it when this war's over, Tom,' she joked, ordering a brandy for herself and a beer for Maude.

'You're splashing out a bit today, Renée,' laughed Tom. 'What's with the brandy? Are they packing you off to a French beach at last?'

'It's my birthday,' proclaimed Renée loudly, 'sweet twenty-five and never been kissed!'

'By hell,' said Tom, 'I wouldn't have put you down as a day less than forty!'

After a couple more brandies, Renée jumped on the back of the bike again, waving and singing all the way up the road.

'Why don't you have a nap for an hour before you go on duty at five?' suggested Maude as soon as they got into the dormitory.

'Aye, maybe I will,' replied an unusually compliant Peddles, already beginning to doze off on the bed.

At precisely half past four, Maude crept downstairs to check that everything was ready, then went back up again to wake her. 'Come on, Peddles,' she said, shaking her shoulder, 'it's time to have a wash and put on a bit of make-up.'

'I don't need a wash' grumbled Renée, 'I'm only going on duty.'

'Yes, you do. Muriel wants you to come downstairs first and have a piece of the birthday cake she's made and Eileen wants to take a photograph. Hurry up. Get in that bathroom and put your face on.'

Renée reluctantly obeyed and the two of them made their way slowly downstairs. As they reached the tiny landing halfway down, at least a hundred voices joined in the loudest rendition of *Happy Birthday* Renée had ever heard. A guard of honour lined the bottom of the stairs and stretched down the long hallway, twenty men in full dress uniform all standing to attention for her. Renée just stood there, speechless for once. Then Maurice and his friend picked her up and carried her into the dining room.

Tears welled in her eyes at the scene in front of her. The centre of the long dining room table was completely covered in primroses, on either side of which were mounds of sandwiches and fancy cakes, a gift from the soldiers who had managed to smuggle them out of their Cliftonville hotels. OP was standing at the far end of the room, grinning, and Muriel was next to her, holding a magnificent birthday cake with twenty five candles, all lit and waiting for Renée to blow out to mark the official start of the festivities.

The party went on all night. Renée, of course, got drunk and Maude helped her up onto the table so she could sing some of her favourite wartime numbers. These were all delivered in a loud, raucous voice, slightly out of tune, with a wide range of accompanying hand movements and facial expressions designed to keep everyone thoroughly entertained. The highlight was her rendition of *Begin the Beguine*, her grandmother's favourite song:

> *When they begin the beguine*
> *It brings back a song of music so tender*
> *It brings back a night of tropical splendour*
> *It brings back a memory evergreen.*

Renée began by making the most of the play on words in the title and then vastly over-dramatised the phrase 'tropical splendour', shaking and wiggling her hips when she delivered the line, as though she were wearing a hula-hula skirt on a South Sea island. At this, everyone fell about in hysterics, the prolonged laughter making their sides ache.

Before they had time to recover, Renée called for silence, deciding that now was the time to formally thank them all for putting on such a wonderful party.

'While I'm up on this table and still just about conscious, I'm going to make a speech, so shut up everybody and show a twenty-five year-old a bit o' respect.'

'Get on with it Renée,' shouted Maurice. 'We don't want to be here all night.'

Ignoring him, Renée continued.

'I want to say that this has definitely been the happiest day of my life. First of all, I've got Maude to thank for being so bloody clever all afternoon and not breathing a word of what you were all up to. And I also want to say a special thank you to Muriel, and everyone that helped her, for making this table I'm standing on look so beautiful. Now then, what was I going to say next?'

'What about thanking me?' called Maurice. 'I nearly put my bloody back out carrying you in here.'

'Oh yes,' Renée went on, suddenly remembering what she had intended to say, 'I can't let the night go by without expressing my appreciation (here, she faltered, pronouncing the 's' in the word *expressing* as 'sh') and deep gratitude to someone we don't often thank. I'm talking about the one and only OP.' As she said this, she gestured towards the commanding officer, Miss Hawkins, who was attempting to keep a low profile in the far corner of the room.

'OP, I want to thank you for your generosity (again the 's' was pronounced 'sh') in giving your permission for us to 'old this party 'ere tonight. You've proved to us all today that you're not such a bad old stick after all...'

At this juncture, Maurice, anticipating that Renée might be about to go too far, led a round of applause and started a final chorus of *Happy Birthday*, thereby bringing a speedy end to her lengthy oration.

The party then continued uninterrupted. Carried away by the carnival atmosphere, even Eileen drank a lot more than she usually did. Halfway through the evening, another batch of men arrived to replace the ones now going back on duty. Among them were Pavel and a group of air force personnel, including Raymond, the young airman Eileen had danced with a few nights earlier. He recognised her at once and came over to talk.

It was a warm night and they stood outside for hours, drinking beer and chatting or rather shouting above the noise of the sing-song coming from inside. Raymond explained he was stationed at RAF Manston. He knew Pavel only slightly, but since he was off duty that night, he had been press-ganged into coming along to Renée's party to make up the numbers.

'I'm so glad, now, that I came along,' he said. 'I had no idea you'd be here.'

Eileen told him about her place at Cambridge and discovered that he had already graduated long before the war started. He had read English at Nottingham University and had been teaching at a grammar school in Guildford for three years when he was called up. Eileen was thrilled to discover a kindred spirit, with whom she could talk freely about literature and discuss ideas. Although life in Margate was wonderful and had given her a new social confidence, she sometimes missed the intellectual stimulation and opportunities for academic debate that she had enjoyed at grammar school.

At two in the morning, with the party still in full swing, Raymond explained that he had to leave because he and his friends were on duty the following morning and needed a few hours' sleep. 'See you in Dreamland on Saturday,' he said, kissing her gently on the cheek in the hallway.

'Yes, till Saturday,' Eileen replied, her heart missing a beat. It was the first time a man other than her father or her Uncle Jack had ever kissed her, and it marked the beginning of their relationship.

The following day, Eileen sat at the table in the dining room to write one of her regular letters to her parents.

Dear mam and dad,

I am writing this just after Renée's surprise party to let you know that everything went really well. We managed to keep it a secret and it was truly wonderful to see her face when we all sang 'Happy Birthday'. I've never ever known her lost for words before! She is such a larger than life character dad, like someone straight out of Dickens, although, having said that, I can't really think of a direct comparison with any of the characters in the novels of his that I've read. I suppose she's like Clara Peggotty, Sam Weller and the reformed Scrooge on Christmas morning, somehow all rolled into one.

I hope you're both as fit and healthy as when you last wrote to me. You mustn't worry about me, mam. Muriel looks after me and there isn't very much danger here at the moment. Margate hasn't been hit anywhere near as badly as Canterbury and is not likely to be.

I still go dancing with the girls in Dreamland on Saturday nights. You'd both love it there. It's so lively and full of people enjoying themselves. I can't wait to play all the latest dance hits for you on the piano when I get home.

Our leave has been cancelled for the foreseeable future so I think that something important is going to happen soon. There are lots of troops around the coast, many of them stationed in the big hotels in Cliftonville.

Must go now. I'm on duty at five. Give my love to Aunty Alice, Uncle Jack and the girls when you next see them and take care of yourselves.

Love from Eileen.

As she was about to insert this letter into its envelope, Eileen realised she had written nothing about Raymond and wondered why. She didn't normally keep anything secret from them. She held the letter between finger and thumb, hesitating about whether or not to add a postscript, but something inside her said that, for the moment, this relationship was best kept to herself.

From the end of April, Eileen began to meet Raymond on a regular basis, although it wasn't always easy to find a time when they were both off duty together. Usually, Raymond would either cycle or catch a bus from his air force base about five miles away and they would meet at the clock tower. Sometimes, they would climb the steep hill towards Cliftonville and sit on a bench together, hand in hand, looking out at the endless rolling sea. More often, they would wander for miles along the beach, talking about new books they had read or authors they particularly liked. Usually, they found their tastes were similar, but if they did happen to disagree about a writer, they enjoyed a good argument and were not afraid to express their opinions forcefully.

'I can't imagine what you see in Virginia Woolf and the rest of that Bloomsbury set,' he said one afternoon in late May as they strolled along the sand. 'They're just a load of toffs sounding off about their pet theories. I hate *stream of consciousness* novels.'

He was becoming animated now, running his fingers through his hair as if spurring himself on, willing himself to concentrate fully on the argument he was developing. 'They pretend to be new and experimental but all they're really doing is telling a story from a particular angle – the writers are just as selective as any old-fashioned omniscient narrator. They try to make us think they're not there, but they can't avoid being there in everything they choose to include or not include.'

'But you've got to admit they've revolutionised the notion of character,' Eileen responded, 'brought us closer to the inner self, to what experience is really like when filtered through a particular mind.'

'I don't admit it at all,' he retorted, his face flushed with anger, his expression slightly peeved.

'Obstinate to the last,' Eliza thought to herself. She decided to say no more, preferring to let the matter drop so that they could enjoy the rest of the day together.

After a few minutes, he calmed down and moved closer to her.

'I'm sorry,' he said, taking her hand in his and smiling. 'Do you forgive me?'

'Of course,' she replied, letting him kiss her gently

on the forehead.

'Why do you love me when I'm such a cad, at times?'

'Oh, lots of reasons,' she laughed. 'But I'm not telling you any of them or you'll get big-headed.'

As they walked on beside the cliffs, she considered what these 'lots of reasons' were. First, of course, there were his good looks, natural charm and easy manner. Then, his intelligence and sensitivity to others. Next, there was his experience of life, so much wider than hers and somehow reassuring. Finally, there was a certain inscrutability at times which, far from finding frustrating, she actually rather liked. It meant he wasn't all surface, there were hidden depths, parts of him yet to be unearthed, some of which, she hoped, might take a whole lifetime to discover.

She tried to imagine a world at peace again, as it had been throughout her childhood, and longed for the time when she and Raymond could be together without the constraints of duty or the ever-present fear of an uncertain future.

'Do you think this war will ever end?' she sighed, as they resumed their walk along the beach.

'It can't be long now, surely,' said Raymond. 'Once we invade France, it should all be over.

Chapter 19

About eight months after her daughter had left for Margate, and once she knew she was happy and settled there, Eliza gave up her morning cleaning job in order to work full time. With most young men in the forces, there were plenty of full time jobs for women and Eliza had more time on her hands now her daughter had gone, time that she was keen to fill purposefully instead of spending much of it in an empty house filled with memories.

She was taken on to check fabrics in the mending room at Lister's mill, which was situated about a mile from the city centre and almost three miles from her home. The extra money would come in handy, she thought, and besides, it was a way of helping the war effort since at that time the mill was making material to be used in parachutes. Although Alice's Dorothy no longer worked there, Eliza had heard from her that the wages were good and what she earned more than made up for what she had to pay in tram fares.

The mill itself was an imposing sandstone building with a long and famous history. Founded in 1838 by Samuel Cunliffe Lister, the business had eventually made its owner a multi-millionaire. Lister's original Manningham mills had been destroyed by a huge fire in 1871 and the buildings where Eliza now worked had replaced the old ones immediately afterwards.

They covered a vast area and reflected the enormous wealth and power of their founder, the most influential textile inventor of his day. As early as 1889, Lister had become world famous for his production of silk and mohair plush, although he was later to be dubbed 'the king of velvet'. His company supplied almost all the velvet for the King George V's coronation, and in its heyday, employed over eleven thousand people on its twenty-seven acre site. The South Shed, where Eliza was taken on her first day, was over a quarter of a mile in length.

The history of Lister's Mill was well known to the people of Bradford, most of whom had some connection with it by way of relatives or friends. Eliza remembered her father telling her about the strike there in 1891, when mill workers refused to accept a proposed pay cut. He used to recount in vivid detail how meetings and rallies were organised by the strikers in Bradford's main squares, and how, when the Durham Light Infantry were sent in by the government to disperse the crowds, riots took place all over the city.

'But Lister broke 'em, the bugger,' she recalled her father saying. 'He just wouldn't back down. In the end, their strike fund ran out and they all had to go back to work for less money.'

The resulting anger had led to the formation of the Bradford Labour Union and ultimately to the foundation of the Independent Labour Party.

As Eliza was to discover after only a short time working there, workers' pay and conditions had improved beyond all recognition since the bitter times of the strike. She was astonished by how different things were compared to her burling and mending days at Salt's. Working hours were much shorter and working conditions far more pleasant and there was a works canteen which produced hundreds of hot meals every day. In addition, the management really looked after its employees. Eliza learned that ten shilling postal orders had been sent to all previous members of the workforce now in German prisoner of war camps, together with a letter assuring them their jobs were safe when they returned home.

It wasn't long before Eliza got used to working in a mill again and she soon made friends with some of the women in her section. The talk was mainly about the war – sometimes cheerful, as when they shared the jokes from the previous night's ITMA radio broadcast, and sometimes sad, when the conversation turned to a husband or son who had gone missing.

In contrast to Eliza's work, Arthur's job had changed little over the years. It consisted of fairly routine, repetitive clerical tasks, for which he was paid a reasonable wage. Capable as he was, he lacked the drive and ambition to take on more responsibility, so when opportunities arose for more senior positions, he let them go by. Eliza had long ago stopped pushing him to go for promotion, reluctantly resigning herself to the fact that he was never going to change. Her life was now centred round Eileen, who seemed to have been fortunate enough to have inherited a mixture of her father's intelligence and her mother's ambition to achieve.

Apart from the occasional drink with colleagues, Arthur spent his weekday evenings reading or listening to the wireless. He and Eliza still went out with Jack and

Alice to the local pub sometimes on Friday nights and were there to help them celebrate the birth of Dorothy's second child, which was born on the twenty-fifth of May and turned out to be a daughter, as they had hoped.

'Here's to little Hilda,' said Arthur raising his glass 'and may she grow up in a world free from war.'

'I'll drink to that,' Jack replied.

'To a world free from war!' called Eliza and Alice in unison.

'How's Dorothy coping with the new little 'un?' Eliza asked.

'Well it's not easy changing nappies when there are no safety pins to be had for love nor money,' replied Alice. 'And in a few months' time, I expect she'll find it hard to get Hilda off to sleep without a dummy. We've been to every shop we can think of, but nobody's got one.'

'My goodness, I'd never thought of that,' said Eliza. 'It's like hair grips and curlers. You can't find any of them these days either.'

'What do you reckon, Arthur?' Jack chuckled. 'It's a bloody good job you're not a woman or a baby!'

Since Eileen had left for Margate, Jack and Arthur

had seen a bit more of each other and had become firm friends. On Saturday afternoons, they either went for a drink together or watched a football match at Valley Parade. Jack had always been a great follower of Bradford City, and even though the football league was suspended during the war, there were still some excellent regional friendly matches to be enjoyed.

Jack would call for Arthur at about two o'clock and they would travel by tram towards the ground. Arthur enjoyed spending a bit of time in the fresh air after being cooped up in his office all week and he and Jack would walk the last quarter of a mile to the entrance, often chatting together about their daughters as they did so.

'Did you know that Evelyn wanted to play for Bradford City when she was little, Jack?' said Arthur one day as they were walking along. 'She used to love their colours, although she could never understand why red and yellow were called claret and amber. I never knew the answer to that and I still don't. She was always asking me questions I couldn't answer.'

'I bet your Eileen asked you a lot of questions as well,' said Jack, not wanting Arthur to dwell too much on

Evelyn and trying to steer him onto a happier topic. 'How's she getting on these days?'

'She's loving every minute of it down there,' Arthur replied. 'We'll hardly know her when she comes back. She'll be that grown up. She writes to us every week without fail, Jack, and she never forgets to pass on her love to you and Alice and the girls.'

'You must be that proud of her,' said Jack warmly. 'She's a credit to you both, she is that.'

Every Sunday morning or evening Arthur went as usual to church, where he continued to be a sidesman. The vicar there, who was now looking distinctly middle-aged, came to visit occasionally. Eliza would get out her best china and offer him a cup of tea. She went to church with Arthur now and then, for appearance's sake, but still found the service hard to get through.

On the Sunday nights that Arthur was on duty at church, Eliza went round to play cards with Mrs Braithwaite and her friends. Alice would sometimes come along too, and over a game of gin rummy they would chat about the latest events in the war. There was usually plenty to talk about, especially when the tide began to turn in Britain's favour.

During the early years of the war, some families had put large maps of Europe on their walls with British and Nazi flags pinned on them to illustrate the latest military positions. They had hoped to chart the British advance by moving their red white and blue over a gradually increasing area of occupied territory. However, when the exact opposite happened, and Hitler appeared to be gaining the upper hand, the maps and flags were soon dismantled and put away in a drawer. Now, despite news of British advances all over Europe, it seemed too late to get them out again. The moment had passed.

From the beginning of May 1944, there had been a steadily increasing feeling that something was about to happen. The sense of impending crisis was felt countrywide, not just on the south coast, where troops had been massing for months. Many northern roads began to be blocked at times, clogged with tanks and armoured vehicles being shunted to strategically important areas in preparation for the allied invasion.

On the morning of the sixth of June, what everyone had been waiting for finally happened. The first news of the D-Day landings was broadcast on the Home Service and it was announced that the same night, after the nine o'clock news, there was to be a new half-hour programme, War Report, which was to broadcast the actual sounds of battle recorded in the field by war correspondents.

At the end of the news, Arthur and Eliza stopped what they were doing and huddled round the wireless, Arthur constantly fiddling with the tuning knob to try and get better reception. They heard the voices of some of the soldiers who were fighting and up-to-the-minute news from the brave correspondents who were witnessing events first-hand. The programme didn't really bring them any closer to an understanding of the horrors of war, but it did make them feel much closer to Eileen, who, they were sure, would be listening, too.

Chapter 20

On the morning of the D-Day landings, the sky was filled with planes providing back-up support to the troops and Eileen stood in the garden of Victoria Homes watching them fly over towards the south coast. Renée's Maurice and the corporal that Nancy Riley had started to go out with had both been part of the advance party shipped off to Normandy and the girls were worried for them. Raymond and Pavel were involved in some of the airborne operations but at least they were able to keep in touch regularly and let Eileen and Muriel know that they were safe.

By September, it was clear that significant advances were being made into France and Belgium, but German resistance remained strong and progress through Normandy was slow. Operation Market Garden was therefore set in motion. This was a plan devised by Field Marshall Montgomery to speed up the allied advance towards Berlin and hence shorten the war. The idea was to drop thousands of troops by parachute across enemy lines and storm a series of key bridges along the Rhine. Neither Pavel nor Raymond said anything about it, but both Muriel and Eileen knew, by their silence, that something was about to happen.

On the morning of the seventeenth of September, hundreds of planes were again seen over the skies of Kent and the home service informed listeners of the latest offensive. Eileen was sure that Pavel and Raymond were part of it and was worried. She remembered only too well what it was like to receive news that someone close had been killed and dreaded being told that Raymond's plane had not returned. For the next two weeks, she found it difficult to sleep, unable to stop herself wondering about Raymond's safety. By the end of the month, however, it was clear that the daring operation had failed, British troops having found it impossible to seize the final bridge at Arnhem.

By the middle of October, therefore, Raymond and Pavel were involved in far fewer operations and began to come over to Dreamland on a regular basis again. One Saturday night, around midnight, Raymond and Eileen went outside together for some fresh air and stood looking up at a clear night sky dotted with stars.

'Things have quietened down at the moment,' he said to her, 'so I'll be able to take a whole day off next week. Maybe we could go out somewhere.'

'Oh yes, that would be wonderful. I'm on nights next week. The only proviso is that I get back by about six so I can have some sleep before the one o'clock shift.'

'Where would you like to go?' he asked. 'Any ideas?'

'Why don't we go to Canterbury?' said Eileen. 'I've always wanted to go there. I read Eliot's *Murder In The Cathedral* at school and I've studied Chaucer, of course. I'd love to see what the place is really like.'

They met at the clock tower the following Wednesday and took the one o'clock bus from Margate, scheduled to arrive about an hour later. On the way, Raymond told her about his last visit to the city two years before, the day after much of it had been destroyed by the Luftwaffe, in reprisal, perhaps, for the earlier allied bombing of Cologne.

'There was dust and rubble everywhere,' he said 'and yet, by some miracle, the cathedral survived. It was amazing. People said that fire wardens had thrown incendiary bombs from the roof onto the grass below to stop them getting through to the interior. Apart from a bit of damage to its library, the building looked just as

317

good as ever. '

'I can't wait to see it,' said Eileen.

They walked around the narrow medieval streets of the city in warm autumn sunlight, a piece of history unfolding at the turn of every corner. Near the Old Weavers' House, they stared at the ancient ducking stool, a grim reminder of the days when suspected witches were hunted down.

'Did they drown witches in that?' Eileen asked.

'Not exactly,' replied Raymond. 'If they thought you might be a witch, they ducked you under the water in it and held you there for several minutes. If you had drowned when they lifted you out, you were pronounced innocent and your name was cleared. If you hadn't died, then it was because you were a witch and so they killed you after that. You couldn't win.'

Eileen shuddered and they moved on. Eventually, they passed through Christchurch Gate into the cathedral precincts and made their way to the great entrance door. Here, Eileen paused to reflect on how the knights might have entered the same way on the morning of the twenty-ninth of December 1170, swords in hand, ready to strike down Thomas Becket in an attempt to rid King Henry II of his 'turbulent priest'. Did they simply walk in unchallenged, she wondered, or did priests really bar the door, as they had in Eliot's play?

Inside, the atmosphere was hushed, reverent. The place was very dark and lacking some of its usual beauty in that much of the stained glass had been removed for safe-keeping at the beginning of the war. Nevertheless, Eileen found the splendour of its architecture quite breathtaking.

They moved along the nave towards the choir stalls, stopping to admire the intricate stonework of the screen and then looking up at the delicate fan vaulting underneath the enormous Bell Harry Tower. Although Becket's shrine had been destroyed under Henry VIII, who had ordered the saint's remains to be removed and his bones cremated, it was still possible to see the spot where the shrine had once stood, a hallowed place, visited by pilgrims over many centuries. Eileen stood in silence there, feeling that she could almost reach out and touch the past. Some recent lines from T.S. Eliot drifted into her mind: *As the light fails on a winter afternoon, history is now and England.*

Raymond left her to her thoughts and went back

into the body of the church. He sat down for a while looking back at her, admiring her tall, slim figure as she stood alone near the shrine. He loved her quiet reflective side and the shyness which masked her intelligence and sharp wit. She possessed an innocence, an extreme sensitivity that he hadn't come across before. As he watched her slowly walk back towards him, her thick dark hair waving down almost to her shoulders, he found himself struggling to breathe, so great was his desire to fold her tightly in his arms and never let go.

They went outside together into the precincts and through a small iron gate into a rose garden reserved specifically for service personnel in uniform. Down one side was a small bench.

'Let's sit here and talk for a bit,' Eileen said, wanting to ask him about his impressions of the cathedral. They discussed its history and architecture for a while and then the conversation became more general. 'Tell me more about your family, Raymond. You don't talk about them very much.'

'Well, I've got a brother, Richard, who's in the navy and a sister, Mary, who's quite a bit younger and still at school in Guildford. I get on with them both all right, I suppose, but I always wanted to be an only child, like you.'

'I wasn't,' said Eileen. 'I had an older sister, once. She was killed in a road accident when she was ten.'

'I'm so sorry, Eileen. I didn't realise. Your parents must have been devastated.'

'They weren't themselves for a long time afterwards,' she admitted. 'But they're better now.'

There was a pause before Eileen continued. 'You haven't said a lot about *your* parents, Raymond. Tell me about them.'

'There's not much to say, really,' he replied. 'They're very ordinary. They own a grocer's shop in Guildford, and like your parents, they couldn't believe it when I won a place at university.'

'Have you told them about me?' she asked.

'Well, not in so many words. I've hinted, I suppose.'

'I'd love to meet them some time,' she said.

'Well maybe when this war finishes, you will,' he replied, looking anxiously at his watch as he did so. 'Come on Eileen, it's nearly five o'clock. Time to get the bus home.'

They juddered over the country roads back to Margate, past cornfields and orchards and pretty oast houses. After a few minutes, Raymond rested his head on Eileen's shoulder and fell fast asleep. An enormous orange sun, like a gigantic eye, was gazing in through the back window seeming to follow them, and as a last ray of light slanted across Raymond's face, Eileen wondered if he realised how deeply she loved him.

Over the next few months, Muriel and Renée noticed the developing intensity of Eileen's relationship with Raymond. Renée thought Raymond was wonderful and was always singing his praises. Muriel liked him too, although she sometimes felt that Eileen might do better to wait and get a bit more experience of life before committing herself to the first man she had ever been out with.

'You really love him, don't you?' she said to Eileen one day.

'Yes, you know I do,' replied Eileen. 'He's kind and brave and intelligent...'

'And bloody handsome as well,' interjected Renée. 'By gum, I wish my Maurice was as good-looking as

Raymond, I do that.'

They all laughed.

'Do you think you and Raymond might get married, Eileen, once this damned war is over and done with?' continued Renée.

'I'd like to think so,' replied Eileen. 'He hasn't talked about marriage yet, though.'

'I expect it won't be long before he does, love,' said Muriel. 'You've been going out together a good while now.'

'How do you fancy a chief bridesmaid with a gammy leg?' joked Renée.

Eileen smiled but said no more.

By the end of October, there was still no news of Renée's Maurice and the girls were beginning to get worried. The corporal going out with Nancy Riley had returned two months earlier, at the end of August. He had no idea what had happened to Maurice, having fought in a different division, but tried to reassure Renée, telling her that many men went missing and subsequently turned up in a prisoner of war camp. In early November though, the Red Cross confirmed that he was dead, and his mother wrote to Renée to give her the sad news.

When he hadn't returned, Renée had guessed that such a letter would probably end up in her hands, but it was still a terrible shock and she found it hard to accept she would never see him again.

The girls rallied round her, of course, though Christmas was a miserable affair without Renée's sparkle to enliven the proceedings. For a few months she was much quieter than her usual self, but she was never one to cry for long, and by early April the girls began to notice that she was beginning to laugh and joke again. Eileen, Maude and Muriel took her out for a quiet drink on her birthday, knowing how difficult it would be for her on this special day. None of them mentioned the previous year's celebrations, but at the end of the evening, Renée proposed a toast to the memory of Maurice.

'To Maurice, my old son,' said quietly, raising her glass. 'I'll be looking out for you when it's my turn to climb up them apples and pears to the golden gates.'

'To Maurice!' her friends responded.

'And to happier times for Renée,' added Muriel, dabbing away a tear.

They all now knew that the war was nearly over and it would soon be time to return home. Anxious to make the most of their last few weeks together, they took every opportunity to go dancing in Dreamland. Although the doors of Victoria Homes were locked on the stroke of midnight, many of the girls managed to stay out much later by asking friends to leave the fire escape exit open for them. In the early hours of the morning, they would then sneak up the iron staircase in the back garden and through the red emergency door, locking it behind them once they had tiptoed inside.

One night, a few days after Renée's birthday, Eileen spent the evening dancing with Raymond in Dreamland. He had ten days' leave starting the next day and was going to visit his parents in Guildford, so Eileen was feeling rather sad.

'Do you have to go away tomorrow?' she pleaded as they moved slowly across the crowded dance floor.

'I really do,' he said. 'I hate the thought of leaving you here all alone, but my mother isn't very well and she's been longing to see me for ages. I can't disappoint her, can I?'

'No, no, of course not,' Eileen agreed. 'I'm just being selfish. But I'll miss you so much.'

'Come on,' said Raymond, 'let's have a few more

drinks and forget all about tomorrow.'

They sat at one of the small round tables and watched their friends foxtrot and quickstep their way past, Raymond refilling their glasses several times before the band struck up for the last waltz, which, of course, they danced together.

Knowing the two of them would probably go for a walk after the ballroom had closed, Eileen asked Muriel to leave the fire escape door open for her, as she had done on a couple of other occasions. Muriel readily agreed, accompanying her and Raymond out of the dance hall and turning back to wave to them as she took a sharp left up the steep road back to the residence.

It was particularly warm for late April and Eileen caught the scent of early wallflowers as they walked slowly towards the beach and over the sands in the direction of the ancient pier. The area was completely deserted, the only sound that of the waves breaking against the shore.

'No more air-raid sirens now,' said Raymond. 'It's almost over.'

'I still can't bear the thought of you going away for ten whole days,' said Eileen, slipping her arm around his waist.

'I know,' said Raymond. He stopped walking now and held her in his arms. 'I don't ever want to leave you Eileen, you know that. Sometimes I wish time would stop and we could stay here like this forever, with only the sea and the stars for company. It's so beautiful tonight. I don't know why, but I keep thinking of some lines from *Othello*, the speech that starts, *If it were now to die.*'

'Yes, I know the speech you mean,' Eileen replied and immediately quoted the lines he was referring to:

> *If it were now to die*
> *'Twere now to be most happy; for I fear*
> *My soul hath her content so absolute*
> *That not another comfort like to this*
> *Succeeds in unknown fate.*

They stood in silence for a while, listening to the relentless surge of the sea and gazing on the vast array of stars in the midnight sky. Then Raymond pulled her closer to him and she knew he wanted to make love to her. He had asked her many times if he could, but she had always refused him, believing it to be wrong. Tonight, though, having drunk much more than usual and feeling thoroughly depressed at the thought of his departure, she was finding it harder and harder to resist him.

'I love you; I love you,' he whispered gently in her ear, drawing her tightly to his chest. 'Just let me show you how much.'

He began to kiss her more passionately than ever and Eileen found herself trembling now, consumed by a rush of physical desire that surprised her with its power and intensity. She returned his kisses, her heart beating faster against his until, unable to fight against his advances any longer, she allowed him to pull her down beside him on the sand. They made love to the rhythm of the lapping waves, watched only by a low-slung moon.

Two hours later, Eileen crept up the fire escape to the door that had been left open for her by Muriel. She slid quietly into bed without speaking, hoping everyone was asleep.

'Are you all right, love?' Muriel whispered, realising her friend had been out much later than on previous occasions.

'Yes, yes, I'm fine,' Eileen whispered back.

In fact, her heart was racing as she turned over in her mind the significance of what had just happened. Guilt mixed with excitement, producing a range of conflicting emotions inside her. She lay completely still, hardly daring to breathe, terrified lest her inner turmoil should somehow communicate itself to Muriel and produce a closer interrogation.

Part of her thought that what she had done was wrong, constituting a betrayal of her Christian beliefs. Another part of her was thrilled to think that now, at last, Raymond would see exactly how much she loved him. Pulled this way and that, unsure of how she should feel, for a long time she struggled to resolve her confusion. Gradually, though, as her pulse slowed, tiredness brought an end to the process and she fell asleep.

Chapter 21

She rose early the next morning and crept outside, walking the half mile down the hill to the sea front. The sea looked so different in the cold grey light of dawn, devoid of the power and beauty of the night before. Raymond was probably already on his way to Guildford to visit his parents, a journey which she knew would take more than three hours. He had told her that he was planning to set off early and intended to spend all his holiday with them, so she had to resign herself to being without him for ten long days. She sighed, wishing she could have gone too and knowing that it would seem an eternity before he returned.

A few gulls were cawing in the distance as she watched the red rim of the sun edge its way above the horizon, spreading ripples of light on the water. She thought about their lovemaking the night before. Although she couldn't regret it, in the cold light of day she resolved not to repeat it, not until they were married, anyway. Perhaps, when he returned, Raymond would ask her to be his wife. She knew without thinking what her answer would be, even if it meant putting Girton on hold.

In a reflective mood, Eileen strolled back in the direction of Victoria Homes. The sun had risen now and the air was full of early morning scents from a host of spring flowers in the neat front gardens of row upon row of tiny Victorian terraces.

'I imagine my mother must have lived in a little house like one of these,' Eileen mused. She had often heard Eliza speak warmly of her childhood in Albert Road and tried hard to picture what her mother must have looked like then. Sadly, there were only a few old photographs from this time – one of her maternal grandparents, one of Uncle George with his wife, and one of Alice's wedding day.

There was also, of course, the photograph that was locked away in her mother's dressing table drawer, the one she took out occasionally to show Eileen. It was of Eliza and Laurie together, just before he went off to the war. Eileen had always been struck by how happy her mother looked, standing arm in arm with this dark, handsome stranger and wondered if she had loved Laurie as much as she herself now loved Raymond.

'Perhaps I should tell her about Raymond soon,' she thought. She had toyed with the idea of telling both her parents about him several months before, during the only brief period of leave she had enjoyed since arriving in Margate, but had decided against it, at least until she was more certain of Raymond's intentions. Now, it was different. Marriage, she was sure, was on the horizon. 'Maybe I'll mention him in my next letter,' she murmured to herself as she mounted the steps to the front door of the residence.

'Where the hell have you been, Eileen?' yelled Renée from the hallway. 'You've nearly missed breakfast!'

By the end of April, it was obvious that the German air-raids had now ceased and an end to the war in Europe was very near. All the fire service girls received a letter informing them that their unit was to be disbanded from the middle of May and that girls not resident in Margate would subsequently be attached to a local fire brigade near their home town, until such time as they were officially demobbed.

The news came as a terrible blow to everyone. Although they had often longed for the war to be over, the thought of leaving Margate to return to civilian life was incredibly depressing.

'It's a black day,' said Renée. 'I don't know what

I'm going to do without you lot to entertain. It's not so bad for you though, Babs. You live here. I wish I bloody did.'

'It won't be the same without all of you,' said Babs. 'It won't ever be the same again.'

The only good news on the horizon was Nancy Riley's engagement to her corporal. They had decided to get married as soon as the war was over and would live with his parents in Rochester until they could afford to rent somewhere.

That night, Muriel rang Pavel with the news of her imminent departure and arranged to meet him the following day to say goodbye. He was sad to hear that Muriel was going but was also pleased for her. 'At least you have a home to go back to,' he said. 'I'm not sure that I have.'

He was referring, of course, to the recent terrible events in Poland following the Warsaw uprising when thousands of his fellow countrymen had been slaughtered by German soldiers. This had happened under the noses of the Russian troops, who merely stood back and watched, knowing that Poland would be easier to carve up at the end of the war if its main fighting force was eliminated.

'What will you do?' asked Muriel, feeling sad and guilty that the very country Britain had gone to war to protect was now under threat again.

'I'm not sure,' he replied. 'Many of my friends want to stay and live here, but I don't think I can do that. My family are all still in Poland and so, I suppose, is my heart.'

He smiled then and removed from his kitbag a large parcel, which he handed to her.

'This is for you and the girls,' he said, 'something to remember me by. Please don't open it until just before you all leave Victoria Homes. You'll understand why when you read the note inside.'

'Good luck, Pavel,' she whispered as she kissed him goodbye. 'One day, your country will be free again. I'm sure of it.'

'Perhaps,' he said, giving her a wistful smile as he got into his truck. 'Perhaps.'

Eileen had arranged to meet Raymond at the clock tower the night after he returned from leave. Desperate to see him again, she arrived a good twenty minutes before the appointed time. Eventually, she saw him cycling towards her in the distance and her heart missed a beat. She watched him dismount, lean his bike against the railings and approach. He walked up to her, kissed her gently on the cheek, then took her by the hand.

They walked along the deserted sea front beyond the harbour wall and sat down on a bench looking back towards the town. The sky was overcast and the afternoon was drawing to a steely close, the sea appearing dark grey and depressing. Eileen immediately told him the news of her forthcoming departure and awaited his response. But Raymond remained strangely silent.

'Well,' she prompted him, 'what do you think? What should we do? I'll have to go home for a while but I suppose I could come back here and get a job till you're demobbed. Then, when I go up to Cambridge, I'll visit you as often as I can, or maybe you could come up from Guildford for weekends and I can show you all round the colleges. You'll love it in Cambridge, I know you will. There's so much to see and do there. And during the long holidays, we could maybe go away somewhere together. What do you think?'

Eileen was gradually conscious that she was

talking to fill a silence and began to feel uneasy. She had never known Raymond to be so quiet and unresponsive.

'What is it?' she asked him eventually. 'There's something wrong, isn't there? Are your parents all right?'

'Yes, I think so,' he replied.

'But you must know,' she said. 'You've just been to see them!'

There was a long pause before he answered her. He gazed out to sea for what seemed to be several minutes, his face white, his lower lip twitching slightly, his eyes strangely blank and emotionless. Eileen was alarmed, now. His expression reminded her of a trapped animal resigning itself to the inevitability of death. Finally, he spoke.

'I lied to you Eileen. I haven't been to see my parents,' he admitted, still gazing out to sea. 'I've been to see my wife.'

Eileen froze, unable to take in what he had said. For a second, she thought he was joking or that she had somehow misheard him, but his troubled anxious face soon made her realise that he was telling the truth. Now, it was her turn to remain quiet. She bowed her head, unable to look at him and unsure of how to deal with the rush of conflicting feelings within her.

Although she showed no obvious signs of emotion, Raymond could sense that she was totally distraught. He had been dreading this moment, had tried to fool himself into thinking that it would never come, yet he had always known it was inevitable. He did love Eileen deeply, but the last ten days had made him absolutely sure that he could never leave his wife for her.

He looked across at the hunched figure beside him, not knowing what to say. If only she had been a bit less serious, a bit more superficial, like the other service girls he had been out with.

'Say something, Eileen,' he pleaded, 'I know you must think I'm a bastard, but I honestly didn't mean this to happen. I didn't mean for us to fall in love, really I didn't. I thought we could just have a bit of fun. Everyone's entitled to have a bit of fun in wartime but then it...'

At this point, Eileen suddenly found her voice.

'A bit of fun. A bit of fun! Is that what I've been to you? Is that all I've meant?'

'No, of course not...' he began, but the anger was welling up inside her now and her voice rose above his.

'You've been lying to me Raymond,' she screamed, 'lying to me for months and months without thinking of anyone but yourself, making me think you loved me, that you were serious and oh so bloody sensitive when all the time you were just a nasty little cheat out for his own ends!'

She turned away from him, embarrassed by the tears welling in her eyes and not wanting to let him see. They were silent for a minute, Raymond not daring to speak again, Eileen trying to gain some control over the fury that had seized her.

At last, Eileen gathered sufficient composure to speak.

'I suppose you have children, as well,' she said, coldly, thinking she was being sarcastic.

'Well, yes, actually... two of them. A boy and a girl.' He was floundering now. 'Does that make any difference?'

'Obviously not to you,' she replied with a bitterness in her voice that she had never heard before. She turned away again and sat completely still for a while, wanting to make him suffer, not wanting him to see that she was suffering, pretending she was staring at a strange cloud formation on the distant horizon.

They both knew instinctively that there was nothing further to be said. After a few more minutes of tense silence, they stood up almost simultaneously and walked slowly back along the front, stopping at the clock tower, where they went through the motions of an awkward goodbye. He made as if to kiss her but she stepped back, shaking her head. She forced herself to watch him stride off and retrieve his bike, forced herself to look at his blond hair blowing in the wind as he rode away and struggled to understand how she could have let herself be deceived for so long. Not until he was a mere speck on the horizon did she allow the tears to return to her eyes.

She hurried back to Victoria Homes in the pouring rain, her mind racing, her emotions in turmoil. Anger had slowly given way to grief and grief to devastation. Embarrassed to show her feelings, she shut herself in the bathroom as soon as she got back. Ten minutes later, Muriel heard her sobbing and knocked on the door to be let in. As they sat together on the bathroom floor, Eileen poured out her heart to her friend, divulging the whole story. Muriel, as always, was sensitive and supportive and promised not to say anything to the others. It was agreed that Eileen would tell them she had finished with Raymond because they'd had a row and leave it at that.

The next morning, Eileen received a letter from home, updating her on all the news. Still tearful and shaky, she tore it open. It was from her father, and although it actually said very little, she found it strangely comforting.

My dear Eileen,

I'm writing this for both of us because your mam is helping Alice look after Dorothy's children for a few days. Poor Dorothy has had a bad bout of the flu but she should be up and about again very soon. No need to worry.

Well, the war is almost over at last and both of us are looking forward to seeing you safe and settled at home. We got your letter saying you'd be coming back in the middle of May. Your mam is going to meet you at the station so make sure you let us know the time of the train. By the way, your mam thinks it would be nice if Renée and Muriel could let her have their mothers' addresses. Maybe they can arrange to meet up at Bradford station and have a cup of tea together while they're waiting for your train to arrive.

There isn't a lot of news our end, really. I went to watch a football match with Uncle Jack on Saturday and he sends you his love. Amy will be back home from Lincolnshire about the same time as you, so you'll be able to meet up with her and share a few stories.

Your Uncle George wrote to us again to say he's definitely going to sell the sheep farm before he and his wife get too old to enjoy their retirement. They are going to stay with his wife's cousin until they find their dream home by the sea. He loved the latest photo of you that we sent him. Thinks you look just like me!

Your mam is still working hard in Lister's Mill but she might find that she's out of a job soon, I shouldn't wonder, once all the troops come back. She won't mind, though. We've got a little bit put by now, so there's no need for her to work, and besides, I'm sure she'd much rather be at home once you're here.

I'm looking forward to showing you my new gramophone, love. I got it cheap from a friend at work and it makes all my old records sound better than ever. I've also dug out that old chess set we got you one Christmas and we can have a game when you feel like it.

All our love – mam and dad.

Several days before the girls were due to leave Margate, news of the end of the war in Europe came through. Some of them, including Maude, went up to London to celebrate what became known as VE Day, but Eileen, Muriel and Renée stayed in, none of them feeling very much like a night on the town after their recent experiences. Eileen wrote back to her father, enclosing the addresses her mother had asked for and confirming the time of the train.

The last day in Victoria Homes was a gloomy affair. Tears flowed as farewells were said and even OP was visibly upset as she kissed Renée goodbye. Before one of the fire service trucks came to collect the party bound for Bradford, Muriel opened Pavel's parcel. Inside were two other parcels, the bigger one addressed to 'the girls', the smaller one to Muriel. The former contained two large boxes of chocolates to be shared between them. Renée opened the note inside and read it aloud to them:

To all the girls in Victoria Homes.
You will never know how much you brightened up the darkest time in my life. Enjoy these chocolates on your way home and please think of me, sometimes, whenever Poland is mentioned in the news. Thank you for everything and good luck.   *Pavel.*

Muriel now opened her present. It was a beautiful solid silver powder compact, with an inscription inside, written in Polish.

'What does it mean and how on earth do you pronounce it?' asked Renée. 'Do you know, Muriel?'

'Yes, as a matter of fact, I do,' she replied. 'He said the same words to me once, not so long ago: *Nigdy nie zapomnij – never forget.*'

The truck arrived shortly afterwards to take Eileen, Muriel and Renée to the station in time to catch the train to Waterloo. OP and the girls waved them off and kept on waving until they had become a tiny speck on the horizon.

'Take us round the clock tower,' Renée instructed the driver as they reached the end of the road. 'I want one last look at it before I go.'

The driver took them along the front as requested and Renée gave her beloved clock tower a final wave as they drove past. 'Goodbye my old pal,' she shouted through the window, the tears streaming down her face. 'You've had the best years of my life.'

Chapter 22

The journey home was long and dismal. The train chugged through the rain, stopping at countless stations lined with happy people still celebrating the end of the war. Muriel, Renée and Eileen said little to each other, just gazed out of the window reliving the Margate years.

Renée thought of Maurice and of how, had he not been attached to the advance landing party on D-Day, he might be sitting beside her now, looking forward to the guided tour of Yorkshire she had always promised him. Muriel thought about Pavel and whether he would write to her or not. She had given him her address in Bradford but sensed that he probably wanted to draw a line under his wartime experiences and move on. Once he was back in Poland, there would be so much to do, so much to catch up on. He would never forget, though, and neither would she, of that she was certain. In Eileen's mind, the final meeting with Raymond kept replaying itself like a scene from a film, the image, of course, always in black and white. In the foreground, Eileen and Raymond were walking slowly along the front, their heads bowed, the gap between their hunched bodies reflecting what had just happened. They were framed by a dull grey sea and sky, the wind ruffling their hair. Beneath them, the pavements were wet, glistening. In the distance, Eileen could make out the curve of the harbour wall and the slight incline beyond, where Holy Trinity Church had stood before it was bombed. The camera followed them from behind as they approached the clock tower, and after that, everything went dark. Gazing out of the carriage window, Eileen feared that this scene would torment her for the rest of her life.

Suddenly, the train pulled into Bradford station, waking them all from their reverie. None of them rushed to get off. They allowed all the other passengers to retrieve their luggage first. Then they hauled their heavy suitcases down the steps of the carriage and hailed a porter to carry them to the end of the platform. They could already see the three eager, excited faces of their mothers peering over the barrier.

'Bloody hell,' said Renée. 'There they are. Hubble, bubble, toil and trouble.'

'Time to look cheerful girls,' said Muriel. 'Come on. Let's try and remember that we've just won the war.'

They followed the porter to the barrier, offering

up a few feeble waves to their waiting mothers as they did so, all of them hoping that their misery wouldn't be too obvious when they got home.

Eliza hugged Eileen as tightly as she could. 'You don't know how much it means to have you back, love,' she said. 'Now we can really start to live again.'

Making the transition from war to peace was far from easy and took time. The girls soon received their demobilisation papers and two weeks later all three of them had found a job and were beginning to adjust to a very different way of life. Renée went to work in an office at the gas board, Muriel found a post in a shoe shop in the centre of Bradford and Eileen, wanting something temporary until she took up her place at Cambridge in October, was offered a summer vacancy in the city's reference library. The fact that they were all working in fairly close proximity meant that it was easy for them to meet up for lunch on a regular basis.

Eileen soon discovered that adjusting to a work routine was easier than adjusting to life at home. Dearly as she loved her parents, she found everything so boring and predictable compared with the excitement of wartime Margate. She tried her best to fit back in, however, and agreed to go with her mother on a few outings.

Eliza had given up her job at Lister's mill, but now that Eileen was paying her own way, the family were not short of money.

'Why don't we go shopping in Leeds on Saturday with Alice and Amy?' said Eliza shortly after Eileen returned. 'It'll be a change from Bradford and you can hear all about how Amy got on in the Land Army.'

Eileen agreed and the four of them met at Bradford station at ten o'clock. The journey to City Square in Leeds took about half an hour, and on the way, Eileen and Amy chatted about Norfolk and Margate, discovering how different their wartime experiences had been. As Amy told of her long days toiling on the land, Eileen realised how lucky she was, not just to have been in the fire service, but to have been in such a lovely seaside town.

They walked out of the station on a bright afternoon in June, the huge statue of The Black Prince on horseback towering above them in the square opposite. Eileen wondered what connection such a statue could possibly have with the city, knowing the figure celebrated was the son of King Edward III and had lived in the fourteenth century, at a time when Leeds was hardly on the map at all.

At the end of Briggate, they turned the corner past the enormous oval building known as The Corn Exchange and then along Vicar Lane towards Kirkgate Market, a favourite haunt of Alice and Eliza before the war. Built in Edwardian times, it was the largest indoor market in Europe and had stalls that sold an amazing range of goods, from fruit and vegetables to baby clothes, from fish and meat to radios and pots and pans. There were several aisles running down the centre of the market, arranged according to the type of product sold, so butchers' row would be full of meat stalls, game row full of poultry and so on. At the end of it, there was an open market selling all kinds of everything, including toys, pet food and even pets.

Eliza and Alice found the whole place a little less impressive than before the war because rationing hadn't yet stopped and food continued to be scarce.

Nevertheless, it was still a hive of activity, echoing with the cries of stallholders and shoppers, assaulting nostrils with the assorted smells of dog biscuits, wet fish, sawdust and mushy peas.

Alice bought some wool so she could knit jumpers for Dorothy's children. Eliza got some Player's cigarettes for Arthur and a doll for her goddaughter, Hilda.

'Why don't we go to Whitelock's for lunch?' suggested Eliza as they came out of the market.

'Aye, that's a good idea,' said Alice. 'We haven't been in there since long before the war. What do you think girls?'

Eileen and Amy were happy to go along with whatever their mothers wanted and followed them down the tiny alleyway off Briggate, past a row of nineteenth century workers' cottages to Turk's Head Yard, where Whitelock's was situated. The busy Victorian pub, originally known as The Turk's Head, was one of the most famous institutions in Leeds. It was long and narrow and full of atmosphere, with sawdust on the floor and a mirrored bar with original brass fittings and shelving that stretched from one end to the other. The etched windows were particularly beautiful, testifying to a period when fine craftsmanship was at its height.

To the right of the bar was a small restaurant with no more than five tables, all of which were usually full, the place being renowned for its excellent food. They had a drink while they were waiting for a table, Eliza surprised by how much Eileen now seemed to know about alcoholic beverages.

'What did you drink in Margate, love?' asked Alice.

'Pale ale, usually,' said Eileen.

'You're not a milk stout fan like your mother then?'

'No,' laughed Eileen, 'I hate the stuff.'

'So do I,' agreed Amy. 'Give me a bottle of Bass anytime.'

They spent the afternoon walking round the shops, ending up at a fashionable department store in The Headrow. Farther down the road, Eileen could see the famous Town Hall and Art Gallery, both of which she would have liked to explore on her own had this been possible. She made a mental note to return without her mother one day and visit them.

During the following week, Eileen's life continued in what she considered to be a somewhat humdrum fashion. Although well-paid, her work at the library was pretty routine and Cambridge still seemed an age away.

Her parents did what they could to help her settle down again at home, but she couldn't help missing the wonderful social life she had enjoyed in Margate and was often bored.

She was still resigning herself to an acceptance of this rather uneventful lifestyle when, in the middle of updating some records in the library, she began to feel rather queasy. Putting it down to the rich pastry on her mother's apple pie the night before, she went over to her desk to sit down, sure that it would quickly pass off. But it didn't. After a few minutes it became much worse. Certain now that she was about to be violently sick, Eileen rushed out of the library to the staff toilet downstairs, desperately hoping she would make it there before the vomiting began.

Seeing her distress, a library colleague followed her down to check that she was all right.

'Come and sit down for a bit,' she said as Eileen, pale and rather shaky now, emerged from the lavatory.

'You look dreadful. Was it something you ate?'

'My mother's apple pie, I think,' Eileen replied, grateful for her colleague's arm to lean on. They found a chair in a secluded part of the library and then someone appeared with a glass of water.

'Don't worry, I'll be fine if you just leave me alone here for a while.'

Once her colleagues had retreated, Eileen began to gather her composure. She sat perfectly still until, gradually, the nauseous sensation wore off and she resumed her work.

It was only as she was leaving the building that night that it dawned on her there could be a connection between the sickness and the fact that she had missed her last two periods. She tried to dismiss the thought, telling herself that she had been under a lot of stress in the last few months and it was all probably due to that. But when she was sick again two days later, she started to be alarmed. The thought that she might possibly be pregnant had never entered her head when she left Margate. Now, it did, and she began to be gripped by an anxiety that wouldn't go away.

On the Monday, she arranged to meet Muriel in Collinson's cafe. As soon as Muriel saw her, she realised something was very wrong. Over a tense lunch, Muriel pressed her friend to tell her what was the matter, and eventually, Eileen plucked up enough courage to confess her fears.

Muriel was shocked and secretly horrified, knowing the dreadful social consequences of any pregnancy out of wedlock. Until it was certain, though, she knew she had to be reassuring and try to calm Eileen down a bit. There was, of course, no way of being certain until she was at least three months gone. Even then, it depended on the doctor's opinion.

'Don't rush to conclusions just yet, love,' she said. 'Any number of things could make you miss a couple of periods. You've had such an upsetting time just lately, what with Raymond and having to leave Margate. It might be down to that. Leave it a few more weeks and see what happens.'

Eileen decided to take her advice and wait a bit longer, but the worry was always at the back of her mind. She found it hard to concentrate on work and even harder to appear cheerful at home. Occasionally, she vomited at work during the morning, though she was now more attuned to the early symptoms of these bouts of sickness and was able to slip down to the staff toilet before anyone noticed there was a problem. They made her panic, though, knowing, as she did, that they were often an early indication of pregnancy.

After a few more weeks had passed, with no sign of a period, Eileen met up with Muriel again.

'I think it *is* time you saw a doctor, love,' her friend said. 'If you've missed three periods, he might be able to tell if you're having a baby or not just by examining you.'

'But what if he thinks I *am* pregnant?' said Eileen, suddenly feeling terrified. 'What on earth do I do then?'

'Let's cross that bridge if we come to it,' said Muriel. 'Look, here's five pounds towards the doctor's fee – try and get an appointment with one as quickly as you can and meet me for lunch again next Friday. You should know something by then.'

Eileen promised to pay her back as soon as possible but Muriel insisted she keep the money.

'I saved up quite a bit in Margate,' she said, 'and there's nothing else I want to do with it. I'd much rather give it to you and know it's doing some good.'

With the five pounds she had already saved from her library work, Eileen had just enough for the consultation fee of ten pounds and sought out a doctor well away from her home area.

His surgery was bleak and depressing, with whitewashed walls and barely enough light to make out the various stern warnings on the faded wartime posters curling off the notice board. A quizzical look from the elderly, overweight receptionist made her feel nervous.

'Does she suspect anything?' thought Eileen. She fastened the top two buttons of her cardigan and lowered her head, feeling awkward and self-conscious.

A few minutes later, there was the distant thud of a door closing and a middle-aged woman in a dark blue jacket hurried down the corridor towards the exit. Soon afterwards, a buzzer sounded, and despite the fact the surgery was completely empty apart from Eileen, the receptionist called her name in a loud voice, as if announcing something of crucial importance.

'Eileen Pendlestone. The doctor is ready to see you now. Go down the corridor. It's the first door on your left.'

Eileen tapped on the door and waited. 'Come in!' the doctor called, his voice sounding cold and forbidding. She paused a moment before entering, taking a deep breath in an effort to calm herself.

The door opened on a small room with an

examination table and a folding screen on the right, a white enamel sink in the corner and a desk immediately in front of her. Behind it sat a silver-haired middle-aged man with thick-rimmed glasses perched on the end of his nose. His manner seemed aloof, somewhat superior.

'What can I do for you my dear?' he began, rather condescendingly.

She explained that it had now been over fourteen weeks since her last period and that she was worried. The doctor asked her various questions and then requested her permission to examine her internally. He got up and drew the screen around the bed.

'Please remove the bottom half of your clothes and then lie down. I'll be back shortly.'

Flustered and afraid, Eileen did as he asked, dreading what was coming next and wondering how long it would take. He returned with a nurse, who stood beside her, attempting to reassure her while the intimate examination took place. It was very painful and Eileen couldn't stop herself wincing or crying out at times.

'All right, get dressed,' the doctor said abruptly as soon as he had finished.

She did so as quickly as she could, anxious to hear

his opinion.

'I gather you're not married Miss Pendlestone,' he began.

'No but I'm engaged to be,' Eileen lied. 'We're getting married soon.'

He raised his eyebrows and gazed at her intently over his glasses, adopting an expression which indicated he had heard many similar stories of such 'engagements' before and therefore wasn't taken in for one minute. He then confirmed that, in his opinion, there was little doubt that she was indeed expecting a child.

'I see,' she replied, frantically trying to appear calm, though her heart was pounding.

She left the surgery without a backward glance, mortified at the thought that, already, she was probably being gossiped about by the nurse or receptionist.

That night, seized by panic, Eileen paced the floor of her bedroom, not knowing what to do next. There was no point telling Raymond, even if she knew where he lived. He was the past, now, and she didn't want the past resurrected. Her parents couldn't possibly be told. It would destroy them. She knew only too well how devastating such news would be, especially to her father, whom she couldn't bear to hurt. There seemed to her no way out, other than to somehow have the baby in secret while she was in Cambridge. She couldn't imagine how this was even remotely feasible, however. Besides, what on earth would she do with the baby once she'd had it?

The next day she met Muriel and gave her the terrible news.

Muriel was silent at first, not knowing how to advise her friend for the best. This was the worst possible thing that could happen. Eileen was about to become an outcast. Many fathers turned their daughters out of the house when such a thing happened, and even if they didn't, life became unbearable with all the gossiping and pointing of fingers.

'You've got to tell your mother,' said Muriel, who had spent a lot of time worrying since they last met. 'She's the only person who can help you, now.'

'I can't,' gasped Eileen. 'I can't possibly tell her. She'll go mad.'

'Of course she will but she's about your only hope. At least you'll have someone else to talk to, someone to share this with. If she loves you Eileen, she won't throw you out. I'm sure she won't.'

Distraught, Eileen dropped her head into her hands, trying to fight back the tears.

'Look, love,' urged Muriel, putting her arm round her friend's shoulder, 'it really is the only thing to do. Please, please promise me you'll tell your mother before this weekend's over.'

'All right,' said Eileen reluctantly, not seeing any alternative. 'I'll try.'

'That's good, that's good,' sighed Muriel. 'Look, I'll meet you in here again at the same time on Tuesday lunchtime and you can tell me how it went.'

That night, Eileen walked home dejectedly, hoping there might be an opportunity to talk with her mother on Saturday afternoon, when her father would be out for a walk and a drink with Jack. Quite how she was going to raise the subject she had no idea, never having spoken much to anyone about personal, private matters. All she could do was hope that, when the time came, she would instinctively know what to say.

Chapter 23

Eliza had noticed a change in Eileen since she had returned from Margate. She seemed much quieter, more subdued, and was nowhere near as excited about going to Cambridge as she expected her to be.

'Maybe she's been more affected by the war than we realise,' she said to Arthur. 'She was always such a sensitive child.'

As Eileen had hoped, Arthur went off with Jack immediately after lunch on Saturday. She deliberately started chatting with her mother as they were doing the washing up, desperately hoping that an appropriate moment to disclose the awful truth would somehow arise as the conversation progressed.

'You don't seem yourself these days, love,' said Eliza as they were putting away the last few dishes. 'Is everything all right?'

'Well no, not really, mam, it isn't.' Eileen's heart was racing now and her mouth felt very dry.

'Oh dear,' said Eliza. 'I've been wondering for a while if there might be something the matter. Let's make a cup of tea and you can sit down and tell me all about it.'

The kettle took an interminable length of time to boil. Eileen watched the tiny puffs of steam rising from its spout and remembered how she used to watch them as a child, used to wait expectantly for the start of the faint whistle that gradually increased in volume until her mother suddenly put a stop to it by lifting the container off the gas. The whole process seemed so wonderfully ordinary then. Now, as if it were calling time on the homely world she had known, the insistent whistle was almost unbearable. It had become the shrill harbinger of a dark, uncertain future.

Eliza finally picked up the kettle and poured its contents into the brown teapot. This she put on the table with two cups and saucers and then sat down next to her daughter.

'Come on then, love,' she said, 'tell me what's wrong.'

'I'm pregnant, mam,' said Eileen abruptly. She hadn't meant it to come out like this, so bluntly without any preparation or preamble, but when it came to it, she simply seized the first opportunity that arose to blurt out the truth.

There was a long pause as a stunned Eliza

struggled to take in what her daughter had just told her.

'You can't be, Eileen. You can't be,' she gasped. She sat back in her chair, dumbfounded, still unable to believe that such a thing could be true. 'Are you sure?'

'Yes, I've seen a doctor and he's confirmed it,' Eileen replied. 'I'm so sorry, mam. I didn't mean it to happen.'

'Didn't mean it? You didn't mean it?' cried Eliza, her voice rising as the reality of her daughter's condition began to dawn on her. She stood up now, anger pulsing through her veins. 'Course you damned well meant it! You're not daft! Who's the father? Tell me who he is! I'll bloody kill him!'

'It doesn't matter who the father is,' said Eileen. 'I can't see him again, anyway. He's married with two children.'

'You've never been going out with a married man!' shouted Eliza, her voice faltering with the shock of this additional revelation. She glared at her daughter, still struggling to believe what she was being told. 'You fool Eileen! You bloody fool!'

'I didn't know he was married, mam, I didn't, honestly,' protested Eileen, who was visibly shaken by the vehemence of her mother's onslaught. 'I finished with him as soon as I found out. I never thought for a minute I'd get pregnant. We only did it the once.'

'Only the once!' screamed Eliza, her face contorted and red with fury. She banged her fist on the table. 'Only the bloody once! You're going to study at Cambridge and you don't even know how you get yourself pregnant! By hell, Eileen, what the bugger did they learn you in that posh school all them years? Nowt that was of any use as far as I can see. You've done for all of us good and proper now, you have that. How the devil are we going to live with this?'

'Don't tell dad,' pleaded Eileen, 'I don't care what you do, mam, but please don't tell dad.'

'Your dad's bound to know soon enough,' her mother cried. 'In another month or two it'll be damned obvious. He'll only have to look at you and he'll be able to tell. How could you do this to us, Eileen? How could you?'

No longer able to control her tears, Eileen ran upstairs to her room and flung herself on the bed. Eliza didn't follow her. It was all she could do to stop herself from lashing out at her daughter, consumed as she was with rage. She paced up and down for several minutes, wringing her hands and feeling as if her head would burst.

When her anger finally began to subside, it was replaced by panic. She thought of what people would say – friends, neighbours, the congregation at church. She knew it would destroy Arthur, and as for Eileen, there would be no Cambridge University now, no career, no future, only a reputation in tatters. It was the end of everything. In her mind's eye, she saw Eileen in a year's time, the laughing stock of the neighbourhood. 'There's that clever girl who was going to Cambridge,' they'd say. 'Look at her now, pushing a pram.'

Eliza sat down at the table and rocked backwards and forwards, trying desperately to think of what to do. She knew in her heart that she couldn't allow this to happen. Not after all they'd been through, all the sacrifices they'd made.

Pouring herself a cup of tea to calm her nerves, she tried to remember a conversation she'd once had with a girl at Salt's mill. She recalled this girl telling her that there were certain women who specialised in helping girls that had got themselves into trouble. In fact, she'd often heard the women in Lister's Mill whisper about them.

Then she cast her mind back to a conversation she'd had with Mrs Braithwaite four or five years back, concerning a friend of hers whose unmarried daughter had fallen pregnant. Mrs Braithwaite had told her how her friend had arranged for somebody to come and 'get rid of the baby' without anyone knowing. Maybe this could be the way out of Eileen's predicament. She resolved to speak to Mrs Braithwaite when she played cards with her the following evening and see what more she could discover.

Feeling a little calmer now, Eliza went upstairs to Eileen, who was still sobbing her heart out on the bed. 'It'll be all right, love,' she said, sitting down next to her. 'Don't worry. I'll think of something.'

Arthur came back home at six and they all had tea together.

'You seem a bit quiet these days, Eileen,' he said. 'Are you feeling all right, love?'

'Yes,' she replied, looking across at her mother for support, 'I'm fine, dad.'

Mrs Braithwaite was in a good mood that Sunday, having heard that her daughter had just given birth to her third child.

'It's lovely when a baby is wanted,' said Eliza, trying to steer the conversation in the desired direction, 'but I can't help feeling sorry for those poor young girls that fall pregnant out of wedlock.'

'Aye, it's a big problem is that,' Mrs Braithwaite agreed.

'Didn't you once have a friend who helped her unmarried daughter to... you know... have some sort of operation on the quiet?'

'Yes, that's right, Mrs Grimshaw in Crossley Street. I think her daughter's happily married now, although I haven't seen her for years.'

Eliza went looking for Mrs Grimshaw the next day. She asked a lady who lived in the end house for the right number, pretending she was a long lost relative who had come to visit. The lady directed her to number fourteen, and after a whispered conversation with Mrs Grimshaw on the doorstep, she was invited inside.

She explained briefly why she had come and asked if there was any way Mrs Grimshaw could put her in touch with someone who might be able to help her daughter out of the mess she found herself in. Guarded and defensive at first, Mrs Grimshaw soon warmed to

Eliza and felt sorry for her. She told her that there *was* somebody in the area, a woman calling herself Cathy, who never divulged her real name or address, for obvious reasons. If Eliza wanted, she would be willing to arrange a time and place for them to meet, but Eliza must swear on her life that she would keep everything completely secret and never tell anyone that Mrs Grimshaw had been involved. Eliza swore solemnly that she would indeed never reveal what had gone on between them, and in turn, Mrs Grimshaw promised to act as a go-between.

'Call round here at the same time on Thursday and I should know more,' she said, showing Eliza out.

Relieved to be doing something at last, Eliza walked home, and for the first time in days, was able to enjoy a cup of tea. When Eileen returned from work, she told her what she was proposing to do. 'Don't worry, love,' she said. 'I'll take care of everything. The lady has done this sort of thing for a lot of other girls, so she'll make sure you're all right.'

'Will it hurt, mam?' asked Eileen, innocently.

'Well, I should think it will at the time but it'll all be over in half an hour. You might have to stay in bed for a while afterwards, but I'll be here to look after you and we can always tell your dad that you're poorly with the flu.'

Eileen wasn't at all sure about her mother's plans. The alternative, however, was even more frightening to contemplate, so she reluctantly agreed. They kept the whole thing secret, being careful to talk about it only when Arthur was out of the house. The only person Eileen did tell was Muriel, whom she knew she could trust.

'Don't worry,' said Muriel. 'I won't tell a soul.'

Chapter 24

The following Thursday, Eliza called to see Mrs Grimshaw as arranged. This time, she wasn't invited in, merely given a slip of paper with a date and time written on it.

'Here you are,' said Mrs Grimshaw, pushing it into her hand. 'Now, go quickly. You mustn't ever come here again.'

Eliza took the paper with her to the end of the street and looked at it. In shaky handwriting was written – *Tuesday. 1.30pm. Ring Of Bells pub off Market Street. I'll be in the snug wearing a black coat and brown headscarf. Cathy.*

Although Eliza had never been in this pub before, she knew where it was. She took the tram into Bradford on the appointed day and slipped nervously through the snug door, pretending to be looking for a friend. The plump middle-aged woman sitting on her own in the corner was instantly recognisable as Cathy. Eliza moved close to her and spoke.

'Is it Cathy?' she said in hushed tones.

'Aye, that's right,' the woman replied. 'Go and get yourself a drink and come and join me.'

Feeling ill at ease on her own in a pub, Eliza went nervously up to the bar, got herself a milk stout and came back to Cathy's table.

'Now then, I hear your daughter's got herself into a bit o' trouble and wants some help to get out of it,' she said brusquely.

They talked quietly for about half an hour. Eliza gathered that Cathy had done many of these operations in her time and was clearly used to secret conversations of this sort. She told Eliza that she charged ten pounds and expected to be paid as soon as she arrived at the house, before the operation took place. The procedure normally took between twenty and forty minutes, depending on the degree of difficulty. Cathy made it clear that she would leave the house immediately the job was finished and could not be contacted again after that. Obviously, her arrival and departure must be kept completely secret. It would be helpful, she thought, if Eliza could be present at the time as her daughter would need to stay in bed and might need looking after for a while afterwards until the bleeding stopped.

It was agreed that Cathy would come to the house the following Tuesday at half past two. Eliza wrote down her address on the slip of paper Cathy gave her and they left the pub together. Once outside, they went their separate ways.

Eliza immediately went to the bank and drew out five pounds. She already had five pounds at home, saved from overtime at the mill, which she kept under the mattress for a rainy day. Cathy's fee was almost the equivalent of three weeks' wages, Eliza thought, but it was well worth it to save them all from ruin.

Instead of going straight home, Eliza went to see Alice. For several days, she had been wondering whether or not to tell her about Eileen. She knew she could trust her implicitly, of course, but up to now had decided to struggle on alone, keeping everything secret if she could. Today's meeting with Cathy had upset her though and she felt she was going to need someone to talk to after the whole sordid business was over. She knew she wouldn't be able to leave Eileen's side immediately after the operation and thought that it would be reassuring to have someone with her in the house, in case anything was needed.

'Come in, love,' said Alice, surprised to see her friend at such a strange hour. 'I'll put the kettle on.'

Alice listened sympathetically to the sad story. 'Are you sure this Cathy knows what she's doing?' she asked. 'How did you find out about her?'

'I can't tell you how I found out about her,' Eliza replied. 'But I do know she's experienced.'

'I bloody hope so,' said Alice.

She enquired no further, sensing that Eliza would never disclose any details about the way she had contacted the woman. Realising that Eliza needed support, though, she agreed to come round to her house at around half past three the following Tuesday, by which time Cathy would be on her way home.

'You know I won't breathe a word of this to anyone,' said Alice, kissing her goodbye, 'not even to Jack.'

Before Arthur arrived home that night, Eliza told Eileen what had been planned for the following Tuesday. She also explained that she had let Alice in on the secret and had asked her to come round afterwards as a bit of extra support.

'You can ring in sick on the Monday and tell them you've got the flu. That way, you'll be able to have the whole week off if you need it. The woman's coming at half past two, so by the time your dad gets back it'll all be over. We'll make out you've felt poorly all day and you need leaving alone to sleep. That should stop him coming up to see you and then there won't be any awkward questions.'

'How much is it all costing, mam?' said Eileen.

'Never you mind that,' said her mother. 'You just concentrate on getting through it and sorting out your life again.'

On the Monday, Eileen rang the library as planned and told them she was ill. She then had the rest of the day to do whatever she wished. Eliza thought her daughter might need this time to prepare herself and would benefit from not having the pressure of work when she already had enough on her mind. She had envisaged they would spend the day together at home, but when it came to it, Eileen couldn't bear to be in the house, feeling she had to get away to try to clear her head. She still wasn't sure she wanted to go through with what her mother had arranged and desperately needed time on her own to think.

'I'm going to take the train to Leeds, mam, and have a look around,' she said. You don't mind, do you?'

'No, of course not, lass,' Eliza replied. 'It'll do you good to get a breath of air.'

Just as she had done a thousand times before, Eliza watched her daughter walk up the slope from their house to the tram stop. Scores of images from the past flashed across her mind – Eileen as a toddler holding her father's hand while Evelyn raced on ahead of them, Eileen as a little girl skipping off to primary school, and later on, running to catch the tram to grammar school in her long blazer with her schoolbag in her hand. She was so innocent and happy then. Now, she looked like a young woman with all the cares of the world on her shoulders.

Stifling a tear, Eliza moved back from the window and went into the kitchen to make a start on the household chores. She put the breakfast dishes in the sink, washed and rinsed each one carefully, then put them on the draining-board to dry. Next came the dusting and polishing. The gateleg table was always first on the list, and, as usual, she removed its dark blue velvet cover and took this into the garden to give it a good shake. Then she went into the kitchen, took out her duster and tin of polish from a wooden shoe-box and returned to the front room, intending to give the table-top its usual healthy shine.

Today, though, she found it impossible to focus on the task. Her hand moved swiftly back and forth across the table, flicking away the dust, but her mind was elsewhere. Halfway through, she stopped, one hand resting on the table, the other pressed against her stomach. She stood like this for some minutes, conscious of a rising tide of fear spreading within her.

'Have I done the right thing?' she kept asking herself. 'What if it doesn't go smoothly and Eileen can't have any more children afterwards?' She had heard that this could happen sometimes if the operation wasn't done properly. But Cathy was experienced, she had been assured of that. She reminded herself how Mrs Grimshaw's daughter had soon recovered and was now happily married with children of her own.

In an attempt to calm her nerves, she made herself a cup of tea but soon found she couldn't settle to drink it and pushed it to one side. Unable to concentrate on the cleaning any longer, she was unsure of what to do next. Panic was surging in her now, unstoppable room-pacing panic that threatened to overwhelm her, a kind of panic she had never experienced before, not even when her Laurie or Evelyn had died.

Realising that being alone in the house was only making things worse, Eliza decided to go out. 'I'll put my coat on and go and see Alice,' she said to herself, thinking it might help her to talk to someone who knew what was going on and would understand how she was feeling.

She walked briskly up the hill and caught the tram to the end of Manningham Lane. The journey took about fifteen minutes and she sat at the front, listening to the conversations of the various groups of people behind her. How normal they all sounded, she thought, with their talk of work and grandchildren and the state of the country after the war. They seemed to inhabit a different world, the kind of world which had once been hers but was hers no longer. For a split second she hated them for not realising how lucky they were.

About a hundred yards from the end of Alice's street, Eliza got off the tram and stood for a moment on the pavement, blinking in the bright August sunshine. Then, taking deep breaths to try to quell her panic, she strode purposefully to her friend's house and knocked on the front door. After a few moments, she knocked again, more insistently. But there was no answer. Eliza could hardly believe it. As far as she knew, Alice had no particular plans for today and this was the first time she had ever visited and found her to be out. She decided to walk to the end of the street and back in the hope that Alice would return soon. This, she did, but there was still no sign of Alice. The sun was getting hotter now and her face was burning. She couldn't imagine why on earth she had put on her coat.

'I can't think straight today,' she muttered as she took it off and folded it over her arm.

She kept an eye out for Alice for almost an hour but finally gave up the quest and caught the two o'clock tram back home.

The rest of the afternoon seemed endless. She forced herself to peel the potatoes, prepare the vegetables and make a shepherd's pie for tea but was constantly looking at the clock, desperate for Eileen to come back. Still finding it hard to keep her rising fears at bay, she opened the small drawer in the sideboard, took out the little bottle of brandy she always kept for medicinal purposes, and with a trembling hand, poured some into a cup of hot water. This seemed to help a bit and prompted her to give herself 'a good talking to'.

'Come on,' she muttered under her breath, 'you've got to pull yourself together or you'll be no good tomorrow when Eileen needs you most. You've done your best for her and Arthur so stop fretting and get on with things. You can't do any more now. Please God it'll soon be over and we can all get on with our lives again.'

She resumed her cleaning, determined that everything should appear normal when her daughter came in from her trip to Leeds. To distract herself, she turned on the radio. Joe Loss and his orchestra were playing some of the old First World War hits, and to Eliza's delight, there was a request for *After The Ball*.

'Happen that's a good omen,' she said, suddenly feeling very close to her parents again.

Eileen soon arrived at City Square in Leeds and found herself once more walking past The Black Prince statue. This time, she went towards the long wide road known as The Headrow, with the large impressive buildings she had glimpsed on her previous visit.

First, she made for the town hall, which, blackened as it was by years of grime from mill chimneys,

378

still remained a glorious testament to the grand architecture of the Victorian era. Eileen mounted its steps and went in through the massive central door, making her way upstairs to the concert hall to have a look around. The auditorium was vast and the huge pipes of the splendid organ were suspended above the stage, with rows of steeply-tiered seats leading up to them. So many famous musicians had played here and she regretted never having been to any of the Saturday concerts. Now the war was over, though, perhaps there would be time. She stood for a while in the balcony, imagining what it would be like to hear the Northern Philharmonic Orchestra conducted by John Barbirolli or Malcolm Sargent, or how thrilling it would be to sit in the audience during the performance of a great oratorio. One day soon, perhaps, she would be able to come back here and enjoy a concert, no longer weighed down by this anxiety that refused to leave her.

Having descended the stairs, she stepped back outside into the warm August sunshine, then took several deep breaths in a vain attempt to suppress her fears and hold back the growing terror that was threatening to overwhelm her at any moment. From the gardens of a square opposite, she could hear the sound of violins. She wandered over, hoping to be distracted from the thought of the ever-present tomorrow.

The two young players were excellent, both students from the nearby college of music. They were playing Bach's double violin concerto in D minor and Eileen sat down on a bench just as the first movement was drawing to a close.

There was a short pause, after which the slow, steady rhythm of the Largo began, the opening high note, played vibrato and sustained, followed by three more notes that descended slowly in stages. It was the start of a piece of music that seemed to Eileen to carry within it all the pain of the world, yet at the same time all its beauty. She listened, entranced, as the dying fall of the opening theme was taken up by each violin in turn. The extraordinary melody soothed her fears, bequeathing her an inner peace. Here was eternal sadness underpinned by eternal love, she thought, as the final notes trembled and faded away. She sighed as she rose from the bench, feeling calmer now, more resigned to whatever lay before her.

She looked for a church where she could sit and

meditate for a while. Noticing one on a road to the left off The Headrow, she walked to the top of its steps and pushed open the heavy wooden door. Once inside, she realised it was a Catholic church. She had never been to a Catholic church before and had been brought up to believe it was somewhere to be avoided. Today, though, was no time to be discriminatory. It was quiet and strangely beautiful there – a good place to sit and think.

Walking down the central aisle, she was struck by how many statues and images there were, each surrounded by a circle of flickering candles. On the left was a small side chapel for prayer and contemplation. She entered it tentatively, wondering if anyone was in there. But it was deserted and seemed exactly the sort of quiet, intimate place she needed. Taking a seat on the front bench beneath the delicately carved wooden crucifix, she tried to reflect calmly on her situation.

A new life was stirring within her, a life created ultimately by God. The thought of destroying it filled her with horror. 'Thou shalt not kill' was central to her philosophy of life. Was it merely cowardice that prevented her from standing up to her mother and refusing this abortion, merely a fear of what people might say about her? If she was serious about her faith, then surely she should be willing to face such ridicule and scorn, in the same way Jesus had done before his crucifixion. And as for her future career or studies at Cambridge, shouldn't she be willing to sacrifice these in order to avoid killing the embryo inside her? Was she not acting purely from selfish motives by going ahead with this abortion?

But in her heart she knew she wasn't simply being selfish. 'Honour thy father and thy mother' was the commandment that had haunted her since the discovery of her pregnancy. The disgrace she would bring on her mother and father by having this baby was unthinkable, too horrific to contemplate. They had loved her so much, had fought so hard to give her all the opportunities denied to them and were desperate to see her do well at Cambridge. They had already suffered terribly after the death of Evelyn, and if they could be spared further suffering, surely it was her duty to spare them. As her mother had said once, God hadn't given her the gift of such intelligence for her to waste it. And she would have to waste it, she knew, if she went ahead with this pregnancy. She would have to scrimp and save and cope with abuse only to bring up a child that would also be abused, called a 'bastard' and scorned or avoided by schoolmates.

'What should I do?' she asked, gazing at the crucifix. She knelt then and prayed. Always in the past she had felt something when she prayed, a closeness to God or an inner sense of what was right or what she should do. Today, there was nothing. Only silence. She waited and waited but still there was no inkling, no hint of guidance or sense of which direction to take. If God was saying anything, it was that this decision was entirely hers.

She seated herself once more on the bench, reviewing the arguments one last time. In the end though, it wasn't arguments that finally decided her. It was the thought of her father's face if he were to discover her pregnancy. She couldn't bear to see the terrible hurt in his eyes, couldn't bear to feel the devastation in his heart. She knew him and loved him more than anyone. She didn't know this unseen baby that hadn't yet developed any thoughts or feelings, hadn't yet looked at her as her father had, with an expression of absolute devotion.

'Forgive me for what I'm about to do,' she whispered, 'but I can do no other.'

She walked to the small altar and lit a candle for the soul of the doomed life within her, then went quickly outside.

The sun was still shining as she descended into the world below and she decided to walk along to the record store she had seen higher up The Headrow. There, she bought a record for her father. It was Paul Robeson singing *All Through The Night,* which she knew to be one of his favourites. He used to sing it to her and Evelyn when they were little, hoping to lull them off to sleep.

On her way back to the station, she stopped at the city art gallery. Its main galleries were still closed, most of its pictures having been removed for safe-keeping at the beginning of the war and not yet returned. There was a small exhibition of student art on the first floor, however, along with various art and craft displays by local people. Eileen ascended the stairs, happy to browse for half an hour before she caught the train home.

On the left side of the room was a motley collection of work set out on trestle tables and manned by elderly enthusiasts. The displays included ships in bottles, model houses made from matchsticks and arrangements of dead butterflies pinned in glass cases. As she passed the butterflies, Eileen shivered, wondering why people ever wanted to pursue such a gruesome hobby. A childhood memory came back of the time she had caught a butterfly. It was a cabbage white and she had trapped it in a small fishing net just after it had settled on one of the sweet peas growing up the canes in the back garden. She remembered putting it in a jam jar and slamming down the lid.

The image of its tiny fragile body came back to her clearly now and she recalled how she had placed it on the window-sill to watch it. It had fluttered frantically for a minute or so, then had rubbed its head slowly against the glass and feebly flapped its wings, sensing it was trapped. She understood exactly now, how it must have felt, and was relieved to think that, after a few minutes, she had set it free to resume its love affair with the flowers. It was strange though, she reflected, how ever since that day, the sight of a butterfly brought back to her the intoxicating scent of sweet peas.

Eileen now moved across to the other side of the room, where students from Leeds College of Art were displaying their work. She wandered round, looking at the various paintings. A brightly coloured oil painting immediately caught her attention. It was entitled *After Derain* and the notes underneath it explained that it was inspired by Derain's *Barges on the Thames*, a painting that, before the war, apparently used to be in the gallery downstairs. Eileen had studied a little art history at school and vaguely remembered that Derain was a contemporary of Matisse and belonged to the Fauvists, a group of artists who used bold, wild colours to create their effects.

She spent several minutes gazing at the work, admiring the way the deep red of the barges and the crane above them contrasted with the bright blue of the bridge and the orange sky beyond. The water of the Thames rippled gold in the sunlight, the exuberant brushstrokes and vivid colours giving the scene a life and energy that she loved. The picture stirred in her a feeling of hope. Suddenly, Cambridge seemed within her reach again, and for a brief moment, she dared to think beyond the present crisis to a brighter future.

On her way out, she passed a series of paintings depicting scenes from the Dales. One was of a bluebell wood, very similar to the wood in Ilkley, discovered so unexpectedly in her childhood. She went over to examine it more closely. Its title, *Bluebells*, together with the name of the artist, was written below but there was no indication of the name of the place that had inspired it. It was beautifully executed, the artist capturing that mysterious intensity of blue her family had encountered on a Sunday walk so long ago. She knew her mother would love it, her father too. The price wasn't high and it was just about affordable if she spent the last bit of the money she had left from the fire service. She dithered for a few seconds, then made up her mind to purchase it.

By now, it was time to go for her train. She caught the five o'clock, reached home by six and went straight into the kitchen to find her mother. Eliza knew by the way Eileen came in that she was feeling better. She looked much more like her old self.

'I've bought dad a record,' she said, placing it gently on the table, 'and here's a present for you, mam.' She gave her mother the picture, which the artist had kindly wrapped in brown paper and tied up with string.

Eliza was pleased. She took some scissors from the kitchen, cut the string and opened it carefully, revealing the bluebell scene.

'It's beautiful, Eileen,' she gasped, 'and just like that place in Ilkley. Wherever did you find it?'

Eileen just smiled, secretly delighted with her mother's response.

As soon as Arthur appeared, Eileen greeted him with a kiss.

'Look what our Eileen's bought me in Leeds,' said Eliza, showing him the painting. 'What does it remind you of, Arthur?'

'The bluebell wood in Ilkley,' said Arthur at once. 'Our little bit of heaven, eh Eileen?'

'There's a present waiting for you as well, dad. It's on the table in the front room,' she said.

'By gum there is an' all,' said Arthur, smiling as he went towards it. He opened up the bag and took out the black shiny record with the EMI label in the middle.

'Nay, love, you shouldn't have,' he said. 'This is grand. I've always wanted him singing this.'

He went across to the gramophone and wound the handle so they could listen to it straight away. The thick point of the silver needle moved steadily across the grooves, the glorious bass-baritone voice of Paul Robeson soaring above the crackles, filling the living room with song. Arthur sat back in his fireside chair, beaming with joy, looking just as Eileen remembered him when she was a little girl. The words of the lullaby came back to her as soon as she heard them, along with memories of Evelyn:

Sleep my love and peace attend thee
All through the night
Guardian angels God will lend thee
All through the night

Soft the drowsy hours are keeping
Hill and dale in slumber sleeping
Love alone his watch is keeping
All through the night.

'By, what a voice that feller's got,' said Arthur, lifting the arm of the gramophone off the end of the record and placing it down again at the start. 'Let's hear it again.'

Later on that evening, Arthur found a picture hook and hung the bluebell painting in the hallway, Eliza advising him on exactly where it should go.

'It's not quite straight, yet, Arthur,' she said.

'What about that?' he asked, standing back a bit and closing one eye to check that the top of the frame was completely level. 'Is that better, do you think?'

'Aye, I reckon it's about right, now. Come and look Eileen.'

Eileen confirmed that it was completely straight and looked perfect in the hallway.

'It's got a bit of a boring title, though, love,' said Arthur smiling. 'Couldn't the painter have thought of something more inspiring than *Bluebells* for such a lovely scene?'

'Oh, I don't know about that,' said Eliza, 'I quite like it. What else could you call it anyway?'

'What would you have called it if you'd painted it Eileen?' asked Arthur.

Eileen thought for a moment, picturing once more their Sunday walk through the wood in Ilkley, recalling how the sunlight filtered through the interwoven branches and cast ribbons of light upon the vast array of flowers that stretched before them, their delicate scents wafting through the air on the warm spring breeze. Although she had been so small at the time, the memory of that afternoon had remained vivid. She could still see herself sitting next to her father, could still hear the delighted cries of Evelyn and her mother as they ran together through the trees. It was a moment of such overwhelming beauty that she was positive she would remember it all her life. The bluebells in the painting were speckled with dappled light in much the same way as the ones in Ilkley had been, but it was the way the artist gave an impression of them swaying in the breeze, as if taking part in a graceful dance, that really reminded her of their time together in the wood.

'What would I have called it, dad?' she replied, smiling. 'I think I would have called it *Sarabande in Blue*.'

'What the hell's a sarabande?' laughed Eliza.

'Don't you remember, mam? When I came back from Cambridge I played you one on the piano and you and dad loved it. It's a sort of brief graceful dance, often with a melody filled with beauty and sadness. A bit like the bluebells, really.'

After listening to this explanation, Arthur and Eliza were both delighted with her suggestion.

'By, it's a grand title is that,' said Arthur. 'We'll call it that from now on.'

At eight o'clock, Eliza prepared to go and play cards with Mrs Braithwaite. She persuaded Eileen to accompany her.

'Come on, love,' she said. 'It'll help to take our mind off things.'

Eileen went upstairs to get her cardigan and Eliza took her arm as they went out.

'We won't be too long, Arthur,' she called, as she closed the front door. 'I think Eileen might be starting a bit of a cold, so she's going to have an early night.'

They chatted with Mrs Braithwaite for a little while and then Alice arrived.

'Where were you today?' asked Eliza, soon after her friend had sat down. 'I called round to see you at lunchtime but you were out.'

Alice looked worried. 'You never did, Eliza. I wish I'd known. What time did you come?'

'About one o'clock. I waited around till nearly two but there was no sign of you.'

'You must have just missed me,' Alice replied. 'Our Dorothy asked me over to her place for lunch. I was back by half past two.'

'Ah well, it doesn't matter, now,' sighed Eliza.

But Alice felt guilty and upset. She knew exactly what Eliza had come to talk to her about and felt dreadful that she hadn't been there when her friend needed her most. They exchanged a knowing look, but with Mrs Braithwaite and Eileen present, they could say no more.

The four of them continued their game of cards for a couple of hours, finishing at around ten. As soon as they got outside, Eliza quietly slipped a spare key to her front door into Alice's hand.

'Here you are,' she whispered. 'Let yourself in when you come tomorrow. I'll probably be busy looking after Eileen upstairs.'

Alice nodded and took the key. She turned to Eileen, then, and gave her a big hug as she said goodbye. 'Good luck tomorrow love,' she whispered. 'I'll see you just after half past three.'

Chapter 25

Tuesday morning passed slowly. As the time for the abortion drew near, Eileen began to realise the enormity of what she was about to have done. Suddenly, she saw the foetus within her womb as a living reality with head and eyes and mouth and limbs, a tiny soul whose delicate hold on life was about to be brutally terminated. 'Perhaps I need more time to consider this again,' she said to herself, beginning to have second thoughts. She turned to her mother.

'Mam, are you sure we're doing the right thing?' she asked.

'Course we are love,' Eliza replied. 'What else is there to do?'

'Well, I suppose I could try and have the baby. Maybe I could get it adopted.'

'Not without everybody knowing about it you couldn't,' said Eliza. 'You can't just go away somewhere and have a baby in secret. Folk would be bound to find out. And what about the shame we'd all have to live with then, all the whispering and pointing of fingers in the street. Think about your dad, Eileen. It would kill him, having to endure all that. I know it would.'

Eileen knew it, too, so remained silent. There definitely seemed to be no way out at all, no way that didn't lead to anguish of one sort or another.

'You've got to go through with it, Eileen,' Eliza said. 'It's all been arranged. There's no turning back now. Once it's over, you'll feel so much easier, love.'

Eileen walked over to the window, knowing that the whole thing was nowhere near as simple as her mother made out. For a while, she stood looking out on a world that seemed so normal and yet so out of reach. She pressed her nose against the pane of glass, longing for someone to take away her pain and misery, to let her fly free again, as if none of this had ever happened. Eventually, with a heavy heart, she went upstairs to the bedroom, fearing that the tiny life that was about to be extinguished would haunt her for the rest of her days.

Cathy arrived promptly at half past two, refusing the cup of tea that Eliza offered her.

'No, let's get on with it,' she said. Her manner was brisk, her tone matter-of-fact. 'Have you got the money for me?'

Eliza gave her the ten pounds and watched her

tuck it into a secret pocket in the lining of her coat. Then she showed her upstairs to the bedroom and introduced her to Eileen, who had already got undressed and was lying on the bed.

The 'procedure', as Cathy called it, involved dilating the cervix by means of sterilised knitting needles and then scraping out the contents of the womb with a crochet hook. She suggested that Eileen might want to cover her face with a pillow to muffle any screams that might inadvertently alert or alarm the neighbours. Then, donning a pair of rubber gloves, she prepared to get on with the task. By now, Eliza was beginning to feel very afraid but she forced herself to appear calm for Eileen's sake, promising to hold her daughter's hand throughout the operation.

After twenty-five minutes, it was all over.

'Let her lie still for the rest of the day,' said Cathy to Eliza, 'till the bleeding eases off. By tomorrow, she'll be feeling a lot better.'

Downstairs, Cathy stood behind the door until she was sure that no one was in the street, then left as abruptly as she had arrived, the soles of her black leather shoes tap tapping quickly along the pavement and up the steep hill.

'Thank God she's gone and it's all over,' said Eliza to herself. She felt faint and leaned against the banister. It had been the most terrible ordeal of her life. She knew that she would never forget the horror of what she had just witnessed and would hear Eileen's screams as long as she lived. But this was no time to stop and think of herself. Taking several deep breaths to try to slow down her pounding heart, she ran upstairs to check on Eileen, who was still haemorrhaging. Eliza brought some old towels from the bathroom for her to hold against herself until the bleeding stopped and went downstairs to make them both a strong cup of tea. Once again, she took out the bottle of brandy from the small drawer in the sideboard and tipped a good measure into each cup. Then she put the cups and saucers on a tray and carried them upstairs.

When she got back to the bedroom, Eileen looked pale and terrified.

'Mam,' she said, 'I'm scared. The bleeding's getting worse.'

Eliza put down the tray of tea next to the bed and rushed off to get more towels to staunch the flow. But

Eileen continued to flood and Eliza, frantic now, started to run to and from the airing cupboard in the bathroom, pulling out all the towels she could find.

She kept holding them tightly against her daughter, praying for the bleeding to show signs of stopping, but nothing that she tried seemed to work and Eileen was becoming increasingly pale. Eliza was running out of towels now and began to rummage through her own wardrobe for some old sheets and pillow-cases.

'Don't worry, my love, don't worry,' she said, returning to her daughter's room with three white sheets and a bolster case in her arms. 'It's only natural to bleed for a bit afterwards. Cathy said so.'

'I feel so cold and faint, mam,' murmured Eileen, 'really faint.'

'I know love, but it'll be all right soon, just you wait and see,' said Eliza reassuringly as she tucked one of the sheets beneath her.

More than half an hour passed, but still the haemorrhaging continued. Eileen had stopped speaking now and seemed barely conscious. Frantic with worry, Eliza rushed into Evelyn's old room and started to trawl through a bedding chest in the hope of finding something else that might serve to stem the relentless tide of blood.

In the middle of this last desperate search, she heard the click of the front door as Alice quietly made her way in, using the spare key she had been given the night before.

'Alice!' screamed Eliza. 'Alice, come up here quick!'

Alarmed, Alice ran upstairs and into the bedroom. She was horrified by the scene that awaited her. Eileen, ashen-faced, was lying on the bed surrounded by a mound of blood-soaked sheets and towels. It was clear that she was still bleeding heavily and that, unless something was done very soon, could be in serious danger.

'I'm going to ring for an ambulance,' cried Alice, rushing out of the room. 'I'll be back as fast as I can.'

'Nay, Alice, don't do that,' pleaded a distraught Eliza. 'We can't have anyone finding out what's gone on. Just help me raise her legs and press these sheets up against her. It's bound to stop soon.'

'No, Eliza,' said Alice, taking charge now, 'something's gone wrong here. I'm phoning for an ambulance and that's that.'

Alice raced downstairs and ran as fast as she could to the phone box at the top of the road, her hand trembling as she dialled the number. The emergency operator put her straight through to the ambulance service.

'There's been an accident and someone's bleeding very badly' she said. 'Whatever we try, we can't stop the blood. Please come. Come quickly.' She gave the address and was assured an ambulance would be there soon.

Alice flew down the hill and shot back upstairs to the bedroom, breathless from her exertions. She ran to the doorway, then stopped, stunned by the scene in front of her.

Eliza was now sitting on the edge of the mattress, cradling her daughter's head in her arms and rocking her backwards and forwards, backwards and forwards. Eileen was completely limp, her face drip white and there was little doubt in Alice's mind that she had died.

For a moment, Alice was unable to take in what she was seeing. Then, struggling to find her voice, she said softly, 'Come on Eliza, love. Let Eileen rest now. She's gone. I think she's gone.'

'No, no, she hasn't gone,' said Eliza, continuing to

rock her daughter back and forth. 'She can't have gone. She's only sleeping, only sleeping.'

For some minutes the scene remained unchanged, Alice standing like a statue in the doorway, Eliza clutching her daughter's lifeless body and whispering words of comfort in her ear, the room strewn with bloody sheets and towels, and on the floor beside the bed, two untouched cups of tea on a silver tray.

When the ambulance men finally came, they realised it was too late to save Eileen. They carefully placed her body on a stretcher and manoeuvred it gently downstairs. Alice and Eliza went with them and sat in the back of the ambulance, Eliza still hoping that Eileen might somehow be revived when she reached the hospital.

Like her sister before her, though, she was pronounced dead on arrival. It was obvious to the doctor concerned that an amateurish abortion had led to a massive haemorrhage and that, in effect, Eileen had bled to death because help had not been called for in time.

Hospital staff immediately sent for the police, and two officers arrived within minutes. Alice and Eliza were both arrested on suspicion of causing Eileen's death and taken away for questioning.

Chapter 26

Arthur walked up the path to the front door just before six, a little earlier than usual. He turned the key in the lock and stepped inside, thinking, as he did so, that the house seemed strangely quiet. There was no sign of the rattle of pots and plates in the kitchen, no sign of Eileen playing the piano or listening to a record on the gramophone. Finding the front room empty, he went through the hall into the kitchen. Here, strangely, there was no indication that Eliza had started to prepare the evening meal. All he could see was the brown teapot, still half full of tea, standing beside the sink. Puzzled, he went out of the back door into the garden to check if either his wife or daughter might for some reason have gone out there. But the garden was also deserted.

Unsure of where to look next, Arthur came back inside again, thinking there must have been some emergency with a neighbour.

'It isn't like Eliza not to leave me a note,' he thought.

Accepting that there was nothing he could do but wait, he went into the hall, thinking of going upstairs for a wash. There, he suddenly noticed that the painting of the bluebells had somehow been knocked askew. He adjusted it carefully, wondering why Eliza hadn't straightened it herself. Then he mounted the stairs but paused on the landing, seeing that Eileen's bedroom door was ajar. Thinking she might have gone for a lie down and perhaps fallen asleep, he quietly pushed the door open to investigate.

His eyes lighted first on the piles of bloody towels and sheets scattered haphazardly across the floor and then on the half-stripped, empty bed, its mattress stained dark crimson. In an instant, the sound of wailing shells and gunfire filled his ears. He was back on the Somme, with dead men's eyes staring blankly up at him and blood frothing in trenches. He stood stock still, completely at a loss and unable to deal with the scene he had stumbled upon.

'Arthur!' called a voice from the hallway. 'Arthur! Are you up there?'

It was Jack. Alice had phoned him earlier from the hospital and told him briefly what had happened, begging him to intercept Arthur before he got home and take him back to their house, at least until she knew what was happening with Eliza. Unfortunately, Jack's tram was delayed so he missed Arthur by a couple of minutes. He ran all the way down the slope and up the path but realised he was too late as soon as he saw that the front door had been left open. He hesitated for a moment on the threshold, then stepped inside.

Receiving no answer to his calls but sensing Arthur's presence in the house, Jack eventually ran upstairs. He found his friend standing in the bedroom doorway, still gazing on the scene of devastation. His face was drained of all colour and his hands were trembling.

'Nay, Arthur,' Jack said, putting his arm around his shoulder. 'You can't stay here. Let's go downstairs. I've ordered a taxi to pick us up at half past six. You're coming back to my place tonight.'

Over a cup of tea, Jack broke the terrible news but Arthur seemed not to hear him, continuing to stare straight ahead, as if he had seen a ghost.

The police arrived before the taxi, wanting to examine Eileen's bedroom. Jack answered the door and showed the two officers upstairs.

'Has anything been touched here, sir?' one of them asked.

'No, I'm sure not,' replied Jack. 'Arthur had only just got home when I arrived and he hadn't actually gone into the room when I found him. He was just standing in the doorway.'

'What's going to happen to him now?' the second officer asked.

'He's coming to stay with me,' said Jack. 'He can't possibly sleep here at the moment.'

'No, no, I understand that. We'll have to seal off this room for a day or so, I'm afraid. If you let me have your phone number, we'll contact Mr Pendlestone and let him know when we've completely finished our examination, so he can come back and get things sorted out.'

'And what about his wife, Eliza?' queried Jack. 'What should I tell him about her?'

'She's staying with us for the moment, sir,' said the first policeman in a tone of voice designed to discourage any further questions on the matter.

Jack took the hint and left them to it. He went into Arthur's bedroom to collect some clothes and a few essential items, which he put into an overnight bag. By this time the taxi was waiting outside. Jack guided a dazed

Arthur to the car and they drove off towards Manningham.

As soon as they got in the house, Jack helped Arthur into a chair in the living room and took out a bottle of brandy from the sideboard. He poured Arthur a large glass and added some hot water.

'There you are, lad,' he said. 'You sit there for a bit and have a drop o' that.'

Arthur sipped it slowly, still unable to speak. Jack sat beside him, one hand on his arm, and waited in silence for Alice to come home.

Amy got in about half an hour later. Jack took her aside in the kitchen and told her what had happened, taking care to speak in hushed tones so that Arthur couldn't hear.

'I'm that worried about your mother,' he said. 'She should have been back hours ago.'

'I'll go to the police station,' said Amy, 'and see if I can find out what's going on.'

Alice had been interrogated for over two hours, the police suspecting her of being the person who had carried out the abortion. It only gradually became apparent to them that she was not. Her story was naturally corroborated by Eliza, but more importantly, neighbours interviewed by police testified to the fact that she was seen walking down the hill to Eliza's house at a few minutes after half past three, around ten minutes before her phone call for an ambulance was received. Clearly, it would not have been possible for her to have performed an abortion in the ten minutes between her arrival and the making of the subsequent phone call.

At around eight o'clock, therefore, just as Amy arrived at the station, the police decided to release Alice, pending further questioning. She and Amy were offered a lift to the end of their road by a policeman about to go off duty.

As soon as she arrived, Alice ran indoors and immediately went to Arthur, putting her arms around him. 'We'll look after you till Eliza gets back, love,' she said. 'You can stay here as long as you want.'

She made sure that Arthur was comfortable in Dorothy's old room and took him a cup of tea up to bed. 'Just give us a shout if you want anything in the night, Arthur,' she said. 'We're only in the room next door.'

Eventually, Alice came down to the kitchen,

where Amy and Jack were waiting for her.

'What the hell's going on Alice?' said Jack. 'What's happening to Eliza? Why hasn't she come back with you?'

'They wouldn't let me see her once we got to the police station,' said Alice. 'We were taken to separate rooms for questioning. I haven't had a chance to talk to her since the doctor told her that Eileen was dead.'

'She must be in a terrible state and there's not a soul with her,' said Amy.

'They must know she's needed here with Arthur at a time like this,' said Jack. 'They'll have to let her go soon, surely.'

'I don't know that they will,' Alice replied. 'I'm worried to death, Jack. I think they might be going to charge her with murder.'

Alice was almost proved right. Despite intense and prolonged interrogation, Eliza refused to disclose where she had met the abortionist or how she had been put in touch with her. In the end, the police realised that she was unlikely ever to talk and feared that the real perpetrator of this terrible crime might never be brought to justice.

After several days of further investigation, they

decided to charge Eliza with manslaughter and she was subsequently remanded in custody.

Chapter 27

Flanked by two officers, Eliza stared blankly up at the gloomy Victorian building ahead of her. Dazed and still incapable of taking in exactly what had happened in the last few days, she was led through a locked iron gate and made to wait outside the main door until the police spoke through the intercom system with one of the warders inside. After a few minutes, Eliza was conscious of the sliding of several bolts and the turning of keys and then the door swung open, revealing a uniformed officer who glanced at them briefly, nodding his approval.

She was taken down a long corridor and into a room at the end, where the necessary preliminaries were gone through. Her clothes and belongings were handed over to the female officer in charge, and after showering, she pulled on the dark grey skirt, blouse and jacket that were to mark her out as a prisoner, possibly for the rest of her life.

'Follow me,' said the officer curtly and led her down yet more corridors, on either side of which were the locked doors of cells where scores of women were confined. As soon as they reached the cell which was to

411

be hers, the officer quickly unlocked the door and ushered her inside.

'You'll be in here until six o'clock. Then you'll be called for breakfast. After that we'll find you some work to do.'

Eliza heard the door slam and the rattle of a key. Then silence.

She sat down on the bed. The cell was small, about nine feet square. Apart from the iron bed with its hard mattress and rather grubby pillow, there was a bucket concealed in a lidded metal container in one corner and a small wooden table and chair in the other. The floor was concrete, the walls were high and there was only one long narrow window with iron bars. There was no form of heating, and even in late summer, the place was cold.

There were a couple of woollen blankets on the bed and Eliza pulled one around her. Tired now and shivering, she lay down and closed her eyes. Part of her still clung to the thought she was having a nightmare, that she would wake up tomorrow beside Arthur as she always did and pop her head round Eileen's door to call her for work before heading into the kitchen to make breakfast.

Half imagining she was still back at home, Eliza finally drifted into sleep, oblivious of the occasional cries of other prisoners, the echoing of footsteps down the corridor and the various unexplained rattles and crashes that were soon to become a regular feature of her endless sleepless nights.

The next day she was woken at six, and after breakfast, was set to work scrubbing floors and corridors. Following a meagre lunch, she was then transferred to the laundry room to wash piles of sheets and blankets. She was classed as an unskilled worker, and as such, received four pence per week, a measly sum which was less than most children of the time received in pocket money and which had to be saved for several weeks in order for her to be able to afford a few basic items from the prison shop. The other inmates were friendly enough and the officers were not as strict as some of the overlookers in the mill, but the place was overcrowded. Also, because of a shortage of prison staff as a result of the war, the warders now worked only one instead of two shifts. From six o'clock at night, therefore, there was just a skeleton staff. This meant that prisoners had to be shut in their cells from early evening until the following morning, alone with their thoughts.

It was this part of the day that Eliza grew to dread. The time passed when she was working but the nights seemed an eternity. This was when the reality of what had happened began to take hold, when she realised how little anything mattered any more. What people said or thought about her in the outside world was irrelevant now, and even Arthur seemed a distant memory.

Shrouded in a dark cloak of numbness, she sat on the bed for hours, surrounded by memories that came back to her as if from another world, somewhere far away that she had once belonged to but could never be a part of again. She felt nothing. All feeling had gone the moment they told her of Eileen's fate, so the remembered scenes were not relived so much as observed from a distance, like the flickering images in the picture house she used to go to with Laurie.

Often, she would watch the light of dusk fade slowly into dark, then go to her tiny window to see the glimmer of the old gas lamps in the streets beyond the prison wall. They were comforting somehow. She thought of them as she tried to sleep, hearing again the sound of their sputtering in Albert Road, along with the clip-clop of the milkman's horse and the faint tapping of Mrs. Lumb's pole on her parents' bedroom window.

Local journalists soon got to hear of Eileen's tragic story and articles began to appear in several papers, usually with the same headline – *Mother Charged With Killing Own Daughter.* Alice and Jack took great care to keep these papers away from Arthur, glad that they were at least able to do something to protect him.

As they had promised, the police rang him after two days to confirm that he could now return to his house whenever he wanted. At Alice's insistence, though, he stayed with her and Jack for one more week. The day after the phone call from the police, Jack and Alice went over to Arthur's house to clear out Eileen's bedroom. They got rid of the old blood-stained mattress and replaced it with a new one. Then they cleaned the carpet thoroughly and Alice put some clean linen on the bed.

'That looks better,' said Jack. 'There'll be enough for Arthur to contend with when he gets back, without having this bedroom to worry about.'

With Eliza in prison, Arthur had the sole responsibility for arranging Eileen's funeral. In this, he was supported as far as possible by the vicar of his church, who had been deeply shocked by the terrible news. He offered to take Arthur to visit his wife in jail so that they could plan the funeral together, but Arthur would have none of it, unable to contemplate even seeing Eliza after what had happened, let alone speaking to her.

It was decided that Eileen would be buried next to her sister in Bowling cemetery, in the plot that Arthur had originally reserved for himself and Eliza, never dreaming that Eileen would be the first to lie in it. The funeral service was delayed for some while as a result of the post-mortem and subsequent inquest, the findings of which were that Eileen had bled to death due to the perforation of her internal organs by a sharp instrument. Had she been taken to the hospital only half an hour earlier, they might have saved her.

Alice and Jack kindly offered to hold the funeral tea in their house, feeling it would be inappropriate for Arthur to invite guests back to where Eileen had so recently died. It was agreed by the prison authorities that Eliza could attend the funeral service if she wanted to, but she declined, not wanting to upset Arthur any further, and conscious of how insensitive it might seem, since she had been the main cause of Eileen's death. She was permitted to visit her daughter in the chapel of rest, however, and was taken there in a prison van the day before the funeral. Handcuffed to a policewoman, she went into the funeral parlour and was escorted to the room where Eileen's body lay. As the undertaker discreetly withdrew, the policewoman unfastened the handcuffs and stood back, allowing Eliza to walk alone to the dark oak coffin.

Still numb and incapable of the slightest hint of emotion, she stood there in silence, looking down at Eileen's pale waxen face and the strands of dark wavy hair that fell across her forehead. She was covered in a long white gown and Eliza wondered why Arthur hadn't given the undertaker her best dress, the one she had worn to Dorothy's wedding. Maybe that would have made her look less pale, given her a bit more colour.

'Ah well, it doesn't matter, now,' she thought.

She moved closer to the coffin, unsure of what to do next. She knew she must say something, must force herself, if only for a moment, to return to the world of yesterday. Bending closer, she stretched out her hand and stroked her daughter's cold forehead.

'Goodbye, my lass,' she whispered, kissing her for the last time. 'I know you'll understand why I can't come to the funeral. Your dad'll see to everything though and make sure it's all done right. They're going to put you next to Evelyn, so you won't be on your own.'

Eliza then turned again to the policewoman, holding out her right hand for the handcuffs to be replaced. Without looking back, she walked beside her out of the room where Eileen lay, allowing the waiting undertaker to close the door behind them. Together, they walked past the quizzical gaze of the receptionist and the drooping white lilies on the table near the exit, their powerful sweet scent coming as a shock to Eliza's nostrils after the foul smells of prison. The policewoman led her quickly outside and into the prison van.

Between the inquest and the funeral, Alice went to see Eliza as often as possible. She tried to engage her in some sort of conversation but Eliza remained impassive, giving only the briefest of automatic responses to her questions, delivered in a lifeless monotone. It was Alice who told her about the arrangements for the funeral, assuring her that Arthur was just about coping,

418

with a bit of help from the vicar.

'I can understand why you feel you shouldn't come to the church,' she said to Eliza, 'but when you're out of here we'll visit her grave together. We'll have a little service of our own and maybe you can lay some flowers.'

Eliza didn't answer. Both sat in silence together until a loud bell signalled the end of visiting time. Alice then kissed her friend goodbye, secretly relieved that another difficult meeting was over.

Many times on subsequent visits, Alice tried to persuade Eliza to tell the police about how she had first contacted Cathy but Eliza always flatly refused, unable to bring herself to betray Mrs Grimshaw, who had been good enough to help her at a time when she was desperate.

'Eliza, you're letting that Cathy walk scot-free,' she remonstrated, 'and she's the one who's really to blame. Think about what she might do to other young girls.'

But Eliza wouldn't budge. All she would ever say was, 'It wasn't Cathy's fault. It was mine.'

In the end, Alice gave up trying to get her to

change her mind, believing it to be a hopeless quest. She never gave up on visiting her, though, despite having to rack her brains every time to think of something to say.

Eventually, the day of the funeral dawned. It was now late September and the leaves on a few of the trees were already beginning to turn yellow.

The service had been planned mainly by Alice and Jack, with the help of the vicar. They had involved Arthur as much as they could, managing to ascertain from him that he had money put away for such an emergency and they were not to worry about the cost. They also discovered from Arthur that Eileen's favourite hymn was *O Love That Wilt Not Let Me Go,* and made sure that this was included in the order of service.

Alice helped Arthur into the back of the funeral car and held his hand all the way to the church. Eileen's coffin, covered now with a mixture of white roses and red and white carnations, was eased gently out of the hearse and carried into the church.

The mourners filed solemnly in behind it, with Arthur, Jack and Alice at the front, followed by Dorothy and Amy. Then came Muriel and Renée from the fire service, Margaret and Bertha, her friends from grammar school, Miss Lucas, her old form teacher and finally Mrs Harris, the librarian at the reference library where Eileen had worked that summer.

As they walked towards the porch, Alice caught a glimpse of a group of women huddled together in the corner of the churchyard, pointing and whispering, the scent of scandal having attracted them.

'Vultures!' she whispered. 'Bloody vultures!'

The service was brief, the vicar paying tribute to Eileen's academic achievements and her commitment to the church in her earlier years. He was understandably reticent to talk about the recent past, referring only to her 'outstanding contribution to the war effort' through her time in the fire service and to her 'tragic early death'.

Alice wondered what Arthur was making of it all. He was sitting perfectly still beside her, lost in his own world, his face blank, his eyes dry, apparently unaware of the significance of what was happening around him.

They stood for the final hymn, *O Love That Wilt Not Let Me Go*. Alice held Arthur's arm, trying desperately to sing for Eileen's sake, but finding that the tears now rolling down her cheeks prevented her from doing so. Renée and Muriel broke down sobbing in the middle of it and everyone there was weeping, except for Arthur.

Twenty minutes later, they all collected round the open grave and watched Eileen's coffin being lowered next to that of her sister, her body, just like Evelyn's, committed to the dust from whence it came.

Alice remained as close as she could to Arthur, who stood at attention throughout, still in a trance, an ashen-faced ghost of his former self. Like a soldier obeying some distant command, he threw a white rose on the coffin now resting in the earth, his movements jerky and mechanical. Alice took out her handkerchief to wipe away the tears that continued to pour down her cheeks. Still unable to fully comprehend the terrible irony of the situation, she kept asking herself how things had come to this. How on earth could it be that Eileen, a girl surrounded by the love of her parents all her life, was denied their tears in death?

The vicar's solemn 'amen' was echoed by the mourners as the burial drew to a close. Head bowed, Arthur allowed himself to be led back to the funeral car. On the way there, he was approached by the undertaker, who came over to express his condolences and to ask him to give some consideration to the wording he wanted to have inscribed on the headstone.

'There's no great hurry, Mr Pendlestone,' he said. 'You can let me know at any time over the next couple of weeks.'

'We'll think about it later,' said Alice, anxious to protect Arthur from further pain.

To her great surprise, Arthur suddenly raised his head, and putting his hand deep in his coat pocket, removed a rather crumpled piece of paper, which he immediately handed over.

'What I want is written down on there,' he said, his voice barely audible and devoid of any emotion.

The undertaker carefully smoothed out the paper and nodded his assent. It read:

In Memory of Eileen,
beloved daughter of Arthur and Eliza,
died aged 21 years.
'Sleep my love and peace attend thee,
all through the night.'

The mourners processed slowly out of the graveyard and everyone went back to Alice's house for a cup of tea. Jack made sure that all the guests were looked after and Alice continued to busy herself in the kitchen, bringing in sandwiches and cakes. Arthur sank back into the trance he had been in before his brief conversation with the undertaker, sitting in silence in the corner, as if he were unable to comprehend why they were all there.

Over tea, Muriel filled Renée in on everything that had happened since they had all met up for lunch only a few weeks before and they both vowed to continue to visit Eileen's parents for as long as they lived, thinking that this was the least they could do for their friend.

As the months passed, Alice and Jack continued to support Arthur and did all they could to help him settle back into some sort of routine. They invited him to stay with them over Christmas and New Year, knowing how unbearable such times must be for him. Meanwhile, Eliza remained in prison, her case having been referred to the next assizes in Leeds.

In early March, the day before Eliza's court appearance, Alice visited the prison again, bringing with her, as requested, a change of clothes.

'I've brought you these so you'll look smart for the judge,' she said, as she handed over a skirt and blouse, together with Eliza's black winter coat and best hat. 'And in this box there's the brooch and hatpin that your mother gave you. Maybe they'll bring you a bit of good fortune at the hearing.'

Eliza thanked her as she handed them over. The prison staff held on to them all, of course, bringing them to her cell for her to change into the following morning.

In the light of a cold watery sun, Eliza got ready to be taken to court to hear her fate. She brushed her hair, greying now and much longer, then put on the blouse and skirt that Alice had brought her. Lastly, she donned the hat and coat, fixing the former in place with the long silver hatpin and then pinning the brooch on her lapel, just as she had done for Alice's wedding more than twenty-seven years before.

The courtroom was cold and forbidding. Eliza was ushered into the dock but found that she was hardly tall enough to see over its semi-circular rail, having to stand on tiptoe in order to get a clear view of the people present. In the crowded public gallery above, she caught a glimpse of Alice smiling down at her encouragingly, while beneath her, the defence lawyer was flicking through his papers. He had been paid for by Arthur who, though not yet able to cope with seeing her, was certainly not prepared to abandon her to her fate.

Eliza had been advised to plead guilty to manslaughter, a crime for which the maximum penalty was life imprisonment. Evidence was presented over two days. The prosecuting counsel referred to hospital reports and asked the judge to consider the brutal nature of the abortion, arranged and paid for by Eliza in full knowledge of both its illegality and the considerable dangers involved. Various medical details were dwelt upon at length and Eliza's slowness in calling an ambulance was condemned, as was the fact that she had consistently refused to disclose the name of the person who had first put her in touch with the abortionist, thereby helping to shield the real culprit from justice. The defence concentrated mainly on Eliza's previously unblemished character and stressed that she had in no way intended to harm her child, let alone kill her.

Throughout the proceedings, Alice sat in the gallery, trying to offer some support. When she got home at night, Jack enquired how it was going.

'I'm not sure, Jack,' she said at the end of the first day. 'It looks a bit grim if you ask me. Eliza doesn't help herself by looking as if she doesn't care what happens and I gather the judge has got a reputation for giving tough sentences. I wish it was all over and done with, I do that.'

On the afternoon of the second day, once all the evidence had been presented and both prosecution and defence counsels had summed up, the judge adjourned proceedings for a short time to deliberate before he passed sentence. Alice went for a quick cup of tea and prepared herself for the worst. She had promised to go round and see Arthur as soon as Eliza was sentenced to let him know the result.

After less than an hour, she heard that the judge was about to return, so she made her way back to the gallery, pushing to the front through the crowds, a strange mix of the morbidly curious, gossip-mongers and members of the press.

Finally, the judge came in and took his seat again. Eliza gazed up at him, watching him carefully adjust the sleeves of his robe and then pause for a moment. He, in turn, gazed down at Eliza, and for the first time, their eyes met. His face softened as he leaned towards her. He said only seven words:

'Mother, I think you have suffered enough.'

Chapter 28

Alice could hardly believe it. Eliza had been set free, the judge exercising his considerable discretion and ruling that the months of imprisonment she had already served were sufficient punishment. The court quickly emptied and Alice was able to hug her friend at last.

'Thank God,' she whispered, clasping Eliza to her breast. 'Thank God for that judge.'

Eliza gave a faint smile and allowed her friend to lead her down the steps of the court. She stood for a moment, surprised by the afternoon sunlight, then Alice hailed a taxi and shepherded her friend into the back. They sped through the streets with the judge's words still ringing in their ears, two old friends reunited but looking out on a world they knew would never be the same again.

Eventually, the taxi drew up outside Eliza's house and Alice went in first to prepare Arthur for the fact that Eliza had been released. After a few minutes, she beckoned Eliza to come in and quickly got back into the taxi herself, instructing the driver to take her home to Manningham.

Arthur put down *David Copperfield* as Eliza entered

the front room and went into the kitchen to put the kettle on. They didn't speak for some while, but as time passed, they worked out a way of coping, neither of them ever mentioning what had occurred, their conversations confined now to the matter-of-fact, the everyday. Since the funeral, Arthur had moved permanently into Evelyn's old room, so Eliza slept alone in their double bed. Eileen's room, of course, remained closed. It had died along with her and was never used again.

Neither Arthur nor Eliza could bear to look at any concrete reminders of their daughter, so nearly all her possessions, including all the photographs of her, were packed away in boxes and stored on top of her wardrobe. Even the coronation mug, which had enjoyed pride of place on the mantelpiece for years, was wrapped in tissue paper and hidden away in a drawer.

Only the painting of the bluebells remained, forever sacred and untouchable, despite the almost unbearable pain it evoked. On many occasions, Arthur went to take it down, but could never quite bring himself to do so. *Sarabande in Blue* thus continued to hang on the wall at the foot of the stairs, a silent testimony to a vanished world.

Three times a week, Alice came round and took Eliza for long walks over the hills and dales, feeling convinced that this was the only way her friend would ever begin to recover from the trauma she had suffered. Unlike the people in the neighbourhood, the hills didn't judge, they were just there, uncompromising, eternal.

'Come on, Eliza,' she'd say. 'Get your hat and coat on, we're going for a walk.'

Dogged in her persistence, Alice refused to take no for an answer and forced Eliza to trek in all weathers across the dark, brooding moors.

Meanwhile, as he had done since Eileen's death, Arthur continued to read his beloved *David Copperfield*. No sooner had he finished the last page than he turned back to the first and started all over again, his obsession with the novel now coming to resemble the obsession of his favourite character, Mr Dick, with the severed head of Charles I. Perhaps it served much the same purpose, protecting him from facing a reality that might otherwise have driven him insane.

Jack did his best to support his friend, still taking him along to Bradford City occasionally or having a drink with him in the local pub, but it was never the same.

430

Arthur was just going through the motions of living. His spirit was somewhere else.

As they had promised, Muriel and Renée regularly called in to see Arthur and Eliza, Renée even managing to make them laugh sometimes about one of her latest escapades. They never forgot Eileen and often brought up her name in conversation knowing that, however painful it might be for her parents, it was better than pretending that she had never lived.

One afternoon in August, almost a year to the day after Eileen's death, Alice came round as usual to take Eliza off for a walk.

'Come on,' she said, smiling. 'We're going somewhere different today. It's a surprise.'

Within the hour, Eliza found herself getting off a bus at the top of Saltaire. She hadn't been back since the day she packed up to go to Bowling. She and Alice wandered down Victoria Road. The old streets looked just the same to them both, even Albert Road hadn't changed at all. How long ago it seemed since they had played their childhood games on its cobbles.

They walked to the gates of the mill, remembering the scores of dark, cold mornings when they used to rush through them to clock on. Smoke was still rising from the gigantic chimney, the windows were still vibrating from the noise of the machines, but as Eliza and Alice both knew, the workers inside inhabited a very different world.

Leaving the familiar building and its memories behind, they crossed the footbridge over the river into the park, passing the bandstand and the spot where the huge statue of Sir Titus Salt stood on his plinth, overlooking the kingdom he had created. Eliza couldn't help thinking of Laurie and how they had met here on the day that he proposed. She could still see his handsome rugged face, and just for a moment, thought she could hear his laughter echoing from behind the boat sheds.

Alice, ahead of her now, turned back and beckoned her to draw alongside again. Taking her arm, she said suddenly, 'Come on, Eliza. Let's go up the glen.'

They climbed slowly up the old steep path beside the tramway and walked past the funfair, its swings still occupied by screaming youngsters pulling on the ropes and daring each other to go higher and higher.

The stones on top of the glen were waiting, as they had been for centuries, and Alice and Eliza sat down on them exactly as they used to, feeling that they had come home at last.

They remained there for several minutes, gazing across at the moors with the wind against their faces, reliving the scenes of their childhood.

'Look!' said Alice, suddenly pointing at something in front of her. She got up and walked across to one of the largest of the ancient rocks, not far from where they were sitting.

'Come and see, Eliza,' she called. 'Here are our initials and the date.'

Eliza went over to her and stared down at them – *EB. AC. 26 August 1906.*

'Aye, so they are,' she said. 'Who would have thought it, after all these years.'

Lost in memories of the past, they stood together beside the stone that still bore witness to the happiness of two little girls on a summer's day so long ago. In the distance, Eliza saw again the purple heather rippling in the breeze. She thought of the painting Eileen had given her, of their day in the sun with the bluebells and of Eileen herself swaying to and fro on the piano stool as she played the solemn melody that would haunt her and Arthur forever.

What was it Eileen had said about it? 'A brief dance filled with beauty and sadness.' That had been her daughter's life, thought Eliza, and the lives of so many others over two world wars. Perhaps that was really all of our lives. The slow, insistent melody of the sarabande floated once more through her mind, speaking to her again as forcibly as it had when Eileen first played it – *no love without the risk of loss*, it said to her again, *no love without the risk of pain.*

Suddenly, without warning, and for the first time since Eileen's death, Eliza felt a stream of hot tears coursing down her cheeks, felt her heart contract and tighten in the grip of the surging tide of emotion sweeping over her. She put her head in her hands and began to sob and sob, her tiny frame shaking uncontrollably as the grief so long denied gushed out with an unstoppable force.

Realising what was happening, Alice moved closer and folded her friend in her arms. She held her tightly, not speaking, but understanding everything, held her for a long time until the storm seemed finally over and the weeping at last subsided.

Alice stepped back then, looking at her friend for

some minutes with a mixture of love and relief.

'By hell,' she said, 'you certainly needed that!'

Eliza gave her the merest hint of a smile and they stood close beside each other, gazing at the lengthening shadows over the moors. Clouds were starting to circle the late afternoon sun, their edges tinged with its gold, and as the two friends watched the changing patterns of light across the distant hills, both were conscious of a deep and growing sense of peace enveloping them.

In that moment, Eliza knew that she had to find the strength to go on. She would never really live again, of course, but she would stick by Arthur, or what was left of him, to her dying day. That's what Eileen would have wanted, she was certain.

Before long, she thought, her life and that of Alice would be forgotten. Only their initials would remain, etched with a thousand others in the rocks, their story left untold, their voices drifting unheard across the bleak, windswept moor.

'Are you ready then?' said Alice, quietly. 'It's getting a bit chilly up here.'

'Aye, I'm ready,' Eliza replied.

They took their leave of the ancient stones and

walked arm in arm down the glen.

Doreen Hinchliffe was born in Yorkshire and taught English there for several years before moving to London, where she now lives. This is her debut novel, although she is an established poet who has already published two poetry collections – *Dark Italics* (Indigo Dreams Publishing, 2017) and *Substantial Ghosts* (Oversteps Books, 2020).

Further details of her publications can be found on her website:

www.doreenhinchliffe.co.uk

www.blossomspringpublishing.com

Printed in Poland
by Amazon Fulfillment
Poland Sp. z o.o., Wrocław